GENA SHOWALTER

MAGGIE SHAYNE
SUSAN KRINARD

Heart of Darkness

HQN™

Recycling programs
for this product may
not exist in your area.

ISBN-13: 978-0-373-77431-9

HEART OF DARKNESS

Copyright © 2010 by Harlequin Books S.A.

The publisher acknowledges the copyright holders of the individual works as follows:

THE DARKEST ANGEL
Copyright © 2010 by Gena Showalter

LOVE ME TO DEATH
Copyright © 2010 by Margaret Benson

LADY OF THE NILE
Copyright © 2010 by Susan Krinard

CONTENTS

THE DARKEST ANGEL   9
Gena Showalter

LOVE ME TO DEATH   145
Maggie Shayne

LADY OF THE NILE   243
Susan Krinard

THE DARKEST ANGEL
Gena Showalter

CHAPTER ONE

FROM HIGH IN THE HEAVENS, Lysander spotted his prey. *At last. Finally, I will end this.* His jaw clenched and his skin pulled tight. With tension. With relief. Determined, he jumped from the cloud he stood upon, falling quickly… wind whipping through his hair…

When he neared ground, he allowed his wings, long and feathered and golden, to unfold from his back and catch in the current, slowing his progress.

He was a soldier for the One True Deity. One of the Elite Seven, created before time itself. With as many millennia as he'd lived, he'd come to learn that each of the Elite Seven had one temptation. One potential downfall. Like Eve with her apple. When they found this…thing, this abomination, they happily destroyed it before it could destroy them.

Lysander had finally found his.

Bianka Skyhawk.

She was the daughter of a Harpy and a phoenix shapeshifter. She was a thief, a liar and a killer who found joy in the vilest of tasks. Worse, the blood of Lucifer—his greatest enemy and the sire of most demon hordes—flowed through her veins. Which meant *Bianka* was his enemy.

He lived to destroy his enemies.

However, he could only act against them when they

broke a heavenly law. For demons, that involved escaping their fiery prison to walk the earth. For Bianka, who had never been condemned to hell, that would have to involve something else. What, he didn't know. All he knew was that he'd never experienced what mortals referred to as "desire."

Until Bianka.

And he didn't like it.

He'd seen her for the first time several weeks ago, long black hair flowing down her back, amber eyes bright and lips bloodred. Watching her, unable to turn away, a single question had drifted through his mind: Was her pearl-like skin as soft as it appeared?

Forget desire. He'd never wondered such a thing about *anyone* before. He'd never cared. But the question was becoming an obsession, discovering the truth a need. And it had to end. Now. This day.

He landed just in front of her, but she couldn't see him. No one could. He existed on another plane, invisible to mortal and immortal alike. He could scream, and she would not hear him. He could walk through her, and she would not feel him. For that matter, she would not smell or sense him in any way.

Until it was too late.

He could have formed a fiery sword from air and cleaved her head from her body, but didn't. As he'd already realized and accepted, he could not kill her. Yet. But he could not allow her to roam unfettered, tempting him, a plague to his good sense, either. Which meant he would have to settle for imprisoning her in his home in the sky.

That didn't have to be a terrible ordeal for him, however. He could use their time together to show her the right way to live. And the right way was, of course, his way. What's more, if she did not conform, if she *did* finally commit that unpardonable sin, he would be there, at last able to rid himself of her influence.

Do it. Take her.

He reached out. But just before he could wrap his arms around her and fly her away, he realized she was no longer alone. He scowled, his arms falling to his sides. He did not want a witness to his deeds.

"Best day ever," Bianka shouted skyward, splaying her arms and twirling. Two champagne bottles were clutched in her hands and those bottles flew from her grip, slamming into the ice-mountains of Alaska surrounding her. She stopped, swayed, laughed. "Oopsie."

His scowl deepened. A perfect opportunity lost, he realized. Clearly, she was intoxicated. She wouldn't have fought him. Would have assumed he was a hallucination or that they were playing a game. Having watched her these past few weeks, he knew how much she liked to play games.

"Waster," her sister, the intruder, grumbled. Though they were twins, Bianka and Kaia looked nothing alike. Kaia had red hair and gray eyes flecked with gold. She was shorter than Bianka, her beauty more delicate. "I had to stalk a collector for days—days!—to steal that. Seriously. You just busted Dom Pérignon White Gold Jeroboam."

"I'll make it up to you." Mist wafted from Bianka's mouth. "They sell Boone's Farm in town."

There was a pause, a sigh. "That's only acceptable if you also steal me some cheese tots. I used to highjack them from Sabin every day, and now that we've left Budapest, I'm in withdrawal."

Lysander tried to pay attention to the conversation, he really did. But being this close to Bianka was, as always, ruining his concentration. Only her skin was similar to her sister's, reflecting all the colors of a newly sprung rainbow. So why didn't he wonder if *Kaia's* skin was as soft as it appeared?

Because she is not your temptation. You know this.

There, atop a peak of Devil's Thumb, he watched as Bianka plopped to her bottom. Frigid mist continued to waft around her, making her look as if she were part of a dream. Or an angel's nightmare.

"But you know," Kaia added, "stealing Boone's Farm in town doesn't help me now. I'm only partially buzzed and was hoping to be totally and completely smashed by the time the sun set."

"You should be thanking me, then. You got smashed last night. And the night before. And the night before that."

Kaia shrugged. "So?"

"So, your life is in a rut. You steal liquor, climb a mountain while drinking and dive off when drunk."

"Well, then yours is in a rut, too, since you've been with me each of those nights." The redhead frowned. "Still. Maybe you're right. Maybe we need a change." She gazed around the majestic summit. "So what new and exciting thing do you want to do now?"

"Complain. Can you believe Gwennie is getting married?" Bianka asked. "And to Sabin, keeper of the demon of Doubt, of all people. Or demons. Whatever."

Gwennie. Gwendolyn. Their youngest sister.

"I know. It's weird." A still-frowning Kaia eased down beside her. "Would you rather be a bridesmaid or be hit by a bus?"

"The bus. No question. That, I'd recover from."

"Agreed."

Bianka did not like weddings? Odd. Most females

craved them. Still. *No need for the bus,* Lysander wanted to tell her. *You will not be attending your sister's wedding.*

"So which of us will be her maid of honor, do you think?" Kaia asked.

"Not it," Bianka said, just as Kaia opened her mouth to say the same.

"Damn it!"

Bianka laughed with genuine amusement. "Your duties shouldn't be too bad. Gwennie's the nicest of the Skyhawks, after all."

"Nice when she's not protecting Sabin, that is." Kaia shuddered. "I swear, threaten the man with a little bodily harm, and she's ready to claw your eyes out."

"Think we'll ever fall in love like that?" As curious as Bianka sounded, there was also a hint of sadness in her voice.

Why sadness? Did she want to fall in love? Or was she thinking of a particular man she yearned for? Lysander had not yet seen her interact with a male she desired.

Kaia waved a deceptively delicate hand through the air. "We've been alive for centuries without falling. Clearly, it's just not meant to be. But I, for one, am glad about that. Men become a liability when you try and make them permanent."

"Yeah," was the reply. "But a fun liability."

"True. And I haven't had fun in a long time," Kaia said with a pout.

"Me, either. Except with myself, but I don't suppose that counts."

"It does the way I do it."

They shared another laugh.

Fun. Sex, Lysander realized, now having no trouble keeping up with their conversation. They were discussing sex. Something he'd never tried. Not even with himself.

He'd never wanted to try, either. Still didn't. Not even with Bianka and her amazing (soft?) skin.

As long as he'd been alive—a span of time far greater than their few hundred years—he'd seen many humans caught up in the act. It looked…messy. As un-fun as something could be. Yet humans betrayed their friends and family to do it. They even willingly, happily gave up hard-earned money in exchange for it. When not taking part themselves, they became obsessed with it, watching others do it on a television or computer screen.

"We should have nailed one of the Lords when we were in Buda," Kaia said thoughtfully. "Paris is hawt."

She could only be referring to the Lords of the Under-world. Immortal warriors possessed by the demons once locked inside Pandora's box. As Lysander had observed them throughout the centuries, ensuring they obeyed heavenly laws—since their demons had escaped hell before those laws were enacted, no one having thought escape possible, they had not been killed but thrust into that box first, and the Lords second—he knew that Paris was host to Promiscuity, forced to bed a new person every day or weaken and die.

"Paris is hot, yes, but I liked Amun." Bianka stretched to her back, mist again whipping around her. "He doesn't speak, which makes him the perfect man in my opinion."

Amun, the host of the demon of Secrets. So. Bianka liked him, did she? Lysander pictured the warrior. Tall, though Lysander was taller. Muscled, though Lysander was more so. Dark where Lysander was light. He was actually relieved to know the Harpy preferred a different type of male than himself.

That wouldn't change her fate, but it did lessen Lysander's burden. He hadn't been sure what he would have done if she'd *asked* him to touch her. That she wouldn't was most definitely a relief.

"What about Aeron?" Kaia asked. "All those tattoos…" A moan slipped from her as she shivered. "I could trace every single one of them with my tongue."

Aeron, host of Wrath. One of only two Lords with wings, Aeron's were black and gossamer. He had tattoos all over his body, and looked every inch the demon he was. What's more, he had recently broken a spiritual covenant. Therefore, Aeron would be dead before the upcoming nuptials.

Lysander's charge, Olivia, had been ordered to slay the warrior. So far she had resisted the decree. The girl was too softhearted for her own good. Eventually, though, she would do her duty. Otherwise, she would be kicked to earth, immortal no longer, and that was not a fate Lysander would allow.

Of all the angels he'd trained, she was by far his favorite. As gentle as she was, a man couldn't help but want to make her happy. She was trustworthy, loyal and all that was pure; she was the type of female who should have tempted him. A female he might have been able to accept in a romantic way. Wild Bianka…no. Never.

"However will I choose between my two favorite Lords, B?" Another sigh returned Lysander's focus to the Harpies.

Bianka rolled her eyes. "Just sample them both. Not like you haven't enjoyed a twofer before."

Kaia laughed, though the amusement didn't quite reach her voice. Like Bianka, there was a twinge of sadness to the sound. "True."

Lysander's mouth curled in mild distaste. Two different partners in one day. Or at the same time. Had Bianka done that, too? Probably.

"What about you?" Kaia asked. "You gonna hook up with Amun at the wedding?"

There was a long, heavy pause. Then Bianka shrugged. "Maybe. Probably."

He should leave and return when she was alone. The more he learned about her, the more he disliked her. Soon he would simply snatch her up, no matter who watched, revealing his presence, his intentions, just to save this world from her dark influence.

He flapped his wings once, twice, lifting into the air.

"You know what I want more than anything else in the world?" she asked, rolling to her side and facing her sister. Facing Lysander directly, as well. Her eyes were wide, amber irises luminous. Beams of sunlight seemed to soak into that glorious skin, and he found himself pausing.

Kaia stretched out beside her. "To co-host *Good Morning America?*"

"Well, yeah, but that's not what I meant."

"Then I'm stumped."

"Well…" Bianka nibbled on her bottom lip. Opened her mouth. Closed her mouth. Scowled. "I'll tell you, but you can't tell anyone."

The redhead pretended to twist a lock over her lips.

"I'm serious, K. Tell anyone, and I'll deny it then hunt you down and chop off your head."

Would she truly? Lysander wondered. Again, probably. He could not imagine hurting his Olivia, whom he loved like a sister. Maybe because she was not one of the Elite Seven, but was a joy-bringer, the weakest of the angels.

There were three angelic factions. The Elite Seven, the warriors and the joy-bringers. Their status was reflected in both their different duties and the color of their wings. Each of the Seven possessed golden wings, like his own. Warriors possessed white wings merely threaded with gold, and the joy-bringers' white wings bore no gold at all.

Olivia had been a joy-bringer all the centuries of her existence. Something she was quite happy with. That was why everyone, including Olivia, had experienced such shock when golden down had begun to grow in her feathers.

Not Lysander, however. He'd petitioned the Angelic Council, and they'd agreed. It had needed to be done. She was too fascinated by the demon-possessed warrior Aeron. Too...infatuated. Ridding her of such an attraction was imperative. As he well knew.

His hand clenched into a fist. He blamed himself for Olivia's circumstances. He had sent her to watch the Lords. To study them. He should have gone himself, but he'd hoped to avoid Bianka.

"Well, don't just lie there. Tell me what you want to do more than anything else in the world," Kaia exclaimed, once again drawing his attention.

Bianka uttered another sigh. "I want to sleep with a man."

Kaia's brow scrunched in confusion. "Uh, hello. Wasn't that what we were just discussing?"

"No, dummy. I mean, I want to sleep. As in, conk out. As in, snore my ass off."

A moment passed in silence as Kaia absorbed the announcement. "What! That's forbidden. Stupid. Dangerous."

Harpies lived by two rules, he knew. They could only eat what they stole or earned, and they could not sleep in the presence of another. The first was because of a curse on all Harpy-kind, and the second because Harpies were suspicious and untrusting by nature.

Lysander's head tilted to the side as he found himself

imagining holding Bianka in his arms as she drifted into slumber. That fall of dark curls would tumble over his arm and chest. Her warmth would seep into his body. Her leg would rub over his.

He could never allow it, of course, but that didn't diminish the power of the vision. To hold her, protect her, comfort her would be…nice.

Would her skin be as soft as it appeared?

His teeth ground together. There was that ridiculous question again. *I do not care. It does not matter.*

"Forget I said anything," Bianka grumbled, once more flopping to her back and staring up at the bright sky.

"I can't. Your words are singed into my ears. Do you know what happened to our ancestors when they were stupid enough to fall asl—"

"Yes, okay. Yes." She pushed to her feet. The faux fur coat she wore was bloodred, same as her lips, and a vivid contrast to the white ice around her. Her boots were black and climbed to her knees. She wore skintight pants, also black. She looked wicked and beautiful.

Would her skin be as soft as it appeared?

Before he realized what he was doing, he was standing in front of her, reaching out, fingers tingling. *What are you doing? Stop!* He froze. Backed several steps away.

Sweet heaven. How close he'd come to giving in to the temptation of her.

He could not wait any longer. Could not wait until she was alone. He had to act now. His reaction to her was growing stronger. Any more, and he *would* touch her. And if he liked touching her, he might want to do more. That was how temptation worked. You gave in to one thing, then yearned for another. And another. Soon, you were lost.

"Enough heavy talk. Let's get back to our boring routine

and jump," Bianka said, stalking to the edge of the peak. "You know the rules. Girl who breaks the least amount of bones wins. If you die, you lose. For, like, ever." She gazed down.

So did Lysander. There were crests and dips along the way, ice bounders with sharp, deadly ridges and thousands of feet of air. Such a jump would have killed a mortal, no question. The Harpy merely joked about the possibility, as if it were of no consequence. Did she think herself invulnerable?

Kaia lumbered to her feet and swayed from the liquor still pouring through her. "Fine, but don't think this is the last of our conversation about sleeping habits and stupid girls who—"

Bianka dove.

Lysander expected the action, but was still surprised by it. He followed her down. She spread her arms, closed her eyes, grinning foolishly. That grin…affected him. Clearly she reveled in the freedom of soaring. Something he often did, as well. But she would not have the end she desired.

Seconds before she slammed into a boulder, Lysander allowed himself to materialize in her plane. He grabbed her, arms catching under hers, wings unfolding, slowing them. Her legs slapped against him, jarring him, but he didn't release his hold.

A gasp escaped her, and her eyelids popped open. When she spotted him, amber eyes clashing with the dark of his, that gasp became a growl.

Most would have asked who he was or demanded he go away. Not Bianka.

"Big mistake, Stranger Danger," she snapped. "One you'll pay for."

As many battles as he'd fought over the years and as many opponents as he'd slain, he didn't have to see to know she had just unsheathed a blade from a hidden slit in her coat. And he didn't have to be a psychic to know she meant to stab him.

"It is you who made the mistake, Harpy. But do not worry. I have every intention of rectifying that." Before she could ensure that her weapon met its intended target, he whisked her into another plane, into his home—where she would stay. Forever.

CHAPTER TWO

BIANKA SKYHAWK GAPED at her new surroundings. One moment she'd been tumbling toward an icy valley, intent on escaping her sister's line of questioning, as well as winning their break-the-least-amount-of-bones game, and the next she'd been in the arms of a gorgeous blond. Which wasn't necessarily a good thing. She'd tried to stab him, and he'd blocked her. Freaking blocked her. No one should be able to block a Harpy's deathblow.

Now she was standing inside a cloud-slash-palace. A palace that was bigger than any home she'd ever seen. A palace that was warm and sweetly scented, with an almost tangible sense of peace wafting through the air.

The walls were wisps of white and smoke, and as she watched, murals formed, seemingly alive, winged creatures, both angelic and demonic, soaring through a morning sky. They reminded her of Danika's paintings. Danika—the All-Seeing Eye who watched both heaven and hell. The floors, though comprised of that same ethereal substance, allowing a view of the land and people below, were somehow solid.

Angelic. Cloud. Heaven? Dread flooded her as she spun to face the male who had grabbed her. "Angelic" described him perfectly. From the top of his pale head to the strength in that leanly muscled, sun-kissed body, to the golden wings stretching from his back. Even the white robe that fell to his ankles and the sandals wrapped around his feet gave him a saintly aura.

Was he an angel, then? Her heart skipped a beat. He wasn't human, that was for sure. No human male could ever hope to compare to such blinding perfection. But damn, those eyes…they were dark and hard and almost, well, empty.

His eyes don't matter. Angels were demon assassins, and she was as close to a demon as a girl could get. After all, her great-grandfather was Lucifer himself. Lucifer, who had spent a year on earth unfettered, pillaging and raping. Only a few females had conceived, but those that had soon gave birth to the first of the Harpies.

Unsure of what to do, Bianka strode around her blond; he remained in place, even when she was at his back, as if he had nothing to fear from her. Maybe he didn't. Obviously he had powers. One, he'd blocked her—she just couldn't get over that fact—and two, he'd somehow removed her coat and all her weapons without touching her.

"Are you an angel?" she asked when she was once again in front of him.

"Yes." No hesitation. As if his heritage wasn't something to be ashamed of.

Poor guy, she thought with a shudder. Clearly he had no idea the crappy hand he'd been dealt. If she had to choose between being an angel and a dog, she'd choose the dog. They, at least, were respectable.

She'd never been this close to an angel before. Seen one, yes. Or rather, seen what she'd thought was an angel but had later learned was a demon in disguise. Either way, she hadn't liked the guy, her youngest sister's father. He considered himself a god and everyone else beneath him.

"Did you bring me here to kill me?" she asked. Not that

he'd have any luck. He would find that she was not an easy target. Many immortals had tried to finish her off over the years, but none had succeeded. Obviously.

He sighed, warm breath trekking over her cheeks. She had accidentally-on-purpose closed some of the distance between them; he smelled of the icecaps she so loved. Fresh and crisp with just a hint of earthy spice.

When she realized that only a whisper separated them, his lips, too full for a man but somehow perfect for him, pressed into a mulish line. Though she didn't see him move, he was suddenly a few more inches away from her. Huh. Interesting. Had he increased the distance on purpose?

Curious, she stepped toward him.

He backed away.

He had. Why? Was he scared of her?

Just to be contrary, as she often was, she stepped toward him again. Again, he stepped away. So. The big, bad angel didn't want to be within striking distance. She almost grinned.

"Well," she prompted. "Did you?"

"No. I did not bring you here to kill you." His voice was rich, sultry, a sin all its own. And yet, there was a layer of absolute truth to it, and she suspected she would have believed anything he said. As if whatever he said was simply fated, meant to be. Unchangeable. "I want you to emulate my life. I want you to learn from me."

"Why?" What would he do if she touched him? The tiny gossamer wings on her own back fluttered at the thought. Her T-shirt was designed especially for her kind, the material loose to keep from pinning those wings as she jolted into super-speed. "Wait. Don't answer. Let's make out first." A lie, but he didn't need to know that.

"Bianka," he said, his patience clearly waning. "This is not a game. Do not make me bind you to my bed."

"Ohh, now that I like. Sounds kinky." She darted around him, running her fingertips over his cheek, his neck. "You're as soft as a baby."

He sucked in a breath, stiffened. "Bianka."

"But better equipped."

"Bianka!"

She patted his butt. "Yes?"

"You will cease that immediately!"

"Make me." She laughed, the amused, carefree sound echoing between them.

Scowling, he reached out and latched on to her upper arm. There wasn't time to evade him; shockingly, he was faster than she was. He jerked her in front of him, and dark, narrowed eyes stared down at her.

"There will be no touching. Do you understand?"

"Do you?" Her gaze flicked to his hand, still clutching her arm. "At the moment, you're the one touching me."

Like hers, his gaze fell to where they were connected. He licked his lips, and his grip tightened just the way she liked. Then he released her as if she were on fire and once again increased the distance between them.

"Do you understand?" His tone was hard and flat.

What was the problem? He should be begging to touch her. She was a desirable Harpy, damn it. Her body was a work of art and her face total perfection. But for his benefit, she said, "Yeah, I understand. That doesn't mean I'll obey." Her skin tingled, craving the return of his. *Bad girl. Bad, bad girl. He's a stupid angel and therefore not an appropriate plaything.*

A moment passed as he absorbed her words. "Are you not frightened of me?" His wings folded into his back, arcing over his shoulders.

"No," she said, raising a brow and doing her best to appear unaffected. "Should I be?"

"Yes."

Well, then, he'd have to somehow grow the fiery claws of her father's people. That was the only thing that scared her. Having been scratched as a child, having felt the acid-burn of fire spread through her entire body, having spent days writhing in agonizing, seemingly endless pain, she would do anything to avoid such an experience again.

"Well, I'm still not. And now you're starting to bore me." She anchored her hands on her hips, glaring up at him. "I asked you a question but you never answered it. Why do you want me to be like you? So much so, that you brought me into heaven, of all places?"

A muscle ticked below one of his eyes. "Because I am good and you are evil."

Another laugh escaped her. He frowned, and her laughter increased until tears were running from her eyes. When she quieted, she said, "Good job. You staved off the boredom."

His frown deepened. "I was not teasing you. I mean to keep you here forever and train you to be sinless."

"Gods, how—oops, sorry. I mean, golly, how adorable are you? 'I mean to keep you here forever and train you,'" she said in her best impersonation of him. There was no reason to fight about her eventual escape. She'd prove him wrong just as soon as she decided to leave. Right now, she was too intrigued. With her surroundings, she assured herself, and not the angel. Heaven was not a place she'd ever thought to visit.

His chin lifted a notch, but his eyes remained expressionless. "I am serious."

"I'm sure you are. But you'll find that you can't keep me anywhere I don't want to be. And me? Without sin? Funny!"

"We shall see."

His confidence might have unnerved her had she been less confident in her own abilities. As a Harpy, she could lift a semi as if it were no more significant than a pebble, could move faster than the human eye could see and had no problem slaying an unwelcome host.

"Be honest," she said. "You saw me and wanted a piece, right?"

For the briefest of moments, horror blanketed his face. "No," he croaked out, then cleared his throat and said more smoothly, "No."

Insulting bastard. Why such horror at the thought of being with her? *She* was the one who should be horrified. He was clearly a do-gooder, more so than she'd realized. *I am good and you are evil,* he'd said. Ugh.

"So tell me again why you want to change me. Didn't anyone ever tell you that you shouldn't mess with perfection?"

That muscle started ticking below his eye again. "You are a menace."

"Whatever, dude." She liked to steal—so what. She could kill without blinking—again, so what. It wasn't like she worked for the IRS or anything. "Where's my sister, Kaia? She's as much a menace as I am, I'm sure. So why don't you want to change her?"

"She is still in Alaska, wondering if you are buried inside an ice cave. And you are my only project at the moment."

Project? Bastard. But she did like the thought of Kaia searching high and low but finding no sign of her, almost like they were playing a game of Hide and Seek. Bianka would totally, finally win.

"You appear…excited," he said, head tilting to the side. "Why? Does her concern not disturb you?"

Yep. A certified do-gooder. "It's not like I'll be here

long." She peeked over his shoulder; more of that wisping white greeted her. "Got anything to drink here?"

"No."

"Eat?"

"No."

"Wear?"

"No."

Slowly the corners of her lips lifted. "I guess that means you like to go naked. Awesome."

His cheeks reddened. "Enough. You are trying to bait me and I do not like it."

"Then you shouldn't have brought me here." Hey, wait a minute. He'd never really told her why he'd chosen her as his *project,* she realized. "Be honest. Do you need my help with something?" After all, she, like many of her fellow Harpies, was a mercenary, paid to find and retrieve. Her motto: if it's unethical and illegal and you've got the cash, I'm your girl! "I mean, I know you didn't just bring me here to save the world from my naughty influence. Otherwise, millions of other people would be here with me."

He crossed his arms over his massive chest.

She sighed. Knowing men as she did, she knew he was done answering that type of question. Oh, well. She could have convinced him otherwise by annoying him until he caved, but she didn't want to put the work in.

"So what do you do for fun around here?" she asked.

"I destroy demons."

Like you, she finished for him. But he'd already said he had no intention of killing her, and she believed him—how could she not? That voice… "So you don't want to hurt me, you don't want to touch me, but you do want me to live here forever."

"Yes."

"I'd be an idiot to refuse such an offer." That she sounded sincere was a miracle. "We'll pretend to be married and spend the nights locked in each other's arms, kissing and touching, our bodies—"

"Stop. Just stop." And, drumroll please, that muscle began ticking under his eye again.

This time, there was no fighting her grin. It spread wide and proud. That tic was a sign of anger, surely. But what would it take to make that anger actually seep into his irises? What would it take to break even a fraction of his iron control?

"Show me around," she said. "If I'm going to live here, I need to know where my walk-in closet is." During the tour, she could accidentally-on-purpose brush against him. Over and over again. "Do we have cable?"

"No. And I cannot give you a tour. I have duties. Important duties."

"Yeah, you do. My pleasure. That should be priority one."

Teeth grinding together, he turned on his heel and strode away. "You will find it difficult to get into trouble here, so I suggest you do not even try." His voice echoed behind him.

Please. She could get into trouble with nothing but a toothpick and a spoon. "If you leave, I'll rearrange everything." Not that there was any furniture to be seen.

Silence.

"I'll get bored and take off."

"Try."

It was a response, at least. "So you're seriously going to leave me? Just like that?" She snapped her fingers.

"Yes." Another response, though he didn't stop walking.

"What about that bed you were going to chain me to? Where is it?"

Uh-oh, back to silence.

"You didn't even tell me your name," she called, irritated despite herself. How could he abandon her like that? He should hunger for more of her. "Well? I deserve to know the name of the man I'll be cursing."

Finally, he stopped. Still, a long while passed in silence and she thought he meant to ignore her. Again. Then he said, "My name is Lysander," and stepped from the cloud, disappearing from view.

CHAPTER THREE

LYSANDER WATCHED AS TWO newly recruited warrior angels—angels under his training and command—finally subdued a demonic minion that had dug its way free from hell. The creature was scaled from head to hoof and little horns protruded from its shoulders and back. Its eyes were bright red, like crystallized blood.

The fight had lasted half an hour, and both angels were now bleeding, panting. Demons were notorious for their biting and scratching.

Lysander should have been able to critique the men and tell them what they had done wrong. That way, they would do a better job next time. But as they'd struggled with the fiend, his mind had drifted to Bianka. What was she doing? Was she resigned to her fate yet? He'd given her several days alone to calm and accept.

"What now?" one of his trainees asked. Beacon was his name.

"You letsss me go, you letsss me go," the demon said pleadingly, its forked tongue giving it a lisp. "I behave. I return. Ssswear."

Lies. As a minion, it was a servant to a demon High Lord—just as there were three factions of angels, there were three factions of demons. High Lords held the most power, followed by Lords, who were followed by the lowest of them all, minions. Despite this one's lack of status, it could cause untold damage among humans. Not only because it was evil, but also because it was a minion of Strife and took its nourishment from the trouble it caused others.

By the time Lysander had sensed its presence on earth, it had already broken up two marriages and convinced one teenager to start smoking and another to kill himself.

"Execute it," Lysander commanded. "It knew the consequences of breaking a heavenly law, yet it chose to escape from hell anyway."

The minion began to struggle again. "You going to lisssten to him when you obviousssly ssstronger and better than him? He make you do all hard work. He do nothing hissself. Lazy, if you asssk me. Kill *him*."

"We do not ask you," Lysander said.

Both angels raised their hands and fiery swords appeared.

"Pleassse," the demon screeched. "No. Don't do thisss."

They didn't hesitate. They struck.

The scaled head rolled, yet the angels did not dematerialize their swords. They kept the tips poised on the motionless body until it caught flame. When nothing but ash remained, they looked to Lysander for instruction.

"Excellent job." He nodded in satisfaction. "You have improved since your last killing, and I am proud of you. But you will train with Raphael until further notice," he said. Raphael was strong, intelligent and one of the best trackers in the heavens.

Raphael would not be distracted by a Harpy he had no hopes of possessing.

Possessing? Lysander's jaw clenched tightly. He was not some vile demon. He possessed nothing. Ever. And when he finished with Bianka, she would be glad of that. There would be no more games, no more racing around him, caressing him and laughing. The clenching in his jaw stopped, but his shoulders sagged. In disappointment? Couldn't be.

Perhaps *he* needed a few days to calm and accept.

HE'D LEFT HER ALONE for a week, the sun rising and setting beyond the clouds. And each day, Bianka grew madder— and madder. And madder. Worse, she grew weaker. Harpies could only eat what they stole (or earned, but there was no way to earn a single morsel here). And no, that wasn't a rule she could overlook. It was a curse. A godly curse her people had endured for centuries. Reviled as Harpies were, the gods had banded together and decreed that no Harpy could enjoy a meal freely given or one they had prepared themselves. If they did, they sickened terribly. The gods' hope? Destruction.

Instead, they'd merely ensured Harpies learned how to steal from birth. To survive, even an angel would sin.

Lysander would learn that firsthand. She would make sure of it. Bastard.

Had he planned this to torture her?

In this palace, Bianka had only to speak of something and it would materialize before her. An apple—bright and red and juicy. Baked turkey—succulent and plump. But she couldn't eat them, and it was killing her. Liter—fucking— ally.

At first, Bianka had tried to escape. Several times. Unlike Lysander the Cruel, she couldn't jump from the clouds. The floor expanded wherever she stepped and remained as hard as marble. All she could do was move from ethereal room to ethereal room, watching the murals play out battle scenes. Once she'd thought she'd even spied Lysander.

Of course, she'd said, "Rock," and a nice-size stone had

appeared in her hand. She'd chucked it at him, but the stupid thing had fallen to earth rather than hit him.

Where was he? What was he doing? Did he mean to kill her like this, despite his earlier denial? Slowly and painfully? At least the hunger pains had finally left her. Now she was merely consumed by a sensation of trembling emptiness.

She wanted to stab him the moment she saw him. Then set him on fire. Then scatter his ashes in a pasture where lots of animals roamed. He deserved to be smothered by several nice steaming piles. Of course, if he waited much longer, *she* would be the one burned and scattered. She couldn't even drink a glass of water.

Besides, fighting him wasn't the way to punish him. That, she'd realized the first day here. He didn't like to be touched. Therefore, touching him was the way to punish him. And touch him she would. Anywhere, everywhere. Until he begged her to stop. No. Until he begged her to continue.

She would make him *like* it, and then take it away.

If she lasted.

Right now, she could barely hold herself up. In fact, why was she even trying?

"Bed," she muttered weakly, and a large four-poster appeared just in front of her. She hadn't slept since she'd gotten here. Usually she crashed in trees, but she wouldn't have had the strength to climb one even if the cloud had been filled with them. She collapsed on the plush mattress, velvet coverlet soft against her skin. Sleep. She'd sleep for a little while.

FINALLY LYSANDER COULD STAND it no more. Nine days. He'd lasted nine days. Nine days of thinking about the female constantly, wondering what she was doing, what she was thinking. If her skin was as soft as it looked.

He could tolerate it no longer. He would check on her, that was all, and see for himself how—and what—she was doing. Then he would leave her again. Until he got himself under control. Until he stopped thinking about her. Stopped wanting to be near her. Her training had to begin sometime.

His wings glided up and down as he soared to his cloud. His heartbeat was a bit…odd. Faster than normal, even bumping against his ribs. Also, his blood was like fire in his veins. He didn't know what was wrong. Angels only sickened when they were infected with demon poison, and as Lysander had not been bitten by a demon—had not even fought one in weeks—he knew that was not the problem.

Blame could probably be laid at Bianka's door, he thought with a scowl.

First thing he noticed upon entering was the food littering the floor. From fruits to meats to bags of chips. All were uneaten, even unopened.

Scowl melting into a frown, he folded his wings into his back and stalked forward. He found Bianka inside one of the rooms, lying atop a bed. She wore the same clothing she'd been clad in when he'd first taken her—red shirt, tights that molded to her perfect curves—but had discarded her boots. Her hair was tangled around her, and her skin worryingly pale. There was no sparkle to it, no pearl-like gleam. Bruises now formed half-moons under her eyes.

Part of him had expected to find her fuming—and out for his head. The other part of him had hoped to find her compliant. Not once had he thought to find her like *this*.

She thrashed, the covers bunched around her. His frown deepened.

"Hamburger," she croaked.

A juicy burger appeared on the floor a few inches from the bed, all the extras—lettuce, tomato slices, pickles and cheese—decorating the edges of the plate. The manifestation didn't surprise him. That was the beauty of these angelic homes. Whatever was desired—within reason, of course—was provided.

All this food, and she hadn't taken a single bite. Why would she request— It wasn't stolen, he realized, and for the first time in his endless existence, he was angry with himself. And scared. For her. He hated the emotion, but there it was. She hadn't eaten in these last nine days because she couldn't. She was truly starving to death.

Though he wanted her out of his head, out of his life, he hadn't wanted her to suffer. Yet suffer she had. Unbearably. Now she was too weak to steal anything. And if he force-fed her, she would vomit, hurting more than she already was. Suddenly he wanted to roar.

"Blade," he said, and within a single blink, a sharp-tipped blade rested in his hand. He stalked to the side of the bed. He was trembling.

"Fries. Chocolate shake." Her voice was soft, barely audible.

Lysander slashed one of his wrists. Blood instantly spilled from the wound, and he stretched out his arm, forcing each drop to fall into her mouth. Blood was not food for Harpies; it was medicine. Therefore her body could accept it. He'd never freely given his blood to another living being and wasn't sure he liked the thought of something of his flowing inside this woman's veins. In fact, the thought actually caused his heartbeat to start slamming against his ribs again. But there was no other way.

At first, she didn't act as if she noticed. Then her tongue

emerged, licking at the liquid before it could reach her lips. Then her eyes opened, amber irises bright, and she grabbed on to his arm, jerking it to her mouth. Her sharp teeth sank into his skin as she sucked.

Another odd sensation, he thought. Having a woman drink from him. There was heat and wetness and a sting, yet it was not unpleasant. It actually lanced a pang of…something unnameable straight to his stomach and between his legs.

"Drink all you need," he told her. His body would not run out. Every drop was replaced the moment it left him.

Her gaze narrowed on him. The more she swallowed, the more fury he saw banked there. Soon her fingers were tightening around his wrist, her nails cutting deep. If she expected some sort of reaction from him, she would not get it. He'd been alive too long and endured far too many injuries to be affected by something so minor. Except for that pang between his legs… *What* was that?

Finally, though, she released him. He wasn't sure if that gladdened him or filled him with disappointment.

Gladdened, of course, he told himself.

A trickle of red flowed from the corner of her mouth, and she licked it away. The sight of that pink tongue caused another lance to shoot through him.

Definitely disap—uh, gladdened.

"You bastard," she growled through her panting. "You sick, torturing bastard."

He moved out of striking distance. Not to protect himself, but to protect her. If she were to attack him, he would have to subdue her. And if he subdued her, he might hurt her. And accidentally brush against her. *Blood… heating…*

"It was never my intent to harm you," he said. And now, even his voice was trembling. Odd.

"And that makes what you did okay?" She jerked to a sitting position, all that dark hair spilling around her shoulders. The pearl-like sheen was slowly returning to her skin. "You left me here, unable to eat. Dying!"

"I know." Was that skin as soft as it looked? He gulped. "And I am sorry." Her anger should have overjoyed him. As he'd hoped, she would no longer laugh up at him, her face lit with the force of her amusement. She would no longer race around him, petting him. Yes, he should have been overjoyed. Instead, the disappointment he'd just denied experiencing raced through him. Disappointment mixed with shame.

She was more a temptation than he had realized.

"You know?" she gasped out. "You know that I can only consume what I steal or earn and yet you failed to make arrangements for me?"

"Yes," he admitted, hating himself for the first time in his existence.

"What's more, you left me here. With no way home."

His nod was stiff. "I have since made restitution by saving your life. But as I said, I am sorry."

"Oh, well, you're sorry," she said, throwing up her arms. "That makes everything better. That makes almost dying acceptable." She didn't wait for his reply. She kicked her legs over the bed and stood. Her skin was at full glow now. "Now you listen up. First, you're going to find a way to feed me. Then, you're going to tell me how to get off this stupid cloud. Otherwise I will make your life a hell you've never experienced before. Actually, I will anyway. That way, you'll never forget what happens when you mess with a Harpy."

He believed her. Already she affected him more than anyone else ever had. That was hell enough. Proof: his mouth was actually watering to taste her, his hands itching to touch her. Rather than reveal these new developments, however, he said, "You are powerless here. How would you hurt me?"

"Powerless?" She laughed. "I don't think so." One step, two, she approached him.

He held his ground. He would not retreat. Not this time. *Assert your authority.* "You cannot leave unless I allow it. The cloud belongs to me and places my will above yours. Therefore, there is no exit for you. You would be wise to curry my favor."

She sucked in a breath, paused. "So you still mean to keep me here forever? Even though I have a wedding to attend?" She sounded surprised.

"When did I ever give you the impression that I meant otherwise? Besides, I heard you tell your sister you didn't want to go to that wedding."

"No, I said I didn't want to be a bridesmaid. But I love my baby sis, so I'll do it. With a smile." Bianka ran her tongue over her straight, white teeth. "But let's talk about you. You like to eavesdrop, huh? That sounds a little demonic for a goody-goody angel."

Over the years he'd been called far worse than demonic. The goody-goody, though… Was that how she saw him? Rather than as the righteous soldier he was? "In war, I do what I must to win."

"Let me get this straight." Her eyes narrowed as she crossed her arms over her middle. Stubbornness radiated from her. "We were at war before I even met you?"

"Correct." A war he would win. But what would he do if he failed to set her on the right path? He would have to destroy her, of course, but for him to legally be allowed to destroy her, he reminded himself, she would first have to commit an unpardonable sin. Though she'd lived a long time, she had never crossed that line. Which meant she would have to be encouraged to do so. But how? Here, away from civilization—both mortal and immortal—she couldn't free a demon from hell. She couldn't slay an angel. Besides him, but that would never happen. He was stronger than she was.

She could blaspheme, he supposed, but he would never—never!—encourage someone to do that, no matter the reason. Not even to save himself.

The only other possibility was for her to convince an angel to fall. As she was *his* temptation, and as he was the only angel of her acquaintance, he was the only one she could convince. And he wouldn't. Again, not for any reason. He loved his life, his Deity, and was proud of his work and all he had accomplished.

Perhaps he would simply leave Bianka here, alone for the rest of eternity. That way, she could live but would be unable to cause trouble. He would visit her every few weeks—perhaps months—but never remain long enough for her to corrupt him.

A sudden blow to the cheek sent his head whipping to the side. He frowned, straightened and rubbed the now-stinging spot. Bianka was exactly as she'd been before, standing in front of him. Only now she was smiling.

"You hit me," he said, his astonishment clear.

"How sweet of you to notice."

"Why did you do that?" To be honest, he should not have been surprised. Harpies were as violent by nature as their inhuman counterparts the demons. Why couldn't she have looked like a demon, though? Why did she have to be so lovely? "I saved you, gave you my blood. I even explained why you could not leave, just as you asked. I did not have to do any of those things."

"Do I really need to repeat your crimes?"

"No." They were not crimes! But perhaps it was best

to change the subject. "Allow me to feed you," he said. He walked to the plate holding the hamburger and picked it up. The scent of spiced meat wafted to his nose, and his mouth curled in distaste.

Though he didn't want to, though his stomach rolled, he took a bite. He wanted to gag, but managed to swallow. Normally he only ate fruits, nuts and vegetables. "This," he said with much disgust, "is mine." Careful not to touch her, he placed the food in her hands. "You are not to eat it."

By staking the verbal claim, the meal did indeed become his. He watched understanding light her eyes.

"Oh, cool." She didn't hesitate to rip into the burger, every crumb gone in seconds. Next he sipped the chocolate shake. The sugar was almost obscene in his mouth, and he did gag. "Mine," he repeated faintly, giving it to her, as well. "But next time, please request a healthier meal."

She flipped him off as she gulped back the ice cream. "More."

He bypassed the French fries. No way was he going to defile his body with one of those greasy abominations. He found an apple, a pear, but had to request a stalk of broccoli himself. After claiming them, he took a bite of each and handed them over. Much better.

Bianka devoured them. Well, except for the broccoli. That, she threw at him. "I'm a carnivore, moron."

She hardly had to remind him when the unpleasant taste of the burger lingered on his tongue. Still, he chose to overlook her mockery. "All of the food produced in this home is mine. Mine and mine alone. You are to leave it alone."

"That'd be great if I were actually staying," she muttered while stuffing the fries in her mouth.

He sighed. She would accept her fate soon enough. She would have to.

The more she ate, the more radiant her skin became. Magnificent, he thought, reaching out before he could stop himself.

She grabbed his fingers and twisted just before contact. "Nope. I don't like you, so you don't get to handle the goods."

He experienced a sharp pain, but merely blinked over at her. "My apologies," he said stiffly. Thank the One True Deity she'd stopped him. No telling what he would have done to her had he actually touched her. Behaved like a slobbering human? He shuddered.

She shrugged and released him. "Now for my second order. Let me go home." As she spoke, she assumed a battle stance. Legs braced apart, hands fisted at her sides.

He mirrored her movements, refusing to admit, even to himself, that her bravery heated his traitorous blood another degree. "You cannot hurt me, Harpy. Fighting me would be pointless."

Slowly her lips curled into a devilish grin. "Who said I was going to try and hurt you?"

Before Lysander could blink, she closed the distance between them and pressed against him, arms winding around his neck and tugging his head down. Their lips met and her tongue thrust into his mouth. Automatically, he stiffened. He had seen humans kiss more times than he could count, but he'd never longed to try the act for himself.

Like sex, it seemed messy—in every way imaginable— and unnecessary. But as her tongue rolled against his, as her hands caressed a path down his spine, his body warmed—far more than it had when he'd simply thought of being here with her—and the tingle he'd noticed earlier bloomed once more. Only this time, that tingle grew and spread. Like the shaft between his legs. Rising…thickening…

He'd wanted to taste her and now he was. She was delicious, like the apple she'd just eaten, only sweeter, headier, like his favorite wine. He should make her stop. This was too much. But the wetness of her mouth wasn't messy in the least. It was electrifying.

More, a little voice said in his head.

"Yes," she rasped, as if he'd spoken aloud.

When she rubbed her lower body against his, every sensation intensified. His hands fisted at his sides. He couldn't touch her. Shouldn't touch her. Should stop this as she'd stopped him, as he'd already tried to convince himself.

A moan escaped her. Her fingers tangled in his hair. His scalp, an area he'd never considered sensitive before, ached, soaking up every bit of attention. And when she rubbed against him again, *he* almost moaned.

Her hands fell to his chest and a fingertip brushed one of his nipples. He did moan; he did grab her. His fingers gripped her hips, holding her still even though he wanted to force her to rub against him some more. The lack of motion didn't slow her kiss. She continued to dance their tongues together, leisurely, as if she could drink from him forever. And wanted to.

He should stop this, he told himself yet again.

Yes. Yes, he would. He tried to push her tongue out of his mouth. The pressure created another sensation, this one new and stronger than any other. His entire body felt aflame. He started pushing at her tongue for an entirely different reason, twining them together, tasting her again, licking her, sucking her.

"Mmm, yeah. That's the way," she praised.

Her voice was a drug, luring him in deeper, making him crave more. More, more, more. The temptation was too much, and he had to—

Temptation.

The word echoed through his mind, a sword sharp enough to cut bone. She was a temptation. She was *his* temptation. And he was allowing her to lead him astray.

He wrenched away from her, and his arms fell to his sides, heavy as boulders. He was panting, sweating, things he had not done even in the midst of battle. Angry as he was—at her, at himself—his gaze drank in the sight of her. Her skin was flushed, glowing more than ever. Her lips were red and swollen. And he had caused that reaction. Sparks of pride took him by surprise.

"You should not have done that," he growled.

Slowly she grinned. "Well, you should have stopped me."

"I wanted to stop you."

"But you didn't," she said, that grin growing.

His teeth ground together. "Do not do it again."

One of her brows arched in smug challenge. "Keep me here against my will, and I'll do that and more. Much, much more. In fact…" She ripped her shirt over her head and tossed it aside, revealing breasts covered by pink lace.

Breathing became impossible.

"Want to touch them?" she asked huskily, cupping them with her hands. "I'll let you. I won't even make you beg."

Holy…Lord. They were lovely. Plump and mouth-watering. Lickable. And if he did lick them, would they taste as her mouth had? Like that heady wine? *Blood… heating…again…*

He didn't care what kind of coward his next action made him. It was either jump from the cloud or replace her hands with his own.

He jumped.

CHAPTER FOUR

LYSANDER LEFT BIANKA alone for another week—
bastard!—but she didn't mind. Not this time. She had
plenty to keep her occupied. Like her plan to drive him
utterly insane with lust. So insane he'd regret bringing her
here. Regret keeping her here. Regret even being alive.

That, or fall so in love with her that he yearned to grant
her every desire. If that was the case—and it was a total
possibility since she was *insanely* hot—she would
convince him to take her home, and then she would finally
get to stab him in the heart.

Perfect. Easy. With her breasts, it was almost too
easy, really.

To set the stage for his downfall, she decorated his
home like a bordello. Red velvet lounges now waited next
to every door—just in case he was too overcome with
desire for her to make it to one of the beds now perched
in every corner. Naked portraits—of her—hung on the
misty walls. A decorating style she'd picked up from her
friend Anya, who just happened to be the goddess of
Anarchy.

As Lysander had promised, Bianka had only to speak
what she wanted—within reason—to receive it. Apparently furniture and pretty pictures were within reason.
She chuckled. She could hardly wait to see him again. To
finally begin.

He wouldn't stand a chance. Not just because of her (magnificent) breasts and hotness—hey, no reason to act as if she didn't know—but because he had no experience. She had been his first kiss; she knew it beyond any doubt. He'd been stiff at first, unsure. Hesitant. At no point had he known what to do with his hands.

That hadn't stopped her from enjoying herself, however. His taste…decadent. Sinful. Like crisp, clean skies mixed with turbulent night storms. And his body, oh, his body. Utter perfection with hard muscles she'd wanted to squeeze. And lick. She wasn't picky.

His hair was so silky she could have run her fingers through it forever. His cock had been so long and thick she could have rubbed herself to orgasm. His skin was so warm and smooth she could have pressed against him and slept, just as she'd dreamed about doing before she'd met him. Even though sleeping with a man was a dangerous crime her race never committed.

Stupid girl! The angel wasn't to be trusted, especially since he clearly had nefarious plans for her—though he still refused to tell her exactly what those plans were. Teaching her to act like him had to be a misdirection of the truth. It was just too silly to contemplate. But his plans didn't matter, she supposed, since he would soon be at her mercy. Not that she had any.

Bianka strode to the closet she'd created and flipped through the lingerie hanging there. Blue, red, black. Lace, leather, satin. Several costumes: naughty nurse, corrupt policewoman, devil, angel. Which should she choose today?

He already thought her evil. Perhaps she should wear the see-through white lace. Like a horny virgin bride. Oh, yes. That was the one. She laughed as she dressed.

"Mirror, please," she said, and a full-length mirror appeared in front of her. The gown fell to her ankles, but there was a slit between her legs. A slit that stopped at the apex of her thighs. Too bad she wasn't wearing any panties.

Spaghetti straps held the material in place on her shoulders and dipped into a deep vee between her breasts. Her nipples, pink and hard, played peek-a-boo with the swooping make-me-a-woman pattern.

She left her hair loose, flowing like black velvet down her back. Her gold eyes sparkled, flecks of gray finally evident, like in Kaia's. Her cheeks were flushed like a rose, her skin devoid of the makeup she usually wore to dull its shimmer.

Bianka traced her fingertips along her collarbone and chuckled again. She'd summoned a shower and washed off every trace of that makeup. If Lysander had found himself attracted to her before—and he had, the size of his hard-on was proof of that—he would be unable to resist her now. She was nothing short of radiant.

A Harpy's skin was like a weapon. A sensual weapon. Its jewel-like sheen drew men in, made them slobbering, drooling fools. Touching it became all they could think about, all they lived for.

That got old after a while, though, which was why she'd begun wearing full body makeup. For Lysander, though, she would make an exception. He deserved what he got. After all, he wasn't just making Bianka suffer. He was making her sisters suffer. Maybe.

Was Kaia still looking for her? Still worried or perhaps thinking this was a game as Bianka had first supposed? Had Kaia called their other sisters and were the girls now searching the world over for a sign of her, as they'd done when Gwennie went missing? Probably not, she thought with a sigh. They knew her, knew her strength and her determination. If they suspected she'd been taken, they would have confidence in her ability to free herself. Still.

Lysander was an ass.

And most likely a virgin. Eager, excited, she rubbed her hands together. Most men kissed the women they bedded. And if she had been his first kiss, well, it stood to reason he'd never bedded anyone. Her eagerness faded a bit. But that begged the question, why hadn't he bedded anyone?

Was he a young immortal? Had he not found anyone he desired? Did angels not often experience sexual need? She didn't know much about them. Fine, she didn't know anything about them. Did they consider sex wrong? Maybe. That would explain why he hadn't wanted to touch her, too.

Okay, so it made more sense that he simply hadn't experienced sexual need before.

He'd definitely experienced it during their kiss, though. She went back to rubbing her hands together.

"*What* are you wearing? Or better yet, not wearing?"

Heart skidding to a stop, Bianka whipped around. As if her thoughts had summoned him, Lysander stood in the room's doorway. Mist enveloped him and for a moment she feared he was nothing more than a fantasy.

"Well?" he demanded.

In her fantasies, he would not be angry. He would be overcome with desire. So…he was here, and he was real. And he was peering at her breasts in open-mouthed astonishment.

Astonishment was better than anger. She almost grinned.

"Don't you like it?" she asked, smoothing her palms over her hips. *Let the games begin.*

"I—I—"

Like it, she finished for him. With the amount of truth that always layered his voice, he probably couldn't utter a single lie.

"Your skin…it's different. I mean, I saw the pearlesque tones before, but now…it's…"

"Amazing." She twirled, her gown dancing at her ankles. "I know."

"You know?" His tongue traced his teeth as the anger she'd first suspected glazed his features. "Cover her," he barked.

A moment later, a white robe draped her from shoulders to feet.

She scowled. "Return my teddy." The robe disappeared, leaving her in the white lace. "Try that again," she told him, "and I'll just walk around naked. You know, like I am in the portraits."

"Portraits?" Brow furrowing, he gazed about the room. When he spotted one of the pictures of her, sans clothing, reclining against a giant silver boulder, he hissed in a breath.

Exactly the reaction she'd been hoping for. "I hope you don't mind, but I turned this quaint little cloud into a love nest so I'd feel more at home. And again, if you remove anything, my redesign will be a thousand times worse."

"What are you trying to do to me?" he growled, facing her. His eyes were narrowed, his lips thinned, his teeth bared.

She fluttered her lashes at him, all innocence. "I'm afraid I don't know what you mean."

"Bianka."

It was a warning, she knew, but she didn't heed it. "I think it's my turn to ask the questions. So where do you go when you leave me?"

"That is not your concern."

Was he panting a little? "Let's see if I can make it my concern, shall we?" She sauntered to the bed and eased onto the edge. Naughty, shameless girl that she was, she spread her legs, giving him the peek of a lifetime. "For every question you answer, I'll put something on," she said in a sing-song voice. "Deal?"

He spun, but not before she saw the shock and desire that played over his harshly gorgeous face. "I do my duty. Watch the gates to hell. Hunt and kill demons that have escaped. Deliver punishment to those in need. Guard humans. Now cover yourself."

"I didn't say what item of clothing I'd don, now did I?" She gave herself a once-over. "One shoe, please. White leather, high heel, open toe. Ties up the calf." The shoe materialized on her foot, and she laughed. "Perfect."

"A trickster," Lysander muttered. "I should have known."

"How did I trick you? Did you ask for specifics? No, because you were secretly hoping I wouldn't cover myself at all."

"That is not true," he said, but for once, she did not hear that layer of honesty in his voice. Interesting. When he lied, or perhaps when he was unsure about what he was saying, his tone was as normal as hers.

That meant she would always know when he lied. Did things get any better than that?

This was going to be even easier than she'd anticipated. "Next question. Do you think about me while you're gone?"

Silence. Thick, heavy.

Wait. She could hear him breathing. In, out, harsh, shallow. He *was* panting.

"I'll take that as a yes," she said, grinning. "But since you really didn't answer, I don't have to add the other shoe."

Again, he didn't reply. Thankfully, he didn't leave, either.

"Onward and upward. Are angels allowed to dally?"

"Yes, but they rarely want to," he rasped.

So she'd been right. He didn't have firsthand knowledge of desire. What he was now feeling had to be confusing him, then. Was that why he'd brought her here? Because he'd seen her and wanted her, but hadn't known how to handle what he was feeling? The thought was almost...flattering. In a stalkerish kind of way, of course. That didn't change her plans, however. She would seduce him—and then she would slice his heart in two. A symbolic gesture, really. An inside joke between them. Well, for herself. He might not get it.

Still, she couldn't deny that she liked the idea of being his first. None of the women after her would compare, of course, and that— Hey, wait. Once he tasted the bliss of the flesh, he would want more. Bianka would have escaped him and stabbed him—and he would have recovered because he was an immortal—by then. He could go to any other female he desired.

He would kiss and touch that female.

"I'm waiting," he snapped.

"For?" she snapped back. Her hands were clenched, her nails cutting her palms. He could be with anyone; it wouldn't bother her. They were enemies. Someone else could deal with his Neanderthal tendencies. But gods, she might just kill the next woman who warmed his bed out of spite. Not jealousy.

"I answered one of your questions. You must add a garment to your body. Panties would be nice."

She sighed. "I'd like the other shoe to appear, please." A moment later, her other foot was covered. "Back to business. Did you return so that I'd kiss you again?"

"No!"

"Too bad. I wanted to taste you again. I wanted to

touch you again. Maybe let you touch me this time. I've been aching since you left me. Had to bring myself to climax twice just to cool the fever. But don't worry, I imagined it was you. I imagined stripping you, licking you, sucking you into my mouth. Mmm, I'm so—"

"Stop!" he croaked out, spinning to face her. "Stop."

His eyes, which she'd once thought were black and emotionless, were now bright as a morning sky, his pupils blown with the intensity of his desire. But rather than stalk to her, grab her and smash his body into hers, he held out his hand, fingers splayed. A fiery sword formed from the air, yellow-gold flames flickering all around it.

"Stop," he commanded again. "I do not want to hurt you, but I will if you persist with this foolishness."

That layer of truth had returned to his voice.

Far from intimidating her, his forcefulness excited her. *I thought you didn't like his Neanderthal tendencies.*

Oh, shut up.

Bianka leaned back, resting her weight against her elbows. "Does Lysandy like to play rough? Should I be wearing black leather? Or is this a game of bad cop, naughty criminal? Should I strip for my body-cavity search?"

He stalked to the edge of the bed, his thick legs encasing her smaller ones, pressing her knees together. He was hard as a rock, his robe jutting forward. Those golden flames still flickering around the sword both highlighted his face and cast shadows, giving him a menacing aura.

Just then, he was both angel and demon. A mix of good and evil. Savior and executioner.

Her wings fluttered frantically, readying for battle— even as her skin tingled for pleasure. She could be across the room before he moved even a fraction of an inch.

Still. She had trouble catching her breath; it was like ice in her lungs. And yet her blood was hot as his sword. This mix of emotions was odd.

"You are worse than I anticipated," he snarled.

If this progressed the way she hoped, he would be very happy about that one day. But she said, "Then let me go. You'll never have to see me again."

"And that will purge you from my mind? That will stop the wondering and the craving? No, it will only make them worse. You will give yourself to others, kiss them the way you kissed me, rub against them the way you rubbed against me, and I will want to kill them when they will have done nothing wrong."

What a confession! And she'd thought her blood hot before... "Then take me," she suggested huskily. She traced her tongue over her lips, slow and measured. His gaze followed. "It'll feel sooo good, I promise."

"And discover if you are as soft and wet as you appear? Spend the rest of eternity in bed with you, a slave to my body? No, that, too, will only make my cravings worse."

Oh, angel. You shouldn't have admitted that. A slave to his body? If that was his fear, he more than craved her. He was falling. Hard. And now that she knew how much he wanted her...he was as good as hers. "If you're going to kill me," she said, swirling a fingertip around her navel, "kill me with pleasure."

He stopped breathing.

She sat up, closing the rest of the distance between them. Still he didn't strike. She flattened her palms on his chest. His nipples were as beaded as hers. He closed his eyes, as if the sight of her, looking up at him through the thick shield of her lashes, was too much to bear.

"I'll let you in on a little secret," she whispered. "I'm softer and wetter than I appear."

Was that a moan?

And if so, had it come from him? Or her? Touching him like this was affecting her, too. All this strength at her fingertips was heady. Knowing this gorgeous warrior wanted her—her, and no other—was even headier. But knowing she was the very first to tempt him, and so strongly, was the ultimate aphrodisiac.

"Bianka." Oh, yes. A moan.

"But if you'd like, we can just lie next to each other." Said the spider to the fly. "We don't have to touch. We don't have to kiss. We'll lie there and think about all the things we dislike about each other and maybe build up an immunity. Maybe we'll stop *wanting* to touch and to kiss."

Never had she told such a blatant lie, and she'd told some big ones over the centuries. Part of her expected him to call her on it. The other part of her expected him to grasp on to the silly suggestion like a lifeline. Use it as an excuse to finally take what he wanted. Because if he did this, simply lay next to her, one temptation would lead to another. He wouldn't be thinking about the things he disliked about her—he would be thinking about the things he could be doing to her body. He would feel her heat, smell her arousal. He'd want—need—more from her. And she'd be right there, ready and willing to give it to him.

She fisted his robe and gently tugged him toward her. "It's worth a try, don't you think? *Anything*'s worth a try to make this madness stop."

When they were nose to nose, his breath trickling over her face, his gaze fastened on her lips, she began to ease backward. He followed, offering no resistance.

"Want to know one of the things I dislike about you?" she asked softly. "You know, to help get us started."

He nodded, as if he were too entranced to speak.

She decided to push a little faster than anticipated. He

already seemed ready for more. "That you're not on top of me." Just a little more persuasion, and that would be remedied. Just a little... "How amazing would it feel to be that close?"

"Lysander," an unfamiliar female voice suddenly called. "Are you here?"

Who the hell? Bianka scowled.

Lysander straightened, jerking away from her as if she had just sprouted horns. He stepped back, disengaging from her completely. But he was trembling, and not from anger.

"Ignore her," she said. "We have important business to attend to."

"Lysander?" the woman called again.

Damn her, whoever she was!

His expression cleared, melted to steel. "Not another word from you," he barked, backing away. "You tried to lure me into bed with you. I don't think you meant to make me dislike you at all. I think you meant to—" A low snarl erupted from his throat. "You are not to try such a thing with me again. If you do, I will finally cleave your head from your body."

Well, this battle was clearly over. Not one to give up, however, she tried a different strategy. "So you're going to leave again? Coward! Well, go ahead. Leave me helpless and bored. But you know what? When I'm bored, bad things happen. And next time you come back here, I just might throw myself at you. My hands will be all over you. You won't be able to pry me off!"

"Lysander," the girl called again.

He ground his teeth. "Return to your *cloud*," he threw over his shoulder. "I will meet you there."

He was going to meet another girl? At her cloud? Alone, private? Oh, hell, no. Bianka hadn't worked him into a frenzy so that someone else could reap the reward.

Before she could inform him of that, however, he said, "Give Bianka whatever she wants." Talking to his own cloud, apparently. "Anything but, escape and more of those…outfits." His gaze intensified on her. "That should stave off the boredom. But I only agree to this on the condition that you vow to keep your hands to yourself."

Anything she wanted? She didn't allow herself to grin, the girl forgotten in the face of this victory. "Done."

"And so it is," he said, then spun and stalked from the room. His wings expanded in a rush, and he disappeared before she could follow. But then, there was no need to follow him. Not now.

He had no idea that he'd just ensured his own downfall. *Whatever she wants*, he'd said. She laughed. She didn't need to touch him or wear lingerie to win their next battle. She just needed his return.

Because then, *he* would become *her* prisoner.

CHAPTER FIVE

HE'D ALMOST GIVEN IN.

Lysander could not believe how quickly he'd almost given in to Bianka. One sultry glance from her, one invitation, and he'd forgotten his purpose. It was shameful. And yet, it was not shame that he felt. It was more of that strange disappointment—disappointment that he'd been interrupted!

Standing before Bianka, breathing in her wicked scent, feeling the heat of her body, all he'd been able to recall was the decadent taste of her. He'd wanted more. Wanted to finally touch her skin. Skin that had glowed with health, reflecting all those rainbow shards. She'd wanted that, too, he was sure of it. The more aroused she'd become, the brighter those colors had glowed.

Unless that was a trick? What did he truly know of women and desire?

She was worse than a demon, he thought. She'd known exactly how to entrance him. Those naked photos had nearly dropped him to his knees. Never had he seen anything so lovely. Her breasts, high and plump. Her stomach, flat. Her navel, perfectly dipped. Her thighs, firm and smooth. Then, being asked to lie beside her and think of what he disliked about her…both had been temptations, and both had been irresistible.

He'd known his resolve was crumbling and had wanted

to rebuild it. And how better to rebuild than to ponder all the things he disliked about the woman? But if he had lain next to her, he would not have thought of what he disliked—things he couldn't seem to recall then or now. He might have even thought about what he *liked* about her.

She was brilliant. She'd had him.

He'd never desired a demon. Had never secretly liked bad behavior. Yet Bianka excited him in a way he could not have predicted. So, what did he like most about her at the moment? That she was willing to do anything, say anything, to tempt him. He liked that she had no inhibitions. He liked that she gazed up at him with longing in those beautiful eyes.

How would she look at him if he actually kissed her again? Kissed more than her mouth? How would she look at him if he actually touched her? Caressed that skin? He suddenly found himself wanting to watch mortals and immortals alike more intently, gauging their reactions to each other. Man and woman, desire to desire.

Just the thought of doing so caused his body to react the way it had done with Bianka. Hardening, tightening. Burning, craving. His eyes widened. That, too, had never happened before. He was letting her win, he realized, even though there was distance between them. He was letting his one temptation destroy him, bit by bit.

Something had to be done about Bianka, since his current plan was clearly failing.

"Lysander?"

His charge's voice drew him from his dark musings. "Yes, sweet?"

Olivia's head tilted to the side, her burnished curls bouncing. They stood inside her cloud, flowers of every kind scattered across the floor, on the walls, even dripping from the ceiling.

Her eyes, as blue as the sky, regarded him intently. "You haven't been listening to me, have you?"

"No," he admitted. Truth had always been his most cherished companion. That would not change now. "My apologies."

"You are forgiven," she said with a grin as sweet as her flowers.

With her, it was that easy. Always. No matter how big or small the crime, Olivia couldn't hold a grudge. Perhaps that was why she was so treasured among their people. Everyone loved her.

What would other angels think of Bianka?

No doubt they would be horrified by her. *He* was horrified.

I thought you were not going to lie? Even to yourself. He scowled. Unlike the forgiving Olivia, he suspected Bianka would hold a grudge for a lifetime—and somehow take that grudge beyond the grave.

For some reason, his scowl faded and his lips twitched at the thought. *Why* would that amuse him? Grudges were born of anger, and anger was an ugly thing. Except, perhaps, on Bianka. Would she erupt with the same amount of unrelenting passion she brought to the bedroom? Probably. Would she want to be kissed from her anger, as well?

The thought of kissing her until she was happy again did *not* delight him.

Usually he dealt with other people's anger the way he dealt with everything else. With total unconcern. It was not his job to make people feel a certain way. They were responsible for their own emotions, just as he was responsible for his. Not that he experienced many. Over the years, he'd simply seen too much to be bothered. Until Bianka.

"Lysander?"

Olivia's voice once more jerked him from his mind. His hands fisted. He'd locked Bianka away, yet she was still managing to change him. Oh, yes. His current plan was failing.

Why couldn't he have desired someone like sweet Olivia? It would have made his endless life much easier. As he'd told Bianka, desire wasn't forbidden, but not many of their kind ever experienced it. Those that did only wanted other angels and often wed their chosen partner. Except in storybooks, he had never heard of an angel pairing with a different race—much less a demon.

"—you go again," Olivia said.

He blinked, hands fisting all the tighter. "Again, I apologize. I will be more diligent the rest of our conversation." He would make sure of it.

She offered him another grin, though this one lacked her usual ease. "I only asked what was bothering you." She folded her wings around herself and plucked at the feathers, carefully avoiding the strands of gold. "You're so unlike yourself."

That made two of them. Something was troubling her; sadness had never layered her voice before, yet now it did. Determined to help her, he summoned two chairs, one for him and one for her, and they sat across from each other. Her robe plumed around her as she released her wings and twined her fingers together in her lap. Leaning forward, he rested his weight on his elbows.

"Let us talk about you first. How goes your mission?" he asked. Only that could be the cause. Olivia found joy in all things. That's why she was so good at her job. Or rather, her former job. Because of him, she was now something she didn't want to be. A warrior angel. But it was for the best, and he did not regret the decision to change her station. Like him, she'd become too fascinated with someone she shouldn't.

Better to end that now, before the fascination ruined her.

She licked her lips and looked away from him. "That's actually what I wanted to speak with you about." A tremor shook her. "I don't think I can do it, Lysander." The words emerged as a tortured whisper. "I don't think I can kill Aeron."

"Why?" he asked, though he knew what she would say. But unlike Bianka, Aeron had broken a heavenly law, so there could be no locking him away and leading him to a righteous path.

If Olivia failed to destroy the demon-possessed male, another angel would be tasked with doing so—and Olivia would be punished for her refusal. She would be cast out of the heavens, her immortality stripped, her wings ripped from her back.

"He hasn't hurt anyone since his blood-curse was removed," she said, and he heard the underlying beseeching.

"He helped one of Lucifer's minions escape hell."

"Her name is Legion. And yes, Aeron did that. But he ensures the little demon stays away from most humans. Those she does interact with, she treats with kindness. Well, her version of kindness."

"That doesn't change the fact that Aeron helped the creature escape."

Olivia's shoulders sagged, though she in no way appeared defeated. Determination gleamed in her eyes. "I know. But he's so…nice."

Lysander barked out a laugh. He just couldn't help himself. "We are speaking of a Lord of the Underworld, yes? The one whose entire body is tattooed with violent, bloody images no less? That is the male you call *nice?*"

"Not all of the etchings are violent," she mumbled, offended for some reason. "Two are butterflies."

For her to have found the butterflies amid the skeletal faces decorating the man's body meant she'd studied him intently. Lysander sighed. "Have you...felt anything for him?" Physically?

"What do you mean?" she asked, but rosy color bloomed on her cheeks.

She had, then. "Never mind." He scrubbed a hand down his suddenly tired face. "Do you like your home, Olivia?"

She blanched at that, as if she knew the direction he was headed. "Of course."

"Do you like your wings? Do you like your lack of pain, no matter the injury sustained? Do you like the robe you wear? A robe that cleans itself and you?"

"Yes," she replied softly. She gazed down at her hands. "You know I do."

"And you know that you will lose all of that and more if you fail to do your duty." The words were harsh, meant for himself as much as for her.

Tears sprang into her eyes. "I just hoped you could convince the council to rescind their order to execute him."

"I will not even try." Honest, he reminded himself. He had to be honest. Which he preferred. Or had. "Rules are put into place for a reason, whether we agree with those reasons or not. I have been around a long time, have seen the world— ours, theirs—plunged into darkness and chaos. And do you know what? That darkness and chaos always sprang from one broken rule. Just one. Because when one is broken, another soon follows. Then another. It becomes a vicious cycle."

A moment passed as she absorbed his words. Then she sighed, nodded. "Very well." Words of acceptance uttered in a tone that was anything but.

"You will do your duty?" What he was really asking: Will you slay Aeron, keeper of Wrath, whether you want to or not? Lysander wasn't asking more of her than he had done himself. He wasn't asking what he *wouldn't* do himself.

Another nod. One of those tears slid down her cheek.

He reached out and captured the glistening drop with the tip of his finger. "Your compassion is admirable, but it will destroy you if you allow it so much power over you."

She waved the prediction away. Perhaps because she did not believe it, or perhaps because she believed it but had no plans to change and therefore didn't want to discuss it anymore. "So who was the woman in your home? The one in the portraits?"

He…blushed? Yes, that was the heat spreading over his cheeks. "My…" How should he explain Bianka? How could he, without lying?

"Lover?" she finished for him.

His cheeks flushed with more of that heat. "No." Maybe. No! "She is my captive." There. Truthful without giving away any details. "And now," he said, standing. If she could end a subject, so could he. "I must return to her before she causes any more trouble." He must deal with her. Once and for all.

OLIVIA REMAINED IN PLACE long after Lysander left. Had that blushing, uncertain, distracted man truly been her mentor? She'd known him for centuries, and he'd always been unflappable. Even in the heat of battle.

The woman was responsible, she was sure. Lysander had never kept one in his cloud before. Did he feel for her what Olivia felt for Aeron?

Aeron.

Just thinking his name sent a shiver down her spine, filling her with a need to see him. And just like that, she was on her feet, her wings outstretched.

"I wish to leave," she said, and the floor softened, turning to mist. Down she fell, wings flapping gracefully. She was careful to avoid eye contact with the other angels flying through the sky as she headed into Budapest. They knew her destination; they even knew what she did there.

Some watched her with pity, some with concern—as Lysander had. Some watched her with antipathy. By avoiding their gazes, she ensured no one would stop her and try and talk sense into her. She ensured she wouldn't have to lie. Something she hated to do. Lies tasted disgustingly bitter.

Long ago, during her training, Lysander had commanded her to tell a lie. She would never forget the vile flood of acid in her mouth the moment she'd obeyed. Never again did she wish to experience such a thing. But to be with Aeron…maybe.

His dark, menacing fortress was perched high on a mountain and finally came into view. Her heart rate increased exponentially. Because she existed on another plane, she was able to drift through the stone walls as if they were not even there. Soon she was standing inside Aeron's bedroom.

He was polishing a gun. His little demon friend, Legion, the one he'd helped escape from hell, was darting and writhing around him, a pink boa twirling with her.

"Dance with me," the creature beseeched.

That was dancing? That kind of heaving was what humans did as they were dying.

"I can't. I've got to patrol the town tonight, searching for Hunters."

Hunters, sworn enemy of the Lords. They hoped to find

Pandora's box and draw the demons out of the immortal warriors, killing each man. The Lords, in turn, hoped to find Pandora's box and destroy it—the same way they hoped to destroy the Hunters.

"Me hate Huntersss," Legion said, "but we needsss practice for Doubtie'sss wedding."

"I won't be dancing at Sabin's wedding, therefore practice isn't necessary."

Legion stilled, frowned. "But we dance at the wedding. Like a couple." Her thin lips curved downward. Was she…pouting? "Pleassse. We ssstill got time to practice. Dark not come for hoursss."

"As soon as I finish cleaning my weapons, I have to run an errand for Paris." Paris, Olivia knew, was keeper of Promiscuity and had to bed a new woman every day or he would weaken and die. But Paris was depressed and not taking proper care of himself, so Aeron, who felt responsible for the warrior, procured females for him. "We'll dance another time, I promise." Aeron didn't glance up from his task. "But we'll do it here, in the privacy of my room."

I want to dance with him, too, Olivia thought. What was it like, pressing your body against someone else's? Someone strong and hot and sinfully beautiful?

"But, Aeron…"

"I'm sorry, sweetheart. I do these things because they're necessary to keep you safe."

Olivia tucked her wings into her back. Aeron needed to take time for himself. He was always on the go, fighting Hunters, traveling the world in search of Pandora's box and aiding his friends. As much as she watched him, she knew he rarely rested and never did anything simply for the joy of it.

She reached out, meaning to ghost a hand through

Aeron's hair. But suddenly the scaled, fanged creature screeched, "No, no, no," clearly sensing Olivia's presence. In a blink, Legion was gone.

Stiffening, Aeron growled low in his throat. "I told you not to return."

Though he couldn't see Olivia, he, too, always seemed to know when she arrived. And he hated her for scaring his friend away. But she couldn't help it. Angels were demon assassins and the minion must sense the menace in her.

"Leave," he commanded.

"No," she replied, but he couldn't hear her.

He returned the clip to his weapon and set it beside his bed. Scowling, he stood. His violet eyes narrowed as he searched the bedroom for any hint of her. Sadly, it was a hint he would never find.

Olivia studied him. His hair was cropped to his scalp, dark little spikes barely visible. He was so tall he dwarfed her, his shoulders so wide they could have enveloped her. With the tattoos decorating his skin, he was the fiercest creature she'd ever beheld. Maybe that was why he drew her so intensely. He was passion and danger, willing to do anything to save the ones he loved.

Most immortals put their own needs above everyone else's. Aeron put everyone else's above his own. That he did so never failed to shock her. And she was supposed to destroy him? She was supposed to end his life?

"I'm told you're an angel," he said.

How had he known what—the demon, she realized. Legion might not be able to see her, either, but as she'd already realized, the little demon knew danger when she encountered it. Plus, whenever Legion left him, she returned to hell. Fiery walls that could no longer confine her but could welcome her any time she wished. Olivia's lack of success had to be a great source of amusement to that region's inhabitants.

"If you are an angel, you should know that won't stop me from cutting you down if you dare try and harm Legion."

Once again, he was thinking of another's welfare rather than his own. He didn't know that Olivia didn't need to bother with Legion. That once Aeron was dead, Legion's bond to him would wither and she would again be chained to hell.

Olivia closed the distance between them, her steps tentative. She stopped only when she was a whisper away. His nostrils flared as if he knew what she'd done, but he didn't move. Wishful thinking on her part, she knew. Unless she fell, he would never see her, never smell her, never hear her.

She reached up and cupped his jaw with her hands. How she wished she could feel him. Unlike Lysander, who was of the Elite, she could not materialize into this plane. Only her weapon would. A weapon she would forge from air, its heavenly flames far hotter than those in hell. A weapon that would remove Aeron's head from his body in a mere blink of time.

"I'm told you're female," he added, his tone hard, harsh. As always. "But that won't stop me from cutting you down, either. Because, and here's something you need to know, when I want something, I don't let anything stand in the way of my getting it."

Olivia shivered, but not for the reasons Aeron probably hoped. Such determination…

I should leave before I aggravate him even more. With a sigh, she spread her wings and leapt, out of the fortress and into the sky.

CHAPTER SIX

"YOU, CLOUD, BELONG TO ME," Bianka said. That was not an attempt to escape, nor another sexy outfit, therefore it was acceptable. "Lysander gave you to me, so as long as I don't touch him, I get what I want. And I want you. I want you to obey me, not him. Therefore, you have to heed my commands rather than his. If I tell you to do something and he tells you not to, you still have to do it. *That's* what I want."

And oh, baby, this was going to be fun.

The more she thought about it, the happier she was that she couldn't touch Lysander again. Really. Seducing—or rather, trying to seduce—him had been a mistake. She'd basically ended up seducing herself. His heat…his scent…his strength… *Give. Me. More.*

Now, all she could think about was getting his weight back on top of her. About how she wanted to teach him where she liked to be touched. Once he'd gotten the hang of kissing, he'd teased and tantalized her mouth with the skill of a master. It would be the same with lovemaking.

She would lick each and every one of his muscles. She would hear him moan over and over again as *he* licked *her.*

How could she want those things from her enemy? How could she forget, even for a moment, how he'd locked her away? Maybe because he was a challenge. A sexy, tempting, frustrating challenge.

Didn't matter, though. She was done playing the role

of sweet, horny prisoner. She still couldn't kill him; she'd be stuck here for eternity. Which meant she'd have to make him want to get rid of her. And now, as master of this cloud, she would have no problem doing so.

She could hardly wait to begin. If he stuck to past behavior, he'd be gone for a week. He'd return to "check on" her. Operation Cry Like A Baby could begin. Tomorrow she'd plan the specifics and set the stage. A few ideas were already percolating. Like tying him to a chair in front of a stripper pole. Like enforcing Naked Tuesdays.

Chuckling, she propped herself against the bed's headboard, yawned and closed her eyes.

"I'd like to hold a bowl of Lysander's grapes," she said, and felt a cool porcelain bowl instantly press atop her stomach. Without opening her eyes, she popped one of the fruits into her mouth, chewed. Gods, she was tired. She hadn't rested properly since she'd gotten here—or even before.

She couldn't. There were no trees to climb, no leaves to hide in. And even if she summoned one, Lysander could easily find her if he returned early—

Wait. No. No, he wouldn't. Not if she summoned hundreds of them. And if he dismissed all the trees, she would fall, which would awaken her. He would not be able to take her unaware.

Chuckling again, Bianka pried her eyelids apart. She polished off the grapes, scooted from the bed and stood. "Replace the furniture with trees. Hundreds of big, thick, green trees."

In the snap of her fingers, the cloud resembled a forest. Ivy twined around stumps and dew dripped from leaves. Flowers of every color bloomed, petals floating from them and dancing to the ground. She gaped at the beauty. Nothing on earth compared.

If only her sisters could see this.

Her sisters. Winning a game or not, she missed them more with every second that passed. Lysander would pay for that, too.

She yawned again. When she attempted to climb the nearest oak, her lingerie snagged on the bark. She straightened, scowled—reminded once again of the way her dark angel had stalked to her, leaned into her, hot breath trekking over her skin.

"I want to wear a camo tank and army fatigues." The moment she was dressed, she scaled to the highest bough, fluttering wings giving her speed and agility, and reclined on a fat branch, peering up into a lovely star-sprinkled sky. "I'd like a bottle of Lysander's wine, please."

Her fingers were clutching a flagon of dry red a second later. She would have preferred a cheap white, but whatever. Hard times called for sacrifices, and she drained the bottle in record time.

Just as she summoned a second, she heard Lysander shout, "Bianka!"

She blinked in confusion. Either she'd been up here longer than she'd thought or she was hallucinating.

Why couldn't she have imagined a Lord of the Underworld? she wondered disgustedly. Oh, oh. How cool would it be if Lysander oil-wrestled a Lord? They'd be wearing loincloths, of course, and smiles. But nothing else.

And she could totally have that! This was her cloud, after all. She and Lysander were now playing by her rules. And, because she was in charge, he couldn't rescind his command that she be obeyed without her permission.

At least, she prayed that was the way this would work.

"Remove the trees," she heard him snap.

She waited, unable to breathe, but the trees remained.

He couldn't! Grinning, she jolted upright and clapped. She'd been right, then. This cloud belonged to her.

"Remove. The. Trees."

Again, they remained.

"Bianka!" he snarled. "Show yourself."

Anticipation flooded her as she jumped down. A quick scan of her surroundings revealed that he wasn't nearby. "Take me to him."

She blinked and found herself standing in front of him. He'd been shoving his way through the foliage and when he spotted her, he stopped. He clutched that sword of fire.

She backed away, remaining out of reach. No touching. She wouldn't forget. "That for me?" she asked, motioning to the weapon with a tilt of her chin. She'd never been so excited in her life and even the sight of that weapon didn't dampen the emotion.

A vein bulged in his temples.

She'd take that for a yes. "Naughty boy." He'd come to kill her, she thought, swaying a little. That was something else to punish him for. "You're back early."

His gaze raked her newest outfit, his pupils dilated and his nostrils flared. His mouth, however, curled in distaste. "And you are drunk."

"How dare you accuse me of such a thing!" She tried for a harsh expression, but ruined it when she laughed. "I'm just tipsy."

"What did you do to my cloud?" He crossed his arms over his chest, the picture of stubborn male. "Why won't the trees disappear?"

"First, you're wrong. This is no longer your cloud. Second, the trees will only leave if I tell them to leave. Which I am. Leave, pretty trees, leave." Another laugh. "Oh my gods. I said leave to a tree. I'm a poet and I didn't know it." Instantly, there was nothing surrounding her and Lysander but glorious white mist. "Third, you're not going anywhere without my permission. Did you hear that, cloud? He stays. Fourth, you're wearing too many clothes. I want you in a loincloth, minus the weapon."

His sword was suddenly gone. His eyes widened as his robe disappeared and a flesh-colored loincloth appeared. Bianka tried not to gape. And she'd thought the forest gorgeous. Wow. Just…wow. His body was a work of art. He possessed more muscles than she'd realized. His biceps were perfectly proportioned. Rope after rope lined his stomach. And his thighs were ridged, his skin sun-kissed.

"This cloud is mine, and I demand the return of my robe." His voice was so low, so harsh, it scraped against her eardrums.

The sweet sound of victory, she thought. He remained exactly as she'd requested. Laughing, she twirled, arms splayed wide. "Isn't this fabulous?"

He stalked toward her, menace in every step.

"No, no, no." She danced out of reach. "We can't have that. I want you in a large tub of oil."

And just like that, he was trapped inside a tub. Clear oil rose to his calves, and he stared down in horror.

"How do you like having your will overlooked?" she taunted.

His gaze lifted, met hers, narrowed. "I will not fight you in this."

"Silly man. Of course you won't. You'll fight…" She tapped her chin with a fingernail. "Let's see, let's see. Amun? No. He won't speak and I'd like to hear some cursing. Strider? As keeper of Defeat, he'd ensure you lost to prevent himself from feeling pain, but that would be an intense battle and I'm just wanting something to amuse me. You know, something light and sexy. I mean, since I can't touch you, I want a Lord to do it for me."

Lysander popped his jaw. "Do not do this, Bianka. You will not like the consequences."

"Now that's just sad," she said. "I've been here two weeks, but you don't know me at all. Of course I'll like the consequences." Torin, keeper of Disease? Watching him fight Torin would be fun, 'cause then he'd catch that black plague. Or would he? Could angels get sick? She sighed. "Paris will have to do, I guess. He's handsy, so that works in my favor."

"Don't you dare—"

"Cloud, place Paris, keeper of Promiscuity, into the tub with Lysander."

When Paris appeared a moment later, she clapped. Paris was tall and just as muscled as Lysander. Only he had black hair streaked with brown and gold, his eyes were electric blue and his face perfect enough to make her weep from its beauty. Too bad he didn't stir her body the way Lysander did. Making out with him in front of the angel would have been fun.

"Bianka?" Paris looked from her to the angel, the angel to her. "Where am I? Is this some ambrosia-induced hallucination? What the hell is going on?"

"For one thing, you're overdressed. You should only be wearing a loincloth like Lysander."

His T-shirt and jeans were instantly replaced with said loincloth.

Best. Day. Ever. "Paris, I'd like you to meet Lysander, the angel who abducted me and has been holding me prisoner up here in heaven."

Instantly Paris morphed from confusion to fury. "Return my weapons and I'll kill him for you."

"You are such a sweetie," she said, flattening a hand over her heart. "Why is it we haven't slept together yet?"

Lysander snarled low in his throat.

"What?" she asked him, all innocence. "He wants to save me. You want to subjugate me for the rest of my long life. But anyway, let me finish the introductions. Lysander, I'd like you to meet—"

"I know who he is. Promiscuity." Disgust layered Lysander's voice. "He must bed a new woman every day or he weakens."

Another grin lifted the corners of her lips, this one smug. "Actually, he can bed men, too. His demon's not picky. I do hope you'll keep that in mind while you guys are rubbing up against each other."

Lysander took a menacing step toward her.

"What's going on?" Paris demanded again, glowering now. Bianka knew he was picky even if his demon wasn't.

"Oh, didn't I tell you? Lysander gave me control of his home, so now I get whatever I want and I want you guys to wrestle. And when you're done, you'll find Kaia and tell her what's happened, that I'm trapped with a stubborn angel and can't leave. Well, I can't leave until he gets so sick of me he allows the cloud to release me."

"Or until I kill you," he snapped.

She laughed. "Or until Paris kills *you*. But I hope you guys will play nice for a little while, at least. Do you have any idea how sexy you both are right now? And if you want to kiss or something while rolling around, don't let me stop you."

"Uh, Bianka," Paris began, beginning to look uncomfortable. "Kaia's in Budapest. She's helping Gwen with the wedding, and thinks you're hiding to get out of your maid of honor duties."

"I am not maid of honor, damn it!" But at least Kaia wasn't worried. *The bitch,* she thought with affection.

"That's not what she says. Anyway, I don't mind fighting another dude to amuse you, but seriously, he's an angel. I need to return to—"

"No need to thank me." She held out her hands. "A bowl of Lysander's popcorn, please." The bowl appeared, the scent of butter wafting to her nose. "Now then. Let's get this party started. Ding, ding," she said, and settled down to watch the battle.

CHAPTER SEVEN

LYSANDER COULD NOT BELIEVE what he was being forced to do. He was angry, horrified and, yes, contrite. Hadn't he done something similar to Bianka? Granted, he hadn't stripped her down. Hadn't pitted her against another female.

There was the tightening in his groin again.

What was wrong with him?

"I will set you free," he told Bianka. And sweet Holy Deity, she looked beautiful. More tempting than when she'd worn that little bit of nothing. Now she wore a green and black tank that bared her golden arms. Were those arms as soft as they appeared? *Don't think like that.* Her shirt stopped just above her navel, making his mouth water, his tongue yearn to dip inside. *What did I just say? Don't think like that.* Her pants were the same dark shades and hung low on her hips.

He'd come here to fight her, to finally force her hand, and judging by that outfit, she'd been ready for combat. That…excited him. Not because their bodies would have been in close proximity—really—and not because he could have finally gotten his hands on her—again, really—but because, if she injured him, he would have the right to end her life. Finally.

But he'd come here and she'd taught him a quick yet unforgettable lesson instead. He'd been wrong to whisk her to his home and hold her captive. Temptation or not. She might be his enemy in ways she didn't understand, but he never should have put his will above hers. He should have allowed her to live her life as she saw fit.

That's why he existed in the first place. To protect free will.

When this wrestling match ended, he would free her as he'd promised. He would watch her, though. Closely. And when she made a mistake, he would strike her down. And she would. Make a mistake, that is. As a Harpy, she wouldn't be able to help herself. He wished it hadn't come to that. He wished she could have been happy here with him, learning his ways.

The thought of losing her did not sadden him. He would not miss her. She'd placed him in a vat of oil to wrestle with another man, for Lord's sake.

There was suddenly a bitter taste in his mouth.

"Bianka," he prompted. "Have you no response?"

"Yes, you will set me free," she finally said with a radiant grin. She twirled a strand of that dark-as-night hair around her finger. "After. Now, I do believe I rang the starting bell."

Her words were slightly slurred from the wine she'd consumed. A drunken menace, that's what she was. And he would not miss her, he told himself again.

The bitterness intensified.

A hard weight slammed into him and sent him propelling to his back. His wings caught on the sides of the pool as oil washed over him from head to toe, weighing him down. He grunted, and some of the stuff—cherry-flavored—seeped into his mouth.

"Don't forget to use tongue if you kiss," Bianka called helpfully.

"You don't lock women away," Paris growled down at

him, a flash of scales suddenly visible under his skin. Eyes red and bright. Demon eyes. "No matter how irritating they are."

"Your friends did something similar to their women, did they not? Besides, the girl isn't your concern." Lysander shoved, sending the warrior hurtling to *his* back. He attempted to use his wings to lift himself, but their movements were slow and sluggish so all he could do was stand.

Oil dripped down his face, momentarily shielding his vision. Paris shot to his feet, as well, hands fisted, body glistening.

"So. Much. Fun," Bianka sang happily.

"Enough," Lysander told her. "This is unnecessary. You have made your point. I'm willing to set you free."

"You're right," she said. "It's unnecessary to fight without music!" Once again she tapped her chin with a nail, expression thoughtful. "I know! We need some Lady Gaga in this crib."

A song Lysander had never heard before was playing through the cloud a second later. Like a siren rising from the sea, Bianka began swaying her hips seductively.

Lysander's jaw clenched so painfully the bones would probably snap out of place at any moment. Clearly there would be no reasoning with Bianka. That meant he had to reason with Paris. But who would ever have thought he'd have to bargain with a demon?

"Paris," he began—just as a fist connected with his face.

His head whipped back. His feet slipped on the slick floor and he tumbled to his side. More of the cherry flavor filled his mouth.

Paris straddled his shoulders, punched him again. Lysander's lip split. Before a single drop of blood could form, however, the wound healed.

He frowned. He now had the right to slay the man, but he couldn't bring himself to do it. He did not blame Paris for this battle; he blamed Bianka. She had forced them into this situation.

Another punch. "Are you the one who's been watching Aeron?" Paris demanded.

"Hey, now," Bianka called. No longer did she sound so carefree. "Paris, you are not to use your fists. That's boxing, not wrestling."

Lysander remained silent, not understanding the difference. A fight was a fight.

Another punch. "Are you?" Paris growled.

"Paris! Did you hear me?" Now she sounded angry. "Use your fists like that again and I'll cut off your head."

She'd do it, too, Lysander thought, and wondered why she was so upset. Could she, perhaps, care for his health? His eyes widened. Was *that* why she preferred the less intensive wrestling to the more violent boxing? Would she want to do the same to him if he were to punch the Lord? And what would it mean if she did?

How would he feel about that?

"Are you?" Paris repeated.

"No," he finally said. "I'm not." He worked his legs up, planted his feet on Paris's chest and pressed. But rather than send the warrior flying, his foot slipped and connected with Paris's jaw, then ear, knocking the man's head back.

"Use your hands, angel," Bianka suggested. "Choke him! He deserves it for breaking my rules."

"Bianka," Paris snapped. He lost his footing and tumbled to his butt. "I thought you wanted me to destroy him, not the other way around."

She blinked over at them, brow furrowed. "I do. I just don't want you to hurt him. That's my job."

Paris tangled a hand through his soaked hair. "Sorry, darling, but if this continues, I'm going to unleash a world of hurt on your frienemy. Nothing you say will be able to stop me. Clearly, he doesn't have your best interests at heart."

Darling? Had the demon-possessed immortal just called Bianka *darling?* Something dark and dangerous flooded Lysander—*mine* echoed through his head—and before he realized what he was doing, he was on top of the warrior, a sword of fire in his hand, raised, descending…about to meet flesh.

A firm hand around his wrist stopped him. Warm, smooth skin. His wild gaze whipped to the side. There was Bianka, inside the tub, oil glistening off her. How fast she'd moved.

"You can't kill him," she said determinedly.

"Because you want him, too," he snarled. A statement, not a question. Rage, so much rage. He didn't know where it was coming from or how to stop the flow.

She blinked again, as if the thought had never entered her mind, and that, miraculously, cooled his temper. "No. Because then you would be like me and therefore perfect," she said. "That wouldn't be fair to the world."

"Stop talking and fight, damn you," Paris commanded. A fist connected with Lysander's jaw, tossing him to the side and out of Bianka's reach. He maintained his grip on the sword and even when it dipped into the oil, it didn't lose a single flame. In fact, the oil heated.

Great. Now he was hot-tubbing, as the humans would say.

"What'd you do that for, you big dummy?" Bianka didn't wait for Paris's reply but launched herself at him. Rather than scratch him or pull his hair, she punched him. Over and over again. "He wasn't going to hurt you."

Paris took the beating without retaliating.

That saved his life.

Lysander grabbed the Harpy around the waist and hefted her into the hard line of his body. Soaked as they both were, he had a difficult time maintaining his grip. She was panting, arms flailing for the demon-possessed warrior, but she didn't try to pull away.

"I'll teach you to defy me, you rotten piece of shit," she growled.

Paris rolled his eyes.

"Send him away," Lysander commanded.

"Not until after I—"

He splayed his fingers, spanning much of her waist. He both rejoiced and cursed that he couldn't feel the texture of Bianka's skin through the oil. "I want to be alone with you."

"You—what?"

"Alone. With you."

With no hesitation, she said, "Go home, Paris. Your work here is done. Thanks for trying to rescue me. That's the only reason you're still alive. Oh, and don't forget to tell my sisters I'm fine."

The sputtering Lord disappeared.

Lysander released her, and she spun around to face him. She was now grinning.

"So you want to be alone with me, do you?"

He ran his tongue over his teeth. "Was that fun for you?"

"Yes."

And she wasn't ashamed to admit it, he realized. Captivating baggage. "Return the cloud to me and I will take you home."

"Wait. What?" Her grin slowly faded. "I thought you wanted to be alone with me."

"I do. So that we can conclude our business."

Disappointment, regret, anger and relief played over her features. One step, two, she closed the distance between them. "Well, I'm not giving you the cloud. That would be stupid."

"You have my word that once you return it to me, I will take you home. I know you hear the truth in my claim."

"Oh." Her shoulders sagged a little. "So we really would be rid of each other. That's great, then."

Did she still not believe him? Or… No, surely not. "Do you want to stay here?"

"Of course not!" She sucked her bottom lip into her mouth, and her eyes closed for a moment, an expression of pleasure consuming her features. "Mmm, cherries."

Blood…heating…

Her lashes lifted and her gaze locked on him. Determination replaced all the other emotions, yet her voice dipped sexily. "But I know something that tastes even better."

So did he. Her. A tremor slid the length of his spine. "Do not do this, Bianka. You will fail." He hoped.

"One kiss," she beseeched, "and the cloud is yours."

His eyes narrowed. Hot, so hot. "You cannot be trusted to keep your word."

"That's true. But I want out of this hellhole, so I'll keep it this time. Promise."

Hold your ground. But that was hard to do while his heart was pounding like a hammer against a nail. "If you wanted out, you would not insist on being kissed."

Her gaze narrowed, as well. "It's not like I'm asking for something you haven't already given me."

"Why do you want it?" He regretted the question immediately. He was prolonging the conversation rather than putting an end to it.

Her chin lifted. "It's a goodbye kiss, moron, but never mind. The cloud is yours. I'll go home and kiss Paris hello. That'll be more fun, anyway."

There would be no kissing Paris! Lysander had his tongue sliding into her mouth before he could convince himself otherwise. His arms even wound around her waist, pulling her closer to him—so close their chests rubbed each time they breathed. Her nipples were hard, deliciously abrading.

"Out of the oil," she murmured. "Clean."

He was still in the loincloth, but his skin was suddenly free of the oil, his feet on soft yet firm mist. The cloud might belong to him once more, but she could still make reasonable demands.

Bianka tilted her head and took his possession deeper. Their tongues dueled and rolled and their teeth scraped. Her hands were all over him, no part of him forbidden to her.

Goodbye, she had said.

This was it, then. His last chance to touch her skin. To finally know. Yes, he planned to see her again, to watch her from afar, to wait for his chance to rid himself of her permanently, but never again would he allow himself to get this close to her. And he had to know.

So he did it.

He glided his hands forward, tracing from her lower back to her stomach. There, he flattened his palms, and her muscles quivered. Dear Deity of Light and Love. She was softer than he'd realized. Softer than anything else he'd ever touched.

He moaned. *Have to touch more.* Up he lifted, remaining under her shirt. Warm, smooth, as he'd already known. Still soft, so sweetly soft. Her breasts overflowed, and his mouth watered for a taste of them. Soon, he told himself.

Then shook his head. This was it; the last time they would be together. Goodbye, pretty breasts. He kneaded them.

More soft perfection.

Trembling now, he reached her collarbone. Her shoulders. She shivered. Still so wonderfully soft. More, more, more, he had to have more. Had to touch all of her.

"Lysander," she gasped out. She dropped to her knees, working at the loincloth before he realized what she was doing.

His shaft sprang free, and his hands settled atop her shoulders to push her away. But once he touched that soft skin, he was once again lost to the sensation. Perfection, this was perfection.

"Going to kiss you now. A different kind of kiss." Warm, wet heat settled over the hard length of him. Another moan escaped him. Up, down that wicked mouth rode him. The pleasure…it was too much, not enough, everything and nothing. In that moment, it was necessary to his survival. His every breath hinged on what she would do next. There would be no pushing her away.

She twirled her tongue over the plump head; her fingers played with his testicles. Soon he was arching his hips, thrusting deep into her mouth. He couldn't stop moaning, groaning, the gasping breaths leaving him in a constant stream.

"Bianka," he growled. "Bianka."

"That's the way, baby. Give Bianka everything."

"Yes, yes." Everything. He would give her everything.

The sensation was building, his skin tightening, his muscles locking down on his bones. And then something exploded inside him. Something hot and wanton. His entire body jerked. Seed jetted from him, and she swallowed every drop.

Finally she pulled away from him, but his body

wouldn't stop shaking. His knees were weak, his limbs nearly uncontrollable. That was pleasure, he realized, dazed. That was passion. That was what human men were willing to die to possess. That was what turned normally sane men into slaves. *Like I am now.* He was Bianka's slave.

Fool! *You knew this would happen.* Fight. It was only as she stood and smiled at him tenderly—and he wanted to tug her into his arms and hold on forever—that a measure of sanity stole back into his mind. Yes. Fight. How could he have allowed her to do that?

How could he still want her?

How could he want to do that to her in return?

How could he ever let her go?

"Bianka," he said. He needed a moment to catch his breath. No. He needed to think about what had happened and how they should proceed. No. He tangled a hand in his hair. What should he do?

"Don't say anything." Her smile disappeared as if it had never been. "The cloud is yours." Her voice trembled with…fear? Couldn't be. She hadn't showed a moment of fear since he'd first abducted her. But she even backed away from him. "Now take me home. Please."

He opened his mouth to reply. What he would say, he didn't know. He only knew he did not like seeing her like that.

"Take me home," she croaked.

He'd never gone back on his word, and he wouldn't start now. He nodded stiffly, grabbed her hand, and flew her back to the ice mountain in Alaska, exactly as he'd found her. Red coat, tall boots. Sensual in a way he hadn't understood then.

He maintained his grip on her until the last possible second—until she slipped away from him, taking her warmth and the sweet softness of her skin with her.

"I don't want to see you again." Mist wafted around her as she turned her back on him. "Okay?"

She...what? After what had happened between them, *she* was dismissing *him?* No, a voice roared inside his head. "Behave, and you will not," he gritted out. A lie? The bitter taste in his mouth had returned.

"Good." Without meeting his gaze, she twisted and blew him a kiss as if she hadn't a care in the world. "I'd say you were an excellent host, but then, you don't want me to lie, do you?" With that, she strolled away from him, dark hair blowing in the wind.

CHAPTER EIGHT

FIRST THING BIANKA DID after bathing, dressing, eating a bag of stolen chips she had hidden in her kitchen, painting her nails, listening to her iPod for half an hour and taking a nap in her secret basement was call Kaia. Not that she had dreaded the call and wanted to put it off or anything. All of those other activities had been necessary. Really.

Plus, it wasn't like her sister was worried about her anymore. Paris would already have told her what was going on. But Bianka didn't want to discuss Lysander. Didn't even want to think about him and the havoc he was causing her emotions—and her body and her thoughts and her common sense.

After making out with him a little, she'd wanted to freaking stay with him, curl up in his arms, make love and sleep. And that was unacceptable.

The moment her sister answered, she said, "No need to throw me a Welcome Home party. I'm not sticking around for long." *Do not ask me about the angel. Do not ask me about the angel.*

"Bianka?" her twin asked groggily.

"You were expecting someone else to call in the middle of the night?" It was 6:00 a.m. here in Alaska. Having traveled between the two places multiple times since Gwen had gotten involved with Sabin, she knew that meant it was 3:00 a.m. there in Budapest.

"Yeah," Kaia said. "I was."

Seriously? "Who?"

"Lots of people. Gwennie, who has become the ultimate bridezilla. Sabin, who is doing his best to soothe the beast but whines to me like I care." She rambled on as if Bianka had never been abducted and she'd never been worried. Sure, she'd thought Bianka was merely shirking her duties, but was a little worry too much to ask for? "Anya, who has decided she deserves a wedding, too. Only bigger and better than Gwen's. William, who wants to sleep with me and doesn't know how to take no for an answer. He's not possessed by a demon so he's not my type. Shall I go on?"

"Yes."

"Shut up."

She imagined Kaia high in a treetop, clutching her cell to her ear, grinning and trying not to fall. "So really, you were *sleeping?* While I was missing, my life in terrible danger? Some loving sister you are."

"Please. You were on vacay, and we both know it. So don't give me a hard time. I had an…exciting day."

"Doing who?" she asked dryly. Only two weeks had passed since she'd last seen Kaia, but suddenly a wave of homesickness—or rather, sistersickness—flooded her. She loved this woman more than she loved herself. And that was a lot!

Kaia chuckled. "I wish it was because of a *who.* I'm waiting for two of the Lords to fight over me. Then I'll comfort them both. So far, no luck."

"Idiots."

"I know! But I mentioned Gwen has become the bride from hell, right? They're afraid I'll act just like her, so no one's willing to take a real chance on me."

"Bride from hell, how?"

"Her dress didn't fit right. Her napkins weren't the right color. No one has the flowers she wants. Whaa, whaa, whaa."

That didn't sound like the usually calm Gwen. "Distract her. Tell her the Hunters captured me and performed a handbotomy on me like they did on Gideon." Gideon, keeper of Lies. A sexy warrior who dyed his hair as blue as his eyes and had a wicked sense of humor.

The thought of seducing him didn't delight her as it once might have. Stupid angel. *Do not think about him.*

"She wouldn't care if you were chopped up into little pieces. You're too much like me and apparently we take nothing seriously so we deserve what we get," Kaia said. "She's driving me freaking insane! And to top off my mountain-o-crap, I was totally losing our game of Hide and Seek. So anyway, why'd you decide to rescue yourself? I'm telling you, you have a better chance of survival in the clouds than here with Gwen."

"Survival schmival. It wasn't fun anymore." A lie. Things had just started to heat up the way she'd wanted. But how could she have known that would scare her so badly?

"Good going, by the way. Allowing yourself to be taken into the clouds where I couldn't get to you. Brilliant."

"I know, *right?*"

"So was it terrible? Being spirited away by a sexy angel?"

She twirled a strand of hair around her finger and pictured Lysander's glorious face. The desire he'd leveled at her while she'd sucked him dry had been miraculous. *You don't want to talk about him, remember?* "Yes. It was terrible." Terribly wonderful.

"You bringing him to Buda for the wedding?"

The words were sneered, clearly a joke, but Bianka found herself shouting, "No!" before she could stop herself. A Harpy dating an angel? Unacceptable!

And anyway, allowing the demon-possessed Lords of the Underworld to surround a warrior straight from heaven would be stupid. Not that she feared for Lysander. Guy could handle himself, no problem. The way he formed a sword of fire from nothing but air was proof of that. But if something were to happen to Gwennie's precious Sabin, like, oh, decapitation, the festivities would be somewhat dimmed.

"I'll be there, though," she added in a calmer tone. "I kinda have to, you know. Since I'm the maid of honor and all."

"Oh, hell, no. I am, remember?"

She grinned slowly. "You told me you'd rather be hit by a bus than be a bridesmaid."

"Yeah, but I want to have a bigger part than you, so…here I am, in Budapest, helping little Gwennie plan the ceremony. Not that she's taking my suggestions. Would it kill her to at least *consider* making everyone come naked?"

They shared a laugh.

"Well, you and I can attend naked," Bianka said. "It'll certainly liven things up."

"Done!"

There was a pause.

Kaia pushed out a breath. "So you're fine?" she asked, a twinge of concern finally appearing in her voice.

"Yeah." And she was. Or would be. Soon, she hoped. All she had to do was figure out what to do about Lysander. Not that he'd tried to stick around, the jerk. He hadn't been able to get away from her fast enough. Sure, she'd pushed him away. But dude could have fought for her attention after what she'd done for him.

"You're gonna make the angel pay for taking you without permission, right? Who am I kidding? Of course you are. If you wait till after the wedding, I can help. Please, please let me help. I have a few ideas and I think you'll like them. Picture this. It's midnight, your angel is strapped to your bed, and we each rip off one of his wings."

Nice. But because she didn't know whether Lysander was watching and listening or not—was he? It was possible, and just the thought had her skin heating—she said, "Don't worry about it. I'm done with him."

"Wait, what?" Kaia gasped out. "You can't be done with him. He abducted you. Held you prisoner. Yeah, he oil-wrestled Paris and I'm pissed I didn't get to see, but that doesn't excuse his behavior. If you let him off without punishment, he'll think it's okay. He'll think you're weak. He'll come after you again."

Yes. Yes, he would, she thought, suddenly trying not to grin. "No, he won't," she lied. *Are you listening, Lysander, baby?*

"Bianka, tell me you don't like him. Tell me you aren't lusting for an angel."

Abruptly her smile faded. This was exactly the line of questioning she'd hoped to avoid. "I'm not lusting for an angel." Another lie.

Another pause. "I don't believe you."

"Too bad."

"Mom thought Gwen's dad was an angel and she regretted sleeping with him all these years. They're too good. Too…different from us. Angels and Harpies are not meant to mix. Tell me you know that."

"Of course I know it. Now, I've gotta go. Tell the bride-zilla to go easy on you. Love you and see you soon," she replied and hung up before Kaia could say anything else.

Despite her fear of what Lysander made her feel, Bianka wasn't done with him. Not even close. But she'd been on his turf before and therefore at a disadvantage. If he wasn't here, she needed to get him here. Willingly.

She'd told him to leave her alone, she thought, and that could be a problem. Except…

With a whoop, she jumped up and spun around. That wouldn't be a problem at all. That was actually a blessing and she was smarter than she'd realized. By telling him to stay away from her, she'd surely become the forbidden fruit. Of course he was here, watching her.

Men never could do what they were told. Not even angels.

So. Easy.

Even better, she'd given him a little taste of what it was like to be with her. He would crave more. But also, she hadn't allowed him to pleasure her. His pride would not allow her to remain in this unsatisfied state for long, while he had enjoyed such sweet completion.

And if that wasn't the case, he wasn't the virile warrior she thought he was and he therefore wouldn't deserve her.

How long till he made an actual appearance? They'd only been apart half a day, but she already missed him.

Missed him. Ugh. She'd never missed a man before. Especially one who wanted to change her. One who despised what she was. One who could only be labeled *enemy*.

You have to avoid him. You want to sleep in his arms. You were protective of him while he fought Paris. He angered you but you didn't kill him. And now you're missing him? You know what this means, don't you?

Her eyes widened, and her excitement drained. Oh, gods. She should have realized…should at least have suspected. Especially when she'd protected him, defended him.

Lysander, a goody-goody angel, was her consort.

Her knees gave out and she flopped onto the floor. As long as she'd been alive, she'd never thought to find one. Because, well, a consort was a meant-to-be husband. Some nights she'd dreamed of finding hers, yes, but she hadn't thought it would actually happen.

Her consort. Wow.

Her family was going to flip. Not because Lysander had abducted her—they'd come to respect that—but because of what he was. More than that, she didn't trust Lysander, would never trust him, and so could never do any actual sleeping with him.

Sex, though, she could allow. Often. Yes, yes, she could make this work, she thought, brightening. She could lure him to the dark side without letting her family know she was spending time with him. Humiliation averted!

Decided, she nodded. Lysander would be hers. In secret. And there was no better time to begin. If he was watching as she suspected, there was only one way to get him to reveal himself.

She dressed in a lacy red halter and her favorite skinny jeans and drove into town. Only reason she owned a car was because it made her appear more human. Flying kind of gave her away. Though her arms and navel were exposed, the frigid wind didn't bother her. Chilled her, yes, but that she could deal with. She wanted Lysander to see as much of her as possible.

She parked in front of The Moose Lodge, a local diner, and strode to the front door. Because it was so early and so cold, no one was nearby. A few streetlamps illuminated her, but she wasn't worried. She unlocked the door—she'd stolen the key from the owner months ago—and disabled the alarm.

Inside, she claimed a pecan pie from the glassed refrigerator, grabbed a fork and dug in while walking to her favorite booth. She'd done this a thousand times before.

Come out, come out, wherever you are. He wouldn't have just left her to her evil ways without thinking to protect the world from her. Right? She wished she could feel him, at least sense him in some way. His scent perhaps, that wild, night sky scent. But as she breathed deeply, she smelled only pecans and sugar. Still. She hadn't sensed him when he'd snatched her from mid-free fall, so it stood to reason she wouldn't sense him now.

Once the pie was polished off, the pan discarded and her fork licked clean, she filled a cup with Dr. Pepper. She placed a few quarters in the old jukebox and soon an erratic beat was echoing from the walls. Bianka danced around one of the tables, thrusting her hips forward and back, arching, sliding around, hands roving over her entire body.

For a moment, only a brief, sultry moment, she thought she felt hot hands replace her own, exploring her breasts, her stomach. Thought she felt soft feathered wings envelop her, closing her in. She stilled, heart drumming in her chest. So badly she wanted to say his name, but she didn't want to scare him away. So…what should she do? How should she—

The feeling of being surrounded evaporated completely.

Damn him!

Teeth grinding, not knowing what else to do, she exited the diner the same way she'd entered. Through the front door, as if she hadn't a care. That door slammed behind her, the force of it nearly shaking the walls.

"You should lock up after yourself."

He was here; he'd been watching. She'd known it! Trying not to grin, she spun around to face Lysander. The sight of him stole her breath. He was as beautiful as she remembered. His pale hair whipped in the wind, little snow crystals flying around him. His golden wings were extended and glowing. But his dark eyes were not blank, as when she'd first met him. They were as turbulent as an ocean—just as they'd been when she'd left him.

"I thought I told you to stay away from me," she said, doing her best to sound angry rather than aroused.

He frowned. "And I told you to behave. Yet here you are, full of stolen pie."

"What do you want me to do? Return it?"

"Don't be crass. I want you to pay for it."

"Moment I do, I'll start to vomit." She crossed her arms over her middle. *Close the distance. Kiss me.* "That would ruin my lipstick, so I have to decline."

He, too, crossed his arms over his middle. "You can also earn your food."

"Yeah, but where's the fun in that?"

A moment passed in silence. Then, "Do you have no morals?" he gritted out.

"No." *No sexual boundaries, either. So freaking kiss me already!* "I don't."

He popped his jaw in frustration and disappeared.

Bianka's arms dropped to her sides and she gazed around in astonishment. He'd left? Left? Without touching her? Without kissing her? Bastard! She stomped to her car.

LYSANDER WATCHED AS Bianka drove away. He was hard as a rock, had been that way since she'd paraded around her cabin naked, had lingered in a bubble bath and then changed into that wicked shirt. His shaft was desperate for her.

Why couldn't she be an angel? Why couldn't she abhor sin? Why did she have to embrace it?

And why was the fact that she did these things—steal, curse, lie—still exciting him?

Because that was the way of things, he supposed, and had been since the beginning of time. Temptation seeped past your defenses, changed you, made you long for things you shouldn't.

There had to be a way to end this madness. He couldn't destroy her, he'd already proven that. But what if he could change *her?* He hadn't truly tried before, so it *could* work. And if she embraced his way of life, they could be together. He could have her. Have more of her kisses, touch more of her body.

Yes, he thought. Yes. He would help her become a woman he could be proud to walk beside. A woman he could happily claim as his own. A woman who would not be his downfall.

CHAPTER NINE

AS LYSANDER HAD NEVER had a…girlfriend, as the humans would say, he had no idea how to train one. He knew only how to train his soldiers. Without emotion, maintaining distance and taking nothing personally. His soldiers, however, *wanted* to learn. They were eager, his every word welcomed. Bianka would resist him at every turn. That much he knew.

So. The first day, he followed her, simply observing. Planning.

She, of course, stole every meal, even snacks, drank too much at a bar, danced too closely with a man she obviously did not know, then broke that man's nose when he cupped her bottom. Lysander wanted to do damage of his own, but restrained himself. Barely. At bedtime, Bianka merely paced the confines of her cabin, cursing his name. Not for a minute did she rest.

How lovely she was, dark hair streaming down her back. Red lips pursed. Skin glowing like a rainbow in the moonlight. So badly he wanted to touch her, to surround her with his wings, making them the only two people alive, and simply enjoy her.

Soon, he promised himself.

She'd given him release, yet he had not done the same for her. The more he thought about that—and think about it he did, all the time—the more that did not sit well with him. The more he thought about it, in fact, the more embarrassed he was.

He didn't know how to touch her to bring her release, but he was willing to try, to learn. First, though, he had to train her as planned. How, though? he wondered again. She seemed to respond well to his kisses—his chest puffed up with pride at that. He'd never rewarded his soldiers for a job well done, but perhaps he could do so for Bianka. Reward her with a kiss every time she pleased him.

A failproof plan. He hoped.

The second day, he was practically humming with anticipation. When she entered a clothing store and stuffed a beaded scarf into her purse, he materialized in front of her, ready to begin.

She stilled, gaze lifting and meeting his. Rather than bow her head in contrition, she grinned. "Fancy meeting you here."

"Put that back," he told her. "You do not need to steal clothing to survive."

She crossed her arms over her middle, a stubborn stance he knew well. "Yeah, but it's fun."

A human woman who stood off to the side eyed Bianka strangely. "Uh, can I help you?"

Bianka never looked away from him. "Nope. I'm fine."

"She cannot see me," Lysander told her. "Only you can."

"So I look insane for talking with you?"

He nodded.

She laughed, surprising him. And even though her amusement was misplaced, he loved the sound of her laughter. It was magical, like the strum of a harp. He loved the way her mirth softened her expression and lit her magnificent skin.

Have to touch her, he thought, suddenly dazed. He took a step closer, intending to do just that. *Have to experience that softness again.* And in doing so, she could begin to know the delights of his rewards.

She gulped. "Wh-what are you—"

"Are you sure I can't help you?" the woman asked, cutting her off.

Bianka remained in place, trembling, but tossed her a glare. "I'm sure. Now shut it before I sew your lips together."

The woman backed away, spun and raced to help someone else.

Lysander froze.

"You may continue," Bianka said to him.

How could he reward her for such rudeness? That would defeat the purpose of her training. "Do you not care what people think of you?" he asked, head tilting to the side.

Her eyes narrowed, and she stopped trembling. "No. Why should I? In a few years, these people will be dead but I'll still be alive and kicking." As she spoke, she stuffed another scarf in her purse.

Now she was simply taunting him. "Put it back, and I'll give you a kiss," he gritted out.

"Wh-what?"

Stuttering again. He was affecting her. "You heard me." He would not repeat the words. Having said them, all he wanted to do was mesh their lips together, thrust his tongue into her mouth and taste her. Hear her moan. Feel her clutch at him.

"You would willingly kiss me?" she rasped.

Willingly. Desperately. He nodded.

She licked her lips, leaving a sheen of moisture behind. The sight of that pink tongue sent blood rushing into his shaft. His hands clenched at his sides. Anything to keep from grabbing her and jerking her against him.

"I—I—" She shook her head, as if clearing her thoughts. Her eyes narrowed again, those long, dark lashes fusing together. "Why would you do that? You, who have tried to resist me at every turn?"

"Because."

"Why?"

"Just put the scarves back." *So the kissing can begin.*

She arched a brow. "Are you trying to bribe me? Because you should know, that won't work with me."

Rather than answer—and lie—he remained silent, chin jutting in the air. Blood...heating.

Still watching him, she reached out, palmed a belt and stuffed it in her purse, as well. "So what do you plan to do to me if I keep stealing? Give me a severe tongue-lashing? Too bad. I *don't* accept."

Fire slid the length of his spine even as his anger spiked. He closed the distance until the warmth of her breath was fanning over his neck and chest. "You could not get enough of me in the heavens, yet now that you are here, you want nothing to do with me. Tell me. Was your every word and action up there a lie?"

"Of course my every word and action was a lie. That's what I do. I thought you knew that."

So...did she desire him or not? Two days ago she'd told her sister, Kaia, that she wanted nothing to do with him. At the time, he'd thought she was merely saying that for Kaia's benefit. Now, he wasn't so sure.

"You could be lying now," he said. At least, that's what he hoped. And who would have thought he'd ever wish for a lie?

Excitement sparked in her eyes and spread to the rest of her features. She patted his cheek, then flattened her palm on his chest. "You're learning, angel."

He sucked in a breath. So hot. So soft.

"Here's a proposition for you. Steal something from this store and *I'll* kiss *you.*"

Wait. Her words from a moment ago drifted through his head. *You're learning, angel. He* was learning? "No," he croaked out. He would not do such a thing. Not even for her. "These people need the money their goods provide. Do you care nothing for their welfare?"

A flash of guilt joined the excitement. "No," she said.

Another lie? Probably. That guilt…it gave him hope. "Why do you need to steal like this, anyway?"

"Foreplay," she said with a shrug.

Blood…heating…again.

"Ma'am, I need you to come with me."

At the unexpected intrusion, they both stiffened. Bianka's gaze pulled from his; together they eyed the policeman now standing beside her.

She frowned. "Can't you see that I'm in the middle of a conversation?"

"Doesn't matter if you're talking to God Himself." The grim-faced officer latched on to her wrist. "I need you to come with me."

"I don't think so. Lysander," she said, clearly expecting him to do something.

Instinct demanded he save her. He wanted her safe and happy, but this would be good for her. "I told you to put the items back."

Her jaw dropped as the officer led her away. And, if Lysander wasn't mistaken, there was pride in her gaze.

ARRESTED FOR SHOPLIFTING, Bianka thought with disgust. Again. Her third time that year. Lysander had watched the policeman usher her in back, empty her purse and cuff her. All without a word. His disapproval had said plenty, though.

She hadn't let it upset her. He'd stood his ground, and she admired that. Was turned on by it. This wouldn't be an easy victory, as she'd assumed. Besides, for the first time in their relationship, he'd offered to kiss her. *Willingly* kiss her.

But only if she replaced her stolen goods, she reminded herself darkly. Didn't take a genius to figure out that he wanted to change her. To condition her to his way of life.

It was exactly what she wanted to do to him. Which meant he wanted her as desperately as she wanted him.

It also meant it was time to take this game to the next level. She, however, would not be the one to cave. The six hours she'd spent behind bars had given her time to think. To form a strategy.

She was whistling as she meandered down the station steps. Lysander had finally posted her bail, but he hadn't hung around to speak with her. Well, he hadn't needed to. She knew he was following her.

At home, she showered, lingering under the hot spray, soaping herself more slowly than necessary and caressing her breasts and playing between her legs. Unfortunately, he never appeared. But no matter.

Just in case her shower hadn't gotten him in the mood, she read a few passages from her favorite romance novel. And just in case *that* hadn't gotten him in the mood, she decorated her navel with her favorite dangling diamond, dressed in a skintight tank and skirt and knee-high boots, and drove to the closest strip club.

"I only have a few days left. Then I'm traveling to Budapest for Gwen's wedding and you are not invited. Do you hear me? Try and come and I'll make your life hell. So, if you want a go at me, now's the time," she said as she got out of the car.

Again, he didn't appear.

She almost screeched in frustration. So far, her strategy sucked. What was he doing?

The night was cold yet the inside of the club was hot and stuffy, the seats packed with men. Onstage, a redhead—clearly not a natural redhead—swung around a pole. The lights were dimmed, and smoke clung to the air.

"You gonna dance, darling?" someone asked Bianka.

"Nope. Got better things to do." She did, however, steal the stranger's wallet, sneak a beer from the bar and settle into a table in the back corner. Alone. "Enjoy," she whispered to Lysander, toasting him with the bottle.

"Have you no shame?" he suddenly growled from behind her.

Finally! Every muscle in her body relaxed, even as her blood heated with awareness. But she didn't turn to face him. He would have seen the triumph in her eyes. "You have enough shame for both of us."

He snorted. "That does not seem to be the case."

"Really? Well, then, let's loosen you up. Do you want a lap dance?" She held up the cash she'd taken. "I'm sure the redhead onstage would love to rub against you."

His big hands settled on her shoulders, squeezing.

"Or maybe you'd like a beer?"

"I would indeed," the stranger she'd stolen from said, now in front of her table. He reached into his back pocket. Frowned. "Hey, my wallet's gone." His gaze settled on the small brown leather case resting on her tabletop. His frown deepened. "That looks like mine."

"How odd," she said innocently. "So do you want me to buy you a beer or not?"

Lysander's grip tightened. "Give him back his wallet and I'll kiss you."

Her breath caught in her throat. Gods, she wanted his

kiss. More than she'd ever wanted anything. His lips were soft, his taste decadent. And if she allowed him to kiss her, well, she knew she could convince him to do other things.

But she said, "Steal his watch and I'll kiss you."

"What are you talking about?" the guy asked, brow furrowed. "Steal whose watch?"

She rolled her eyes, wishing she could shoo him away.

Lysander leaned down and cupped her breasts. A tremor moved through her, her nipples beading, reaching for him. Sweet heaven. Her stomach quivered, jealous of her breasts, wanting the touch lower.

"Give him back the wallet."

Suddenly she wanted to do just that. Anything for more of Lysander and this sultry side of him. She didn't need the money, anyway. Wait. *What are you doing? Caving?* She straightened her spine. "No, I—"

"I'll kiss you all over your body," Lysander added.

Oh… Hell. He'd decided to take their game to the next level, as well.

Damn, damn, damn. She couldn't lose. If she did, he would control her with sex. He would expect her to be good like him. All the damn time. There would be no more stealing, no more cursing, no more *fun*. Well, except when they were in bed—but would he expect her to be good there, too?

Life would become boring and sinless, everything a Harpy was taught to fight against.

She stood to shaky legs and turned, finally facing him. His hands fell away from her. She tried not to moan in disappointment. His expression was blank.

She blanked hers, as well, reached out and cupped *him*. Though he showed no emotion, he couldn't hide his hardness. "Steal something, anything at all, and I'll kiss *you* all over." Her voice dipped huskily. "Remember last time? You came in my mouth, and I loved every moment of it."

His nostrils flared.

"Yes!" the guy behind her exclaimed. "Give me five minutes and I'll have stolen something."

"You aren't trainable, are you?" Lysander asked stiffly.

"No," she said, but suddenly she didn't feel like smiling. There'd been resignation in his tone. Had she pushed him too far again? Was he going to leave her? Never return? "That doesn't mean you should stop trying, though."

"Wait. Trying what?" the stranger asked, confused.

Gods, when would he leave?

"Lysander," she prompted.

"That's not my name."

"Get lost," she growled.

Lysander's gaze lifted, narrowed on the human. Then Bianka heard footsteps. Her angel hadn't said anything, hadn't revealed himself, but had somehow managed to make the human leave. He had powers she hadn't known about, then. Why was that even more exciting?

"If you won't give the wallet back and I won't steal anything, where does that leave us?" he asked.

"At war. I don't know about you, but I do my best fighting in bed," she said, and then threw her arms around his neck.

CHAPTER TEN

WIND WHIPPED THROUGH Bianka's hair, and she knew that Lysander was flying her somewhere with those majestic wings. She had her eyes closed, too busy enjoying him— finally!—to care where he took her. His tongue made love to hers. His hands clutched her hips, fingers digging sharply. Then she was tipping over, a cool, soft mattress pressing into her back. His weight pinned her deliciously.

And it shouldn't have been delicious. This was not a position she allowed. Ever. It caged her wings, and her wings were the source of her strength. Without them, she was almost as weak as a human. But this was Lysander, honest to a fault, and she'd wanted him forever, it seemed. And as wary as he'd been about this sort of thing, she was afraid any type of rebuke would send him flying away.

Besides, he could do anything he wanted to her like this…

"No one is to enter," he said roughly.

Moaning, she wound her legs around his waist, tilted her head to receive his newest kiss and enjoyed a deeper thrust of his tongue. White lightning, the man was a fast learner. Very fast. He was now an expert at kissing. The best she'd ever had. By the time she finished with him, he'd be an expert at *everything* carnal.

His cock, hard and long and thick, rode the apex of her thighs. She could feel every inch of him through the softness of his robe. His arms enveloped her, and when she opened her eyes—they were inside his cloud, she realized—she saw his golden wings were spread, forming a blanket over them.

She tangled her hands in his hair and pulled from the kiss. "Are you going to get into trouble for this?" she asked, panting. Wait. What? Where had that thought come from?

His eyes narrowed. "Do you care?"

"No," she lied, forcing a grin. No, no, no. That wasn't a lie. "But that adds a little extra danger, don't you think?" There. Better. That was more like her normal self. She didn't like his goodness, didn't want to preserve it and keep him safe.

Did she?

"Well, I will not get into trouble." He flattened his palms at her temples, boxing her in and taking the bulk of his own weight. "If that is the only reason you are here, you can leave."

How fierce he appeared. "So sensitive, angel." She hooked her fingers at the neck of his robe and tugged. The material ripped easily. But as she held it, it began to weave itself back together. Frowning, she ripped again, harder this time, until there was a big enough gap to shove the clothing from his shoulders and off his arms. "I was only teasing."

His chest was magnificent. A work of art. Muscled and sun-kissed and devoid of any hair. She lifted her head and licked the pulse at the base of his neck, then traced his collarbone, then circled one of his nipples. "Do you like?"

"Hot. Wet," he rasped, lids squeezed tight.

"Yeah, but do you like?"

"Yes."

She sucked a peak until he gasped, then kissed away the sting. A tremor of pleasure rocked him, which caused a lance of pride to work through her. "Why do you desire me, angel? Why do you care if I'm good or not?"

A pause. A tortured, "Your skin…"

Every muscle in her body stiffened, and she glared up at him. "So any Harpy will do?" She tried to hide her insult, but didn't quite manage it. The thought of another Harpy—hell, any other woman, immortal or not—enjoying him roused her most vicious instincts. Her nails lengthened, and her teeth sharpened. A red haze dotted her line of vision. *Mine,* she thought. She would kill anyone who touched him. "We all have this skin, you know?" The words were guttural, scraping her throat.

His lashes separated as his eyes opened. His pupils were dilated, his expression tightening with…an emotion she didn't recognize. "Yes, but only yours tempts me. Why is that?"

"Oh," was all she could first think to say, her anger draining completely. But she needed to respond, had to think of something light, easy. "To answer your question, you want me because I'm made of awesome. And guess what? I will make you so happy you said that, warrior."

Warrior, rather than angel. She'd never called him that before. Why? And why now?

"No. I will make *you* happy." He ripped her shirt just as she had done his robe. She wasn't wearing a bra, and her breasts sprang free. Another tremor moved through him as he lowered his head.

He licked and sucked one nipple, as she had done to him, then the other, feasting. Savoring. Soon she was arching and writhing against him, craving his mouth elsewhere. Her skin was sensitized, her body desperate for release. Yet she didn't want to rush him. She was still afraid of scaring him away. But damn him, if he didn't hurry, didn't touch her between her legs, she was going to die.

"Lysander," she said on a trembling breath.

His wings brushed both her arms, up and down, tickling, caressing, raising goosebumps on her flesh. Holy hell, that was good. So damn good.

He lifted from her completely.

"Wh-what are you doing? I wasn't going to tell you to leave," she screeched, bracing her weight on her elbows.

"I do not want anything between us." He shoved the robe down his legs until he was gloriously naked. Moisture gleamed at the head of his cock, and her mouth watered. Reaching out, he gripped her boots and tore them off. Her jeans quickly followed. She, of course, was not wearing any panties.

His gaze drank her in, and she knew what he saw. Her flushed, glowing skin. The aching juncture between her legs. Her rose-tinted nipples.

"I want to touch and taste every inch," he said and just kind of fell on her, as if his will to resist had abandoned him completely.

"Touch and taste every inch next time." Please let there be a next time. She tried to hook her legs around his waist again. "I need release *now*."

He grabbed her by the knees and spread her. Her head fell back, her hair tangling around her, and he kissed a path to her breasts, then to her stomach. He lingered at her navel until she was moaning.

"Lysander," she said again. Fine. She'd jump on this grenade if she had to; if he wanted to taste, he could taste. "More. I need more."

Rather than give it to her, he stilled. "I…took care of myself before following you this day," he admitted, cheeks pinkening. "I thought that would give me resistance against you."

Her eyes widened, shock pouring through her. "You pleasured yourself?"

A stiff nod.

"Did you think of me?"

Another nod.

"Oh, baby. That's good. I can picture it, and I love what I see." His hand on his cock, stroking up and down, eyes closed, features tight with arousal, body straining toward release. Wings spread as he fell to his knees, the pleasure too much. Her, naked in his mind. "What did you think about doing?"

Another pause. A hesitant response. "Licking. Between your legs. Tasting you, as I said."

She arched her back, hands skimming down her middle to her thighs. Although he already held her open, she pushed her legs farther apart. "Then do it. Lick me. I want it so bad. Want your tongue on me. See how wet I am?"

He hissed in a breath. "Yes. Yes." Leaning down, he started at her ankles and kissed his way up, lingering at the back of her knees, at the crease of her legs.

"Please," she said, so on edge she was ready to scream. "Please. Do it."

"Yes," he whispered again. "Yes." Finally he settled over her, mouth poised, ready. His tongue flicked out. Then, sweet contact.

She expected the touch, but nothing could have prepared her for the perfection of it. She did scream, shivered. Begged for more. "Yes, yes, yes. Please, please, please."

At first, he merely lapped at her, humming his approval at her taste. Thank the gods. Or God. Or whoever was responsible for this man. If he hadn't liked her in that way, she wasn't sure what she would have done. In that moment, she wanted—needed—to be everything *he* wanted—needed. She wanted him to crave every part of her, as she craved every part of him.

Even his goodness?

Yes, she thought, finally admitting it. Yes. Just then, she had no defenses; she'd been stripped to her soul. His goodness somehow balanced her out. She'd fought against it—and still had no plans to change—but they were two extremes and actually complemented each other, each giving the other what he or she lacked. In her case, the knowledge that some things were worth taking seriously. In his, that it wasn't a crime to have fun.

"Bianka," he moaned. "Tell me how…what…"

"More. Don't stop."

Soon his tongue was darting in and out of her, mimicking the act of sex. She grasped at the sheets, fisting them. She writhed, meeting his every thrust. She screamed again, moaned and begged some more.

Finally, she splintered apart. Bit down on her bottom lip until she tasted blood. White lights danced over her eyes—from her skin, she realized. Her skin was so bright it was almost blinding, glowing like a lamp, something that had never happened before.

Then Lysander was looming above her. "You are not fertile," he rasped. Sweat beaded him.

That gave her fuzzy mind pause. "I know." Her words were as labored as his. Harpies were only fertile once a year and this wasn't her time. "But how do you know that?"

"Sense it. Always know that kind of thing. So…are you ready?" he asked, and she could hear the uncertainty in his voice.

He must not know proper etiquette, the darling virgin.

He would learn. With her, there was no etiquette. Doing what felt good was the only thing that drove her.

"Not yet." She flattened her hands on his shoulders and pushed him to his back, careful of his wings. He didn't protest or fight her as she straddled his waist and gripped his cock by the base. Her wings fluttered in joy at their freedom. "Better?"

He licked his lips, nodded. *His* wings lifted, enveloped her, caressing her. Her head fell, the long length of her hair tickling his thighs. He trembled.

Would he regret this? she suddenly wondered. She didn't want him to hate her for supposedly ruining him.

"Are *you* ready?" she asked. "There's no taking it back once it's done." If he wasn't ready, well, she would...wait, she realized. Yes, she would wait until he *was* ready. Only he would do. No other. Her body only wanted him.

"Do not stop," he commanded, mimicking her.

A grin bloomed. "I'll be careful with you," she assured him. "I won't hurt you."

His fingers circled her hips and lifted her until she was poised at his tip. "The only thing that could hurt me is if you leave me like this."

"No chance of that," she said, and sank all the way to the hilt.

He arched up to meet her, feeding her his length, his eyes squeezing shut, his teeth nearly chewing their way through his bottom lip. He stretched her perfectly, hit her in just the right spot, and she found herself desperate for release once more. But she paused, his enjoyment more important than her own. For whatever reason.

"Tell me when you're ready for me to—"

"Move!" he shouted, hips thrusting so high he raised her knees from the mattress.

Groaning at the pleasure, she moved, up and down, slipping and sliding over his erection. He was wild beneath her, as if he'd kept his passion bottled up all these years and it had suddenly exploded from him, unstoppable.

Soon, even that wasn't enough for him. He began hammering inside her, and she loved it. Loved his intensity. All she could do was hold on for the ride, slamming down on him, gasping. Her nails dug into his chest, her moans blended with his. And when her second orgasm hit, Lysander was right there with her, roaring, muscles stiffening.

He grabbed her by the neck and jerked her down, meshing their lips together. Their teeth scraped as he primitively, savagely kissed her. It was a kiss that stripped her once more to her soul, left her raw, agonized. Reeling.

He was indeed her consort, she thought, dazed. There was no denying it now. He was it for her. Her one and only. Necessary. Angel or not. She laughed, and was surprised by how carefree it sounded. Tamed by great sex. It figured. After this, no other man would do. Ever. She knew it, sensed it.

She collapsed atop him, panting, sweating. Scared. Suddenly vulnerable. How did he feel about her? He didn't approve of her, yet he had gifted her with his virginity. Surely that meant he liked her, just as she was. Surely that meant he wanted her around.

His heart thundered in his chest, and she grinned. Surely.

"Bianka," he said shakily.

She yawned, more replete than she'd ever been. *My consort.* Her eyelids closed, her lashes suddenly too heavy to hold up. Fatigue washed through her, so intense she couldn't fight it.

"Talk…later," she replied, and drifted into the most peaceful sleep of her life.

CHAPTER ELEVEN

FOR HOURS LYSANDER HELD Bianka in the crook of his arm while she slept, marveling—this was what she'd craved most in the world and *he* had given it to her—and yet, he was also worrying. He knew what that meant, knew how difficult it was for a Harpy to let down her guard and sleep in front of another. It meant she trusted him to protect her, to keep her safe. And he was glad. He *wanted* to protect her. Even from herself.

But could he? He didn't know. They were so different.

Until they got into bed, that is.

He could not believe what had just happened. He had become a creature of sensation, his baser urges all that mattered. The pleasure…unlike anything he'd ever experienced. Her taste was like honey, her skin so soft he wanted it against him for the rest of eternity. Her breathy moans—even her screams—had been a caress inside his ears. He'd loved every moment of it.

Had he been called to battle, he wasn't sure he would have been able to leave her.

Why her, though? Why had *she* been the one to captivate him?

She lied to him at every opportunity. She embodied everything he despised. Yet he did not despise her. For every moment with her, he only wanted more. Everything she did excited him. The pleasure she'd found in his arms...she had been unashamed, uninhibited, demanding everything he had to give.

Would he have been as enthralled by her if she had led a blameless life? If she had been more demure? He didn't think so. He liked her exactly as she was.

Why? he wondered again.

By the time she stretched lazily, sensually against him, he still did not have the answers. Nor did he know what to do with her. He'd already proven he could not leave her alone. And now that he knew all of her, she would be even more impossible to resist.

"Lysander," she said, voice husky from her rest.

"I am here."

She blinked open her eyes, jolted upright. "I fell asleep."

"I know."

"Yeah, but I feel asleep." She scrubbed a hand down her beautiful face, twisted and peered down at him with vulnerable astonishment. "I should be ashamed of myself, but I'm not. What's wrong with me?"

He reached up and traced a fingertip over her swollen lips. How hard had he kissed her? "I'm...sorry," he said. "I lost control for a moment. I shouldn't have taken you so—"

She nipped at his finger, her self-recrimination seeming to melt away in favor of amusement. "Do you hear me complaining about that?"

He relaxed. No, he did not hear her complaining. In fact, she appeared utterly sated. And he had done that. He had given her pleasure. Pride filled him. Pride—a foolish emotion that often led to a man's downfall. Was that how Bianka would make him fall? For as his temptation, she *would* make him fall.

With a sigh, she flopped back against him. "You turned serious all of the sudden. Want to talk about it?"

"No."

"Do you want to talk about *anything?*"

"No."

"Well, too bad," she grumbled, but he heard a layer of satisfaction in her tone. Did she enjoy making him do things he didn't want to do—or didn't think he wanted to do? "Because you're going to talk. A lot. You can start with why you first abducted me. I know you wanted to change me, but why me? I still don't know."

He shouldn't tell her; she already had enough power over him, and knowing the truth would only increase that power. But he also wanted her to understand how desperate he'd been. Was. "At the heart of my duties, I am a peacekeeper, and as such, I must peek into the lives of the Lords of the Underworld every so often, making sure they are obeying heavenly laws. I…saw you with them. And as I have proven with my actions this day, I realized you are my one temptation. The one thing that can tear me from my righteous path."

She sat up again, faced him again. Her eyes were wide with…pleasure? "Really? I alone can ruin you?"

He frowned. "That does not mean you should try and do so."

Laughing, she leaned down and kissed him. Her breasts pressed against his chest, once again heating his blood in that way only she could do. But he was done fighting it, done resisting it. "That's not what I meant. I just like being important to you, I guess." Her cheeks suddenly bloomed with color. "Wait. That's not what I meant, either. What I'm trying to say is that you're forgiven for whisking me to your palace in the sky. I would have done the same thing to you had the situation been reversed."

He had not expected forgiveness to come so easily.

Not from her. Frown intensifying, he cupped her cheeks and forced her to meet his gaze. "Why were *you* with *me?* I know I am not what your kind views as acceptable."

She shrugged, the action a little stiff. "I guess you're my temptation."

Now he understood why she'd grinned over his proclamation. He wanted to whoop with satisfied laughter.

"If we're going to be together—" She stopped, waiting. When he nodded, she relaxed and continued, "Then I guess I could only steal from the wicked."

It was a concession. A concession he'd never thought she would make. She truly must like him. Must want more time with him.

"So listen," she said. "My sister is getting married in a week, as I told you before. Do you want to, like, come with me? As my guest? I know, I know. It's short notice. But I didn't intend to invite you. I mean, you're an angel." There was disgust in her voice. "But you make love like a demon so I guess I should, I don't know, show you off or something."

He opened his mouth to reply. What he would say, he didn't know. They could not tell others of their relationship. Ever. But a voice stopped him.

"Lysander. Are you home?"

Lysander recognized the speaker immediately. Raphael, the warrior angel. Panic nearly choked him. He couldn't let the man see him like this. Couldn't let any of his kind see him with the Harpy.

"We must discuss Olivia," Raphael called. "May I enter your abode? There is some sort of block preventing me from doing so."

"Not yet," he called. Was his panic in his voice? He'd never experienced it before, so didn't know how to combat it. "Wait for me. I will emerge." He sat up and slipped from the bed, from Bianka. He grabbed his robe, or rather, the pieces of it, from the floor and wrapped it around himself. Immediately it wove back together to fit his frame. The material even cleaned him, wiping away Bianka's scent.

The latter, he inwardly cursed. *For the best.*

"Let him in," Bianka said, fitting the sheet around her, oblivious. "I don't mind."

Lysander kept his back to her. "I do not want him to see you."

"Don't worry. I've covered my naughty nakedness."

He gave no reply. Unlike her, he would not lie. And if he did not lie to her, he would hurt her. He did not want to do that either.

"So call him in already," she said with a laugh. "I want to see if all angels look like sin but act like saints."

"No. I don't want him inside right now. I will go out to meet him. You will stay here," he said. Still he couldn't face her.

"Wait. Are you jealous?"

He gave no reply.

"Lysander?"

"Stay silent. Please. Cloud walls are thin."

"Stay…silent?" A moment passed in the very silence he'd requested. Only, he didn't like it. He heard the rustle of fabric, a sharp intake of breath. "You don't want him to know I'm here, do you? You're ashamed of me," she said, clearly shocked. "You don't want your friend to know you've been with me."

"Bianka."

"No. You don't get to speak right now." With every word, her voice rose. "I was willing to take you to my sister's wedding. Even though I knew my family would laugh at me or view me with disgust. I was willing to give you a chance. Give us a chance. But not you. You were going to hide me away. As if *I'm* something shameful."

He whirled on her, fury burning through him. At her, at himself. "You *are* something shameful. I kill beings like you. I do not fall in love with them."

She didn't say anything. Just looked up at him with wide, hurt-filled eyes. So much hurt he actually stumbled back. A sharp pain lanced *his* chest. But as he watched, her hurt mutated into a fury that far surpassed his.

"Kill me, then," she growled.

"You know I will not."

"Why?"

"Because!"

"Let me guess. Because deep down you still think you can change me. You think that I will become the pure, virtuous woman you want me to be. Well, who are you to say what's virtuous and what isn't?"

He merely arched a brow. The answer was obvious and didn't need to be stated.

"I told you that from now on I'd only hurt the wicked, right? Well, surprise! That's what I've done since the beginning. The pie you watched me eat? The owner of that restaurant cheats at cards, takes money that doesn't belong to him. The wallet I stole? I took it from a man cheating on his wife."

He blinked down at her, unsure he'd heard correctly. "Why would you have kept that from me?"

"Why should it change how you feel about me?" She tossed back the cover and stood, glorious in her nakedness. Her skin was still aglow, multihued light reflecting off it—he'd touched that skin. Dark hair cascaded around her—he'd fisted that hair.

"I want to be with you," he said. "I do. But it has to be in secret."

"I thought the same. Until what we just did," she said as she hastily dressed. Her clothes were not like his, did not repair on their own, and so that ripped shirt revealed more than it hid.

He tried again. Tried to make her understand. "You are everything my kind stands against, Bianka. I train warriors to hunt and kill demons. What would it say to them were I to take you as my companion?"

"Here's a better question. What does it say to them that you hide your sin? Because that's how you view me, isn't it? Your sin. You are such a hypocrite." She stormed past him, careful not to touch him. "And I will not be with a hypocrite. That's worse than being an angel."

He thought she meant to race to Raphael and flaunt her presence. Shockingly enough, she didn't. And because he hadn't commanded her to stay, when she said, "I want to leave," the cloud opened up at her feet.

She disappeared, falling through the sky.

"Bianka," he shouted. Lysander spread his wings and jumped after her. He passed Raphael, but at that point, he didn't care. He only wanted Bianka safe—and that hurt and fury wiped away from her expression.

She'd turned facedown to increase her momentum. He had to tuck his wings into his back to increase his own. Finally, he caught her halfway and wrapped his arms around her, her back pressed into his stomach. She didn't flail, didn't order him to release her, which he'd been prepared for.

When they reached her cabin, he straightened them, spread his wings and slowed. Snow still covered the ground and crunched when they landed. She didn't pull away. Didn't run. Something else he'd been prepared for.

Clearly he knew very little about her.

"It's probably best this way, you know," she said flatly,

keeping her back to him. The wind slapped her hair against his cheeks. "That was my afterglow talking earlier, anyway. I never should have invited you to the wedding. We're too different to make anything work."

"I was willing to try," he said through gritted teeth. *Don't do this,* he projected. *Don't end us.*

She laughed without humor, and he marveled at the difference between this laugh and the one she'd given inside his cloud. Marveled and mourned. "No, you were willing to hide me away."

"Yes. Therefore I was *trying* to make something work. I want to be with you, Bianka. Otherwise I would not have followed you. I would have left you alone from the first. I would not have tried to show you the light."

"You are such a pompous ass," she spat. "Show me the light? Please! You want me to be perfect. Blameless. But what happens when I fail? And I will, you know? Perfection just isn't in me. One day I will curse. Like now. Fuck you. One day I will take something just because it's pretty and I want it. Would that ruin me in your eyes?"

"It hasn't so far," he spat back.

She laughed again, this one bleaker, grim. "The scarves I took were made by child laborers. So I haven't really done anything too terrible yet. But I will. And you know what? If you were to do something nauseatingly righteous, I wouldn't have cared. I would still have wanted to take you to the wedding. That's the difference between us. Evil or not, good or not, I wanted you."

"I want you, too. But that was not always the case, and you know it. You *would* care." He tightened his grip on her. "Bianka. We can work this out."

"No, we can't." Finally, she twisted to face him. "That would require giving you a second chance, and I don't do second chances."

"I don't need a second chance. I just need you to think about this. To realize our relationship must stay hidden."

"I'm not going to be your secret shame, Lysander."

His eyes narrowed. She was trying to force his hand, and he didn't like it. "You steal in secret. You sleep in secret. Why not this?"

"That you don't know the answer proves you aren't the warrior I thought you were. Have a nice life, Lysander," she said, jerking from his hold and walking away without a backward glance.

CHAPTER TWELVE

LYSANDER SAT IN THE BACK of the Budapest chapel, undetectable, watching Bianka help her sisters and their friends decorate for the wedding. She was currently hanging flowers from the vaulted ceiling. Without a ladder.

He'd been following her for days, unable to stay away. One thing he'd noticed: she talked and laughed as if she was fine, normal, but the sparkle was gone from her eyes, her skin.

And he had done that to her. Worse, not once had she cursed, lied or stolen. Again, his fault. He'd told her she was unworthy of him. He'd been—*was,* right?—too embarrassed of her to tell his people about her.

But he couldn't deny that he missed her. Missed everything about her. That much he knew. She excited him, challenged him, frustrated him, consumed him, drew him, made him *feel.* He did not want to be without her.

Something soft brushed his shoulder. He barely managed to tear his gaze from Bianka to turn and see that Olivia was now sitting beside him.

What was wrong with him? He hadn't heard her arrive. Normally his senses were tuned, alert.

"Why did you summon me here?" she asked. She glanced around nervously. Her dark curls framed her face, rosebuds dripping from a few of the strands.

"To Budapest? Because you are always here anyway."

"As are you these days," she replied dryly.

He shrugged. "Did you just come from Aeron's room?"

She gave a reluctant nod.

"Raphael came to me," he said. The day he'd lost Bianka. The worst day of his existence.

"Those flowers aren't centered, B," the redheaded Kaia called, claiming his attention and stopping the rest of his speech to his charge. "Shift them a little to the left."

Bianka expelled a frustrated sigh. "Like this?"

"No. *My* left, dummy."

Grumbling, Bianka obeyed.

"Perfect." Kaia beamed up at her.

Bianka flipped her off, and Lysander grinned. Thank the One True Deity he had not killed all of her spirit.

"I think they're perfect, too," her youngest sister, Gwendolyn, said.

Bianka released the ceiling panels and dropped to the floor. When she landed, she straightened as if the jolt had not affected her in any way. "Glad the princess is finally happy with something," she muttered. Then, more loudly, "I don't understand why you can't get married in a tree like a civilized Harpy."

Gwen anchored her hands on her fists. "Because my dream has always been to be wed in a chapel like any other normal person. Now, will someone please remove the naked portraits of Sabin from the walls? Please."

"Why would you want to get rid of them when I just spent all that time hanging them?" Anya, goddess of Anarchy and companion to Lucien, keeper of Death, asked, clearly offended. "They add a little something extra to what would otherwise be very boring proceedings. *My* wedding will have strippers. Live ones."

"Boring? Boring!" Fury passed over Gwen's features, black bleeding into her eyes, her teeth sharpening.

Lysander had watched this same change overtake her multiple times already. In the past hour alone.

"It won't be boring," Ashlyn, companion to Maddox, the keeper of Violence, said soothingly. "It'll be beautiful."

The pregnant woman rubbed her rounded belly. That belly was larger than it should have been, given the early state of her pregnancy. No one seemed to realize it, though. They would soon enough, he supposed. He just hoped they were ready for what she carried.

What would a child of Bianka's be like? he suddenly wondered. Harpy, like her? Angel, like him? Or a mix of both?

A pang took root and flourished in his chest.

"Boring?" Gwen snarled again, clearly not ready to let the insult slide.

"Great!" Bianka threw up her arms. "Someone get Sabin before Gwennie kills us all in a rage."

A Harpy in a rage could hurt even other Harpies, Lysander knew. As Gwen's consort, Sabin, keeper of Doubt, was the only one who could calm her.

With that thought, Lysander's head tilted to the side. He had never seen Bianka erupt, he realized. She'd viewed everything as a game. Well, not true. Once, she had gotten mad. The time Paris had punched him. Lysander had been her enemy, but she'd still gotten mad over his mistreatment.

Lysander had calmed her.

The pang grew in intensity, and he rubbed his breastbone. Was he Bianka's consort? Did he want to be?

"No need to search me out. I'm here." Sabin strode through the double doors. "As if I'd be more than a few feet away when she's so sensitiv—uh, just in case she needed my help. Gwen, baby." There at the end, his tone had lowered, gentled. He reached her and pulled her into his arms; she snuggled against him. "The most important thing tomorrow is that we'll be together. Right?"

"Lysander," Olivia said, drawing his attention from the now-cooing couple. "The wait is difficult. Raphael came to you and…what?"

Lysander sighed, forcing himself to concentrate. "Answer a few questions for me first."

"All right," she said after a brief hesitation.

"Why do you like Aeron when he is so different from you?"

She twisted the fabric of her robe. "I think I like him *because* he is so different from me. He has thrived amid darkness, managing to retain a spark of light in his soul. He is not perfect, is not blameless, but he could have given in to his demon long ago and yet still he fights. He protects those he loves. His passion for life is…" She shivered. "Amazing. And really, he only hurts people when his demon overtakes him—and only if they are wicked, at that. Innocents, he leaves alone."

It was the same with Bianka. Yet Lysander had tried to make her ashamed of herself. Ashamed when she should only be proud of what she had accomplished, thriving amid darkness, as Olivia had said. "And you are not embarrassed for our kind to know of your affection for him?"

"Embarrassed of Aeron?" Olivia laughed. "When he is stronger, fiercer, more alive than anyone I know? Of course not. I would be proud to be called his woman. Not that it could ever happen," she added sadly.

Proud. There was that word again. And this time, something clicked in his mind. *I'm not going to be your secret shame, Lysander,* Bianka had said. He'd reminded her that she committed all her other sins in secret. Why not him? She hadn't told him the answer, but it came to him now. Because she'd been proud of him. Because she'd wanted to show him off.

As he should have wanted to show *her* off.

Any other man would have been proud to stand beside her. She was beautiful, intelligent, witty, passionate and lived by her own moral code. Her laughter was more lovely than the song of a harp, her kiss as sweet as a prayer.

He'd considered her the spawn of Lucifer, yet she was a gift from the One True Deity. He was such a fool.

"Have I answered your questions sufficiently?" Olivia asked.

"Yes." He was surprised by the rawness of his voice. Had he ruined things irreparably between them?

"So answer a few now for me."

Unable to find his voice, he nodded. He had to make this right. Had to try, at least.

"Bianka. The Harpy you watch. Do you love her?"

Love. He found her among the crowd and the pang in his chest grew unbearable. She was currently adding a magic marker mustache to one of Sabin's portraits while Kaia added…other things down below. Kaia was giggling; Bianka looked like she was just going through the motions, taking no joy.

He wanted her happy. Wanted her the way she'd been.

"You think you are embarrassed of her," Olivia continued when he gave no response.

"How do you know?" He forced the words to leave him.

"I am—or was—a joy-bringer, Lysander. It was my job to know what people were feeling and then help them see the truth. Because only in truth can one find real joy. You were never embarrassed of her. I know you. You are embarrassed by nothing. You were simply scared. Scared that *you* were not what *she* needs."

His eyes widened. Could that be true? He'd tried to change her. Had tried to make her what he was so that she, in turn, would *like* what he was? Yes. Yes, that made sense, and for the second time in his existence, he hated himself.

He had let Bianka get away from him. When he should have sung her praises to all of the heavens, he had cast her aside. No man was more foolish. Irreparable damage or not, he had to try and win her back.

He jumped to his feet. "I do," he said. "I love her." He wanted to throw his arms around her. Wanted to shout to all the world that she belonged to him. That she had chosen him as her man.

His shoulders slumped. Chosen. Key word. Past tense. She would not choose him again. She did not give second chances, she'd said.

She often lies…

For the first time, the thought that his woman liked to lie caused him to smile. Perhaps she had lied about that. Perhaps she would give him a second chance. A chance to prove his love.

If he had to grovel, he would. She was his temptation, but that did not have to be a bad thing. That could be his salvation. After all, his life would mean nothing without her. Same for her. She had told him that he was her own temptation. He could be *her* salvation.

"Thank you," he told Olivia. "Thank you for showing me the truth."

"Always my pleasure."

How should he approach Bianka? When? Urgency flooded him. He wanted to do so now. As a warrior, though, he knew some battles required planning. And as this was the most important battle of his existence, plan his attack he would.

If she forgave him and decided to be with him, they

would still have a tough road ahead. Where would they live? His duties were in the heavens. She thrived on earth, with her family nearby. Plus, Olivia was destined to kill Aeron, who would essentially be Bianka's brother-in-law after tomorrow. And if Olivia decided not to, another angel would be chosen to do the job.

Most likely, that would be Lysander.

One thing his Deity had taught him, however, was that love truly could conquer all. Nothing was stronger. They could make this work.

"I've lost you again," Olivia said with a laugh. "Before you rush off, you must tell me why you summoned me. What Raphael said to you."

Some of his good mood evaporated. While Olivia had just given him hope and helped him find the right path, he was about to dash any hopes of a happily-ever-after for her.

"Raphael came to me," he repeated. *Just do it; just say it.* "He told me of the council's unhappiness with you. He told me they grow weary of your continued defiance."

Her smile fell away. "I know," she whispered. "I just…I haven't been able to bring myself to hurt him. Watching him gives me joy. And I deserve to experience joy after so many centuries of devoted service, do I not?"

"Of course."

"And if he is dead, I will never be able to do the things I now dream about."

His brow furrowed. "What things?"

"Touching him. Curling into his arms." A pause. "Kissing him."

Dangerous desires indeed. Oh, did he know their power. "If you never experience them," he offered, "they are easier to resist." But he hated to think of this wonderful female being without something she wanted.

He could petition the council for Aeron's forgiveness, but that would do no good. A decree was a decree. A law had been broken and someone had to pay. "Very soon, the council will be forced to offer you a choice. Your duty or your downfall."

She gazed down at her hands, once again twisting the fabric of her robe. "I know. I don't know why I hesitate. He would never desire me, anyway. The women here, they are exciting, dangerous. As fierce as he is. And I am—"

"Precious," he said. "You are precious. Never think otherwise."

She offered him a shaky smile.

"I have always loved you, Olivia. I would hate to see you give up everything you are for a man who has threatened to kill you. You do know what you would be losing, yes?"

That smile fell away as she nodded.

"You would fall straight into hell. The demons there will go for your wings. They always go for the wings first. No longer will you be impervious to pain. You will hurt, yet you will have to dig your way free of the underground—or die there. Your strength will be depleted. Your body will not regenerate on its own. You will be more fragile than a human because you were not raised among them."

While he thought he could survive such a thing, he did not think Olivia would. She was too delicate. Too…sheltered. Until this point, every facet of her life had dealt with joy and happiness. She had known nothing else.

The demons of hell would be crueler to her than they would be even to him, the man they feared more than any other. She was all they despised. Wholly good. Destroying such innocence and purity would delight them.

"Why are you telling me this?" Her voice trembled. Tears streaked down her cheeks.

"Because I do not want you to make the wrong decision. Because I want you to know what you're up against."

A moment passed in silence, then she jumped up and threw her arms around his neck. "I love you, you know."

He squeezed her tightly, sensing that this was her way of saying goodbye. Sensing that this would be the last time they were offered such a reprieve. But he would not stop her, whatever path she chose.

She pulled back and smoothed her trembling hands down her glistening white robe. "You have given me much to consider. So now I will leave you to your female. May love always follow you, Lysander." As she spoke, her wings expanded. Up, up she flew, misting through the ceiling—and Bianka's flowers—before disappearing.

He hoped she'd choose her faith, her immortality, over the keeper of Wrath, but feared she would not. His gaze strayed to Bianka, now walking down the aisle toward the exit. She paused at his row, frowned, before shaking her head and leaving. If he'd been forced to pick between her and his reputation and lifestyle, he would have picked her, he realized.

And now it was time to prove it to her.

CHAPTER THIRTEEN

I'VE GOT TO PULL MYSELF from this funk, Bianka thought. This was her youngest sister's wedding day. She should be happy. Delighted. If she were honest, though, she was a tiny bit—aka a *lot*—jealous. Gwen's man, a demon, loved her. Was proud of her.

Lysander considered Bianka unworthy.

She'd thought about proving herself to him, but had quickly discarded the idea. Proving herself worthy—his idea of worthy, that is—would entail nothing more than a lie. And Lysander hated lies. So, according to him, she would never be good enough for him. Which meant he was stupid, and she didn't date stupid men. Plus, he didn't deserve her.

He deserved to rot in his unhappiness. And that's what he'd be without her. Unhappy. Or so she hoped.

"So much for our plan to go naked," Kaia muttered beside her. "Gwen saw me leave my room that way and almost sliced my throat."

"Did not," the bride in question said from behind them.

They turned in unison. Bianka's breath caught as it had every time she'd seen her youngest sister in her gown. It was a princess cut, which was fitting, the straps thin, the beautiful white lace cinching just under her breasts before flowing to her ankles. The material covering her legs was sheer, allowing glimpses of thigh and those gorgeous red heels.

Her strawberry curls were half up, half down, diamonds glittering through the strands. There was so much love and excitement in her gold-gray eyes it was almost blinding.

"I almost pushed you out a window," Gwen added.

They laughed. Even stoic Taliyah, their oldest sister, who had her arm wrapped through Gwen's. Since it turned out Gwen's father was the Lords' greatest enemy, and Gwen's mom had disowned her years ago, Taliyah was escorting Gwen down the aisle.

"Hence the reason I'm now wearing this." Kaia motioned to her own gown, an exact match to Bianka's. A buttercup yellow creation with more ribbons, bows and sequined rose appliqués than anyone should wear in an entire lifetime. They even wore hats with orange streamers.

Gwen shrugged, unrepentant. "I didn't want you looking prettier than me, so sue me."

"Weddings suck," Bianka said. "You should have just had Sabin tattoo your name on his ass and called it good." That's what she would have done. Not that Lysander ever would have agreed to such a thing. Whether they were together or not.

Which they never would be. Bastard.

"I did. Have him tattoo my name on his ass," Gwen said. "And his arm. And his chest. And his back. But then I casually mentioned how much I'd always wanted a big wedding, and well, he told me I had four weeks to plan it or he'd take over and do it himself. And everyone knows men can't plan shit. So…" She shrugged again, though the excitement and love on her face had intensified. "Are they ready for us yet?"

Bianka and Kaia turned back to the chapel, peeking through the crack in the closed doors.

"Not yet," Bianka said. "Paris is missing."

Paris, who had gotten ordained over the Internet, would be presiding over the nuptials.

"He better hurry," she added grumpily. "Or I'll find a way to make him oil-wrestle again."

"You've been so depressed lately. Missing your angel?" Kaia asked her, pinkie-waving to Amun, who stood in the line of groomsmen beside Sabin at the altar.

Amun shouldn't have been able to see her, but somehow he did. He nodded, a smile twitching at the corners of his lips.

"Of course not. I hate him." A lie. She hadn't told her sisters why she and Lysander had parted, only that they had. Forever. If they knew the truth, they'd want to kill him. And as all but Gwen were paid killers, immensely good at their job, she'd find herself the proud owner of Lysander's head.

Which she didn't want.

She just wanted him. Stupid girl.

"I only would have teased you for a few years, you know," Kaia said. "You should have kept him around. It might have been fun to corrupt him."

He didn't want to be corrupted any more than she wanted to be purified. They were too different. Could never make anything work. Their separation was for the best. So why couldn't she get over it? Why did she feel his gaze on her, every minute of every day? Even now, when she looked like a Southern belle on crack?

"So Sabin doesn't have a last name," she said to Gwen, drawing attention away from herself. "Are you going to call yourself Gwen Sabin?"

"No, nothing like that. I'm going to call myself Gwen Lord."

"What's Anya plan to call herself? Anya Underworld?" Kaia asked with a laugh.

"Knowing our goddess, she'll demand Lucien take *her* last name. Trouble. Or is that her middle name?"

"I here, I here," a voice suddenly screeched. Legion pushed her way in front of Bianka and Kaia. She was wearing a yellow dress, as well. Only hers had more ribbons, bows and sequins. A basket of flowers was clutched in her hands, her too-long nails curling around the handle. Best of all, she wore a tiara. Because she didn't have hair, it had had to be glued to her scaled head. "We begin now."

She didn't wait for permission but shouldered her way through the door. The crowd—which consisted of the Lords of the Underworld, their companions and some gods and goddesses Anya knew—turned and gasped when they saw her. Well, except for Gideon. He'd recently been captured and tortured by Hunters, the Lords' nemeses, and was currently missing his hands. (His feet weren't in the best of shape, either.) Because of his injuries, he was beyond weak, so he lay in his gurney, barely conscious. He'd insisted on coming, though.

From his pew, Aeron smiled indulgently as Legion tossed pink petals in every direction. Just as she reached the front, Paris raced to the podium. He looked harried, pale, and Sabin punched him in the shoulder.

Sabin looked amazing. He wore a black tux, his hair slicked back, and when he turned to face the door, watching for Gwen, his entire face lit. With love. With pride. Bianka's jealousy increased. She wanted that. Wanted her man to find her perfect in every way.

Was that too much to ask?

Apparently so. Stupid Lysander.

"Go, go, go," Gwen ordered, giving them a little push.

Bianka kicked into motion, heading toward Strider, her appointed groomsman. He smiled at her when she reached him. He would be proud to call her his woman, she thought. She tried to make herself return the gesture, but her eyes were too busy filling with tears. She looked around, trying to distract herself.

The chapel really was beautiful. The glittery white flowers she'd hung from the ceiling were thick and lush and offered a canopy, a haven. They were the best part of the decor, if you asked her. Candles flickered with golden light, twining with shadows.

Kaia approached her side, and everyone except for Gideon stood. The music changed, slowing down to the bridal march. Gwen and Taliyah appeared. Sabin's breath caught. Yes, that was the way a man should react to the sight of his woman.

What makes you think you were ever Lysander's woman?

Because she was his one temptation. Because of the reverent way he had touched her. Because she liked how he made her feel. Because they balanced each other. Because he completed her in a way she hadn't known she needed. He was the light to her darkness.

He was willing to show you that light. Over and over again.

Perhaps she should have fought for him. That's what she was, after all. A fighter. Yet she'd given in as if he meant nothing to her when he had somehow become the most important thing in her life.

Bianka didn't mean to, but she tuned out as Paris gave his speech and the happy couple recited their vows, her thoughts remaining focused on Lysander. Should she try and fight for him now? If so, how would she go about it?

Only when the crowd cheered did she snap out of her haze, watching as Sabin and Gwen kissed. Then they were marching down the aisle and out the doors together. The rest of the bridal party made their way out, as well.

"Shall we?" Strider asked, holding out his arm for her.

"She can't." Paris grabbed her arm. "You're needed in that room." With his free hand, he pointed.

"Why?" Was he planning revenge against her for forcing him to oil-wrestle Lysander? He hadn't mentioned it in the days since her return to Buda, but he couldn't be happy with her. He should be thanking her, for gods' sake. He'd gotten to touch all of Lysander's hawtness.

Paris rolled his eyes. "Just go before your boyfriend decides he's tired of waiting and comes out here."

Her boyfriend. Lysander? Couldn't be. Could it? But why would he have come? Heart drumming in her chest, she walked forward. She didn't allow herself to run, though she wanted to soooo badly. She reached the door. Her hand shook as she turned the knob.

Hinges creaked. Then she was staring into—an empty room. Her teeth ground together. Paris's revenge, just as she'd figured. Of course. That rat bastard piece of shit was going to pay. She wasn't just going to make him oil-wrestle. She was going to—

"Hello, Bianka."

Lysander.

Gasping, she whipped around. Her eyes widened. In an instant, the chapel had been transformed. No longer were her sisters and friends inside. Lysander and his kind occupied every spare inch. Angels were everywhere, light surrounding them and putting Gwen's candles to shame.

"What are you doing here?" she demanded, not daring to hope.

"I came to beg your forgiveness." His arms spread. "I came to tell you that I am proud to be your man. I brought my friends and brethren to bear witness to my proclamation."

She swallowed, still not letting hope take over. "But I'm evil and that's not going to change. I'm your temptation. You could, I don't know, lose everything by being with me." The thought hit her, and she wanted to wilt. He could lose everything. No wonder he had wanted to destroy her. No wonder he had wanted to hide her.

"No, you are not evil. And I don't want you to change. You are beautiful and intelligent and brave. But more than that, you are my everything. I am nothing without you. Not good, not right, not complete. And do not worry. I will not lose everything as you said. You have not committed an unpardonable sin."

She gulped. "And if I do?"

"I will fall."

Okay. A small kernel of hope managed to seep inside her. But no way would she let him fall. Ever. He loved being an angel. "What brought this on?"

"I finally pulled my head out of my ass," he said dryly.

He'd said *ass*. Lysander had just said the word *ass*. More hope beat its way inside and she had to press her lips together to keep from smiling. And crying! Tears were springing in her eyes, burning.

Could they actually make their relationship work? Just a little bit ago, she'd been grateful—or pretending to be grateful—that they were apart, since so many obstacles existed.

"I only hope you can love so foolish a man. I am willing to live wherever you desire. I am willing to do anything you need to win you back." He dropped to his knees. "I love you, Bianka Skyhawk. I would be proud to be yours."

He was proud of her. He wanted her. He loved her. It was everything she'd secretly dreamed about this past week. Yes, they could make this work. They would be together, and that was the most important thing. But she told him none of that.

"Now?" she screeched instead. "You decided to introduce me to your friends now? When I look like this?" Scowling, she peeked over his shoulder at them and saw their stunned expressions. "I usually look better than this, you know. You should have seen me the other day. When I was naked."

Lysander stood. "That's all you have to say to me?"

She focused back on him. His eyes were as wide as hers had been, his arms crossed over his middle. "No. There's more," she grumbled. "But I will never live this yellow gown thing down, you know."

"Bianka."

"Yes, I love you, too. But if you ever decide I'm unworthy again, I'll show you just how demonic I can be."

"Deal. But you don't have to worry, love," he said, a slow smile lifting those delectable lips. "It is I who am unworthy. I only pray you never learn of this."

"Oh, I know it already," she said, and his grin spread. "Now c'mere, you." She cupped the back of his neck and jerked him down for a kiss.

His arms banded around her, holding her close. She'd never thought to be paired with an angel, but she couldn't regret it now. Not when Lysander was the angel in question.

"Are you sure you're ready for me?" she asked him when they came up for air.

He nipped at her chin. "I've been ready for you my entire life. I just didn't know it until now."

"Good." With a whoop, she jumped up and wound her legs around his waist. A wave of gasps circled the room.

They were still here? "Ditch your friends, I'll blow off my sister's reception and we'll go oil-wrestle."

"Funny," he said, wings enveloping her as he flew her up, up and into his cloud. "That's exactly what I was thinking."

* * * * *

Look for more LORDS OF THE UNDERWORLD
adventures coming soon from
Gena Showalter and HQN Books:
INTO THE DARK, May 2010
THE DARKEST PASSION, June 2010
THE DARKEST LIE, July 2010

LOVE ME TO DEATH
Maggie Shayne

PROLOGUE

Valentine's Day, Twenty-two Years Ago
Port Lucinda, Maine

DAVID TOOK A LONG PULL from the bottle. It was only wine, and it was cheap wine lifted from the back of Brad's older brother's Jeep before he left on his road trip. He wouldn't even notice it was missing until he got to Miami. It tasted like hell, but beggars (or thieves, in this case) couldn't be choosers, and none of the five boys currently sucking down the wine were old enough to have bought it legally. So they'd take what they could get.

They deserved a good drunk after what they'd been through. It was David's first one ever, though he wouldn't admit that to the other guys if his life depended on it.

And then Brad said, "Damn, I'm dizzy. And I think my lips are going numb. Is this normal?"

"What?" Kevin asked. "You never been drunk before?"

"Hell no."

Kevin grinned crookedly and said, "Me neither," and then they all started laughing as if it was the funniest thing they'd ever heard in their lives.

They were standing in a small circle outside the old Muller place, passing the fourth and final wine bottle around. David didn't know why it was called the old Muller place. He'd never known any Mullers to live in Port

Lucinda—never known anyone to live in that old house, period.

He looked at the place now, its weathered gray boards and broken windows and sagging roof. Some of the shutters were missing, while others hung from one hinge, ready to fall off.

"I can't believe she did this to me," Mark moaned, wiping his mouth with the back of his hand as he passed the bottle to the right. "I mean, right before Valentine's Day."

"I know, man." David slapped his friend's shoulder. "It must have sucked walking in on her making out with that jock."

"Big time."

"At least Sally had the courtesy to dump me to my face," Brad said. "Not that it sucks any less. Dumped is dumped."

Kevin nodded. "I guess I'm the lucky one. Mine's only out of town for two months."

David looked at Randy, who was silent, and drinking more deeply than any of them. His girlfriend's family had moved to Hong Kong when her father's company offered him a huge promotion if he would transfer there. Hong Kong. It might as well be the moon.

"Still no word from Sierra?" Mark asked him.

David blinked and felt his throat go tight at the mention of her name. Unlike the other guys, he hadn't been dumped or left behind or betrayed. He'd spent his entire sophomore year trying to work up the nerve to ask Sierra to go out with him. Last week he'd finally been ready to do it. He'd made his plan, figured out what to say, how to do it and when. And that day, she hadn't shown up for school.

No one had seen or heard from Sierra Terrence since.

And no one knew where she was. The cops had been in and out of school all week, questioning students and teachers and staff. But no one knew shit.

"Dave?" Mark nudged him with an elbow, handed him the bottle.

"No, nothing. I mean, there are all kinds of rumors, but no one knows a damn thing."

"Yeah," Kevin said. "I heard her dad was abusing her and she ran away, but hell, if the cops thought that, her old man would be in jail by now."

"I heard she ran off with an older guy—a college guy," Brad said, and when Randy elbowed him hard, he rushed on. "Not that I believe it. No way."

"What do you think happened to her, Dave?" Mark asked.

"I don't know. I don't want to talk about it." He took a big pull from the bottle, draining it, and then tossed it onto the old house's lawn and took a few unsteady steps forward, eyeing the thing. "This place is a freakin' eyesore." Only it sounded like "eyeshore."

"Sure as hell not worth the whole town fighting over, is it?" Mark asked. "Historical Society—led by Davey's mom—trying to save it. Like it's worth saving? I mean, look at it."

"It's gonna fall down on its own pretty soon," Kevin said. "Then the town council won't have to keep fighting to have it condemned so they can do the honors."

"It's all my mom ever talks about," David said. "I'm sick as hell of hearing about it."

"We all are." Brad marched a few steps nearer. Then he picked up the empty wine bottle and turned it in his hand. "I think we should do something about it."

David frowned. "Like what?"

Brad met his eyes and smiled. "All we need is this bottle, a rag and some kerosene."

"And a lighter," Mark said, his face splitting in a broad smile.

"There's kerosene at my house," Randy put in. It was one of the few times he'd spoken all night. "It's only around the corner. I can go get it and be back in five minutes."

"Yeah. Yeah, let's do this. Let's torch this freaking old hulk and get it over with," Mark said, grinning from ear to ear. "Go, Randy."

Randy took off at an unsteady trot, but after a few steps, it slowed to a walk. An uneven, swaying walk. David bit his lower lip. "I don't know about this, guys."

"What? Where's the harm?" Mark looked to the left and right of the old house. "There's not another house close enough to catch a spark or anything, right? There's no one around. Shit, David, I'd think you would want to do this more than anyone. It would at least stop your mother from running around town like some kind of televangelist, trying to convert everybody to her way of thinking."

"That really must be embarrassing." Kevin looked at Dave as if he felt sorry for him. "Shit, just last week she was standing in front of the town courthouse with a bullhorn. A bullhorn, for crying out loud."

David cringed inwardly. It *was* embarrassing. His mom and a handful of local housewives had latched on to this cause as if it were a shot at world peace or something. And she was so involved with it, she didn't even care that his heart was broken, or that the girl he'd let himself fall for was missing.

She didn't have time to care.

He sat down in the grass. The others joined him there, one by one. They all sat in a row, in the dead of night, staring at the crooked, falling down nightmare of a house.

"Little kids are scared to walk by this place," Brad said. "We'd be doing this whole town a favor."

David sighed, and they sat there a while longer, all of them adding their arguments as to why this would be a good idea, when the truth was that it would just be a good way to vent their frustration. And fun, to boot.

Randy came staggering back with a small kerosene can, and without waiting for anyone to say anything, he filled the empty wine bottle. Then he took a red bandanna from his back pocket, twisted it up and stuffed it into the bottle.

He held it up, and the others all rose from the ground, one by one.

"Who's got a lighter?" he asked.

"Here." Mark dug in his jeans pocket and pulled out a little green disposable job. He handed it to Randy.

Randy shook his head. "No way, I'm not throwing it. I got the kero. One of you guys has to toss this baby in."

"Which one?"

Brad said, "Let's draw for it." He reached for the backpack he'd used to carry the stolen wine. David had assumed it was empty, but Brad pulled a deck of playing cards from a zipped pocket.

"Jeez, you got a kitchen sink in there, too?" David asked. He was feeling nervous as hell and he didn't know why.

Brad shrugged. "I snagged the backpack from my brother's Jeep, wine and all. He must've stuck the cards in there. Anyway, who cares?" He took the cards from their box, shuffled them a few times. As he did, one fell from the deck and landed, face up, on the sidewalk.

Ace of spades.

David felt a chill go up his spine.

"Low card throws the bottle," Brad said. "Draw." He fanned the cards, facedown, and held them out.

Each of the others drew a card, including Brad himself, though David wondered if he'd cheated. He was too drunk to notice if he had.

Anyway, it didn't matter. He'd drawn a two. And it didn't get any lower than that.

As each boy flipped his card to reveal it, he hoped for a tie, but it wasn't to be. A king, a seven, a nine and a jack surrounded him.

Randy flicked the lighter, lit the rag and handed him the bottle. "Throw it."

David closed his hand around the cool bottle, smelled the kerosene, thought about everyone having a blast tonight at the Valentine's Day Ball, where he'd expected to be. He and his four friends, as well. Tonight was supposed to be a big deal. They were not supposed to be standing outside in the freezing cold of a Maine February night, shivering and drinking sour, cheap wine while their hearts bled out.

It wasn't *fair.*

A sudden rush of anger surged up, and he let it move him. He drew back, took aim and hurled the bottle with all his might.

It sailed right through an already broken window and landed inside. And almost as one, the five boys ran away from the house—but only a few steps away. They stopped and turned, looking back, waiting, but seeing no results.

Five full minutes they waited there, staring at that dark window. But nothing. "Damn," Randy said. "It must have gone out."

"No, wait!" Mark pointed. "Look!"

There was light, dancing and flickering light. It grew bigger fast, though, and soon flames were shooting up. The old place was like tinder, dry and dead inside, and the fire quickly raged, showing its face in every window they could see.

"How the hell did it spread so fast?" David muttered.

"Come on. Someone's gonna see it and call it in any second now, if they haven't already. We've gotta get out of here," Mark said, tugging on his arm.

But David couldn't take his eyes from the flames.

Kevin punched him in the shoulder, *hard*. "Come on, David."

"Yeah," David said. "All right." And turning, he joined the others as they ran. And ran. And within a few yards, he felt as if he were being pursued, and he ran even faster as panic nipped an icy path up his spine.

They didn't stop until they were outside Randy's house again, the only house where no parents were at home that night, and they crowded inside, closed the door and stood there, looking at each other.

David heard sirens and swore under his breath. "That was the stupidest thing we've ever done."

"Only if we get caught," Mark said. "Randy, we need to wash up, get the wine smell off our breath."

"They're gonna know it was us," David said. "Everyone else is at the damn dance. They're gonna know."

Randy clasped his shoulder. "No one's gonna know, because we're not gonna tell them. We take an oath, right here, right now. None of us are ever going to say a word about what we did tonight. On our lives. Swear?" He thrust a fist out.

One by one the other guys clapped their right hands over his fisted one. "Swear," they each muttered.

"Good. Bathroom's through there. Let's clean up."

And so they washed up, and they went home, and they acted as if nothing had happened and pretended it was all going to be just fine, even though David had a sick feeling in his gut that told him it wasn't.

When the cops showed up at school the next day, he

knew it wasn't. And when the principal called an emergency assembly in the gym, he was sure someone was going to point a finger right at his face and say, "He did it!"

But that wasn't what happened. What happened was that Principal O'Malley stood at a podium in the front of the gym and told them that Sierra Terrence had been found, and that she was dead. She'd run away, and apparently had been hiding out in the old Muller house. Last night that house had been gutted by fire. She'd been trapped inside, and had died of smoke inhalation. Arson was suspected and if anyone knew anything about any of this, they needed to come to him privately, and in complete confidence.

David barely kept from throwing up right there. He managed to hold on until the assembly was dismissed, and then he ran straight to the boys' room and vomited until he thought he'd puked out his insides.

When he rinsed his mouth at the sink and lifted his head to look into the mirror through burning, wet eyes, there was a cop standing behind him.

Raising his chin, David turned and met the officer's steady gaze. He didn't even wait for the man to ask him the question. He didn't care that he was breaking the vow he'd made to his friends. And he didn't intend to rat them out. He was the one, anyway. He was the one who'd thrown that molotov cocktail into the old Muller house.

It was him.

"It was me," he said aloud. "I started the fire. I…I killed Sierra."

CHAPTER ONE

DAVID NICHOLS LIFTED the visor of his helmet and stood gazing at the sodden, still smoldering pile of rubble that used to be a diner, wishing his crew had been able to do more. The business owner, a man who probably looked like a biker most of the time, stood silently, holding his wife as big fat tears rolled down his face. The wife's grief wasn't as silent. She was sobbing openly.

His fellow firefighters were rolling up hoses, gathering equipment. He went to the couple, taking his helmet off as he did. "I'm so sorry. If we'd gotten here sooner—"

"My fault," the man said. "The alarm system went haywire last week. I should have had it fixed, but I put it off, and now—" He looked at the wreckage that had been his livelihood and shook his head.

"You're insured, right?" David said, relieved when the woman nodded. "I know it looks bad now, but you'll be okay. You will. I've seen enough of this to know. And really, thank your lucky stars no one was inside. No one was hurt or killed. It could've been a lot worse."

"We know you did all you could," the woman said.

He nodded and moved aside as the couple were surrounded by friends or loved ones who'd rushed to the scene. They would be okay.

As for him, hell, he never would. It wouldn't have made a difference if he had saved the structure. He would still feel the black knot in his stomach that had never quite gone away. No matter how many kids or pets he'd carried out of burning buildings, no matter how many lives he'd saved, he would never erase the stain from his soul.

The two years he'd spent at juvenile detention hadn't come close to being a fair price to pay for what he'd done as a kid. But Sierra had been poor, and of mixed blood—her mother was East Indian and had left Sierra and her white-trash father before Sierra's death, to return to her family in Delhi—while he and the guys had all been upper-crust white boys on their way to college. So they'd been tried as minors, sent off to juvie until they turned eighteen, and then set free with their records wiped clean. A fresh start. A second chance.

It was more than Sierra Terrence had been given.

He walked back to the truck, shrugging out of his heavy yellow coat as he did. Climbing into the driver's seat, he saw that his cell phone, lying on the dash, had *Missed Call* shining from its face.

Frowning, he picked it up, recognized the number and hit the voicemail button.

But it wasn't his old friend Mark's voice on the recording.

"David, it's Janet. Mark's been in an accident. It's… serious." That word emerged as if it barely fit through her throat. And her voice was tighter, deeper after that. "He's asking for you. All of you. Please come…soon."

That was it. There was nothing more. All of you, she'd said. All of you. And that could only mean his closest friends and himself. They'd bonded twenty-two years ago. Oh, they'd been friends, good friends, before the drunken debacle that had cost a young woman her life. But afterward, their friendship had taken on a depth David figured few men experienced in their lives. When he, David, had confessed, he hadn't given up any of the others. But they had all come forward, one by one, to shoulder their share of the blame. And then in juvie, hours from Port Lucinda and surrounded by really messed up young men, they'd needed each other just to stay sane—and safe.

And while they no longer lived in close proximity, they still kept in close touch, and got together on all the important occasions. Weddings. Kids being born. Summer holidays. Mark was the only one who'd stayed in Port Lucinda—he'd taken over his father's little grocery store there.

So when Janet said, "All of you," she could only have meant Randy, Kevin, Brad and him. The reformed arsonists who would never wash the blood of a sixteen-year-old girl off their hands.

His phone was ringing again. He glanced at the screen, and saw his assumption confirmed. It was Randy. He answered with the words, "Janet called you, too?"

"Yeah. Did she tell you what happened?" Randy asked.

"Accident, she said."

"He was hit by a truck, Dave."

"What?"

"Right outside the store. I got the feeling his prognosis isn't good."

"Yeah, I got that, too," David admitted, though even saying the words brought a lump to his throat. "So when are you coming?"

"I'm flying out tonight, overnight flight. Changing planes in Detroit, and I'll land early tomorrow morning.

Kevin and Brad have early flights tomorrow, so I'm just going to rent a car and wait for them at the airport, and we'll all drive into Port Lucinda together."

"You going to room together or—"

"My dad still has the cottage there," Randy said. "He said we could use it. There's plenty of room for all four of us. And it's only twenty minutes from the hospital."

He nodded, recalling the "cottage" of which Randy spoke. It was a two-story house perched on the cliffs, overlooking the rocky Atlantic shore. Breathtaking place. Randy's parents had lived in an ordinary house in town, and rented the cottage out to summer visitors to make extra money. David had never understood how anyone could own a home like that one and not want to live in it.

"Thanks, Randy. I'd actually love to stay in the cottage with you guys. I can't think of a better place, in fact. Listen, I've got an overnight shift to finish, then I'm going to pack up a few things and hit the road. I'll drive in—it's only a few hours from here. I should be there by nine, nine-thirty tomorrow."

"You're not going to sleep?"

"I don't think I could if I wanted to—not knowing, you know?" David had to swallow again; his throat kept clenching up.

"Yeah," Randy replied. "Listen, just be careful. I don't want to have two friends to visit in the hospital tomorrow, okay?"

"You, too. I'll see you in the morning."

David ended the call, lowered his head, thought about Mark and Janet. They had twin sons, both seniors in high school. And while Janet was not the girl Mark had been pining over the night they'd been such idiots, she was the love of his life. Hell, *none* of the guys had ended up with the girls they'd been so wrought up over back then. Brad had met his wife Cindy in college. She was a nurse in his booming chiropractic practice in Philly. Kevin had been married and divorced three times now, and was currently into dating bone-thin fashion models. He lived in New York, made a living doling out financial advice to the wealthy and powerful. Randy had a successful career writing commercial jingles, though he really wanted to be a rock star. At thirty-eight, he still couldn't admit that wasn't going to happen. He'd come out of the closet a year after they all got out of detention. He lived with his partner, Albert, in San Francisco.

David had never married. He'd become a firefighter, and he didn't need a shrink to tell him that he did it as some kind of self-imposed penance for his past mistakes. Maybe that was why he stayed single, too. He didn't feel he deserved to fall in love, get married, have kids—all those things Sierra Terrence would never have the chance to do. So he devoted himself to work, engaged in one-night stands now and then, and aside from his four best friends, never let himself get close to anyone. And he was fine with that. He'd chosen it, and it was fine.

Now, though, one of them was facing mortality. And dammit, David knew what Mark must be feeling right now. That he didn't want to die without having made up for what he'd done—he didn't want to face judgment with that girl's death on his side of the scale.

David knew it. Because he felt the same thing every time he walked into a burning building. Every single time. Dying didn't scare him. But the thought of seeing Sierra again—of looking into those dark, deep eyes of hers and having to explain why he killed her—that thought terrified him. Kept him awake nights.

Haunted him—especially lately. He'd been dreaming—

For just an instant, the recurring dream flooded his mind, pulling him into its depths. Sierra, all draped in flowing white, floating toward him, more beautiful than ever. And as he reached out for her, she said, "I'm coming back, David. I'm coming back."

He snapped out of the fantasy with a gasp, just as he had for the last five consecutive mornings. Why? God, why now?

Maybe because of Mark.

Poor Mark. If he was dying, and knew it, he must be suffering the fires of a thousand hells right now. And there wasn't a damned thing that David or any of the other guys were going to be able to do to ease that. They could only know that they would all face exactly the same thing, in the end.

CHAPTER TWO

DAVID DROVE HIS JEEP Wrangler past the big wooden "Welcome to Port Lucinda, The Town Where Time Stands Still" sign, and shook his head at how appropriate the nickname was. Hell, he'd never realized just how stuck in time his hometown was, until he'd grown up and done some traveling.

The storefronts hadn't changed. The green-and-white striped awnings, the old-fashioned lettering, the fact that the drugstore still served fountain sodas and root beer floats. A lot of the buildings had expanded backward rather than sideways, not wanting to mess up the quaint look of the storefronts. Hell, the salon that today offered hot stone massages, manicures, pedicures, facials and anything and everything related to hair still had an antique barber pole guarding the front door. During tourist season, a quartet of moustached locals showed up to sing in harmony beside that pole every Friday, Saturday and Sunday afternoon.

Not so in February.

He passed Potter's Grocery. Mark's father had handed it down to him, just as his grandfather had passed it on to his dad, and he was pretty sure his granddad had taken over from his own family. It had been Potter's for as long as anyone could remember. But Mark's boys weren't even out of high school yet. God, it wasn't time for them to have to take over.

Within a couple of minutes, David was driving out of the village and passing by the last place officially a part of it.

The old Muller House. Of course, now it was called Sierra House, in honor of the girl who'd died there so long ago. It served as a community center, for the most part. A place to hold dances, talent shows, host everything from local bands to bake sales. But it was also a resource for troubled teens. Twice a month, there were crisis counselors on duty there. Kids with problems could come and talk confidentially, and they'd be steered to the resources they needed. They'd be listened to and helped.

The fire hadn't burned the old Muller place to the ground. It had only gutted it, and spurred the townsfolk to stop fighting over it and agree it was worth saving. The restoration had begun that very spring.

David pulled the Jeep onto the snowy shoulder of the road and sat there for a moment. There was a picket fence surrounding the house now. There hadn't been before. The sidewalk had been buckled and cracked—he remembered tripping on it as they ran from the blossoming flames that night. In fact, it was almost impossible for him to look at the place—all freshly painted with new shutters and curtains in the windows—and see anything other than the sagging, peeling menace it had been back then. He hated the Muller House. He hated the town for not tearing it down to begin with.

He hated himself for blaming the house, or the town, or anyone for what happened. It was no one's fault but his own.

God, he could almost see her face in the upstairs window, staring out at him, flames leaping up around her as she cried and pounded on the window glass.

He hadn't seen that, not then, not now. It wasn't a

memory, it was his mind torturing him. And he couldn't stop thinking about the life he'd taken away.

Or the woman she would have become.

He'd been with that woman again the other night, in dreams so vivid they left him shaken and more exhausted than before he'd slept at all. Sierra. A little older, a little more beautiful. Sierra. God, how she haunted him.

He shook himself, dragged his attention away from the girl whose soul seemed to live inside his own and shifted the Jeep into gear, glancing into the mirror. And then he froze, because for just the barest instant, he saw her in his rearview mirror—Sierra Terrence, standing on the opposite side of the road, slightly behind where he was parked, and staring at that house just the way he'd been doing. It was a glimpse, no more. She stood there in faded jeans, enveloped in a big heavy parka, but its hood was down and her long dark hair was moving with the winter wind.

There, and then not there.

He slammed the Jeep into Park and twisted around in his seat to look again. But there was no one there.

He took a couple of open-mouthed breaths, scanning the sidewalks up one side of the street and down the other. Looking for her. Because that hadn't been his mind, or his imagination. Maybe the resemblance had—but there had been somebody there.

Or else he was hallucinating.

Damn, he had been without sleep for close to twenty hours. That was probably all it had been. But it had sure as hell felt real. Real enough that his heart was still racing. Sierra. God, would he ever get over her?

So he drove on, up the winding road that led to The Heights, which was what the locals had unofficially named the seaside portion of Port Lucinda. Not creative, but certainly accurate.

As Randy's father's cottage came into view, David noticed a green SUV in the wide driveway and knew his friends had already arrived. Moments later he was pulling in next to it.

Randy, Kevin and Brad came out the front door before he was even out of the Jeep, and then they were all around him, clapping him on the shoulders, pumping his hand. Brad had gained weight and lost hair. Kevin still looked like a male model. And Randy, who'd barely changed at all, hugged him hard. David wasn't ashamed to hug back. These were more than friends to him. More than brothers, even.

"My bag's in the back," he began.

"Why don't you leave it, for now?" Randy said.

David frowned, and Kevin added, "We just got a call from Janet. She said we should hurry."

"Aw, hell. Is he—?"

"She wouldn't say. Just said he was asking for us. To get there, fast. So we're going."

"Okay. So we're going."

As one, they trooped to the SUV and piled in.

"OH, THANK GOD. THANK GOD you're all here." Janet rose from the chair beside her husband's bed and met the four men halfway across the hospital room. And David wanted to look at her, to acknowledge her, but for the life of him, he couldn't take his eyes from Mark. Because he didn't look like Mark at all.

His face was red, swollen, bruised to hell and gone. His head was swathed in bandages that went under his chin and encircled his entire skull like a nun's wimple. His left leg was casted all the way to his groin, and suspended from a rack over the bed. There were IV lines running into one arm, an oxygen tube taped to his nose and other electronics wired to his chest and his head.

Janet had been hugging each of them, and finally it was his turn. He returned her embrace and as she stepped away, he looked at her and thought she'd aged ten years since he'd seen the two of them last summer—Independence Day. How long ago was that? Seven months? No one aged ten years in seven months. He suspected the weariness and stress he saw in her now had occurred in the last forty-eight hours.

He cupped the side of her face. "What can we do for you, Jan? What do you need?"

She shook her head. "You came. That's all he's wanted—insisted on. Maybe he'll relax a little bit now that you're here."

"How is he, Janet?" Randy asked. "Really?"

She met Randy's eyes, and then just shook her head, very slightly. As if to say they didn't expect Mark to live. And David knew she wouldn't want to say that out loud, not in the same room with him.

"Is he asleep?" David asked.

"I don't know," she whispered. "His eyes are too swollen to open. Come on."

She gripped his arm and tugged him closer to the bed. Behind him, he heard the door open again, heard a nurse insisting that only two visitors were allowed at a time and heard Brad telling her she'd need more help if she wanted to remove any of them. Then Randy said, "We won't stay long, we promise."

There was a sigh, then the door swinging closed. The nurse must have withdrawn. And then Kevin was standing at his side, Randy and Brad on the opposite side of the bed, all of them staring down at Mark.

"What the hell happened?" Brad asked. "Randy said he was hit by a *truck?*"

Janet's voice was so lifeless it was nearly a monotone.

"The driver says he just came sprinting out of nowhere, and right into his path. Everyone's been asking him why, but he said he couldn't talk to anyone but the four of you."

"Don't let that hurt you, hon," Randy said, sending Janet a fond look. "We really bonded in the detention center. It was hell there, you know. We needed each other."

"I know," she said. "I know what you all went through together. And I know he's never gotten over it. I'm just so glad you came." Leaning over the bed, cupping her husband's face, she said, "Hey, baby. The guys are here, just like you asked. Can you hear me? Dave, Brad, Kevin and Randy. They're all here. They came just as fast as they could."

His head moved very slightly. His mouth seemed to tense, then his lips parted and he spoke with effort. "Guys?"

"Right here, Mark," David said softly, and he laid a hand over one of Mark's, so he could feel him there. Only then did he realize Mark's eyes actually were open, mere slits between his swollen lids.

Mark nodded very slightly, and shifted what there was of his gaze toward Janet. "I need you…to wait…"

"You want privacy. I understand." There was hurt in her tone, but she didn't argue. She leaned down and kissed an exposed part of his face, then hurried from the room and closed the door.

"Okay, we're alone, pal," Brad said. "What's going on?"

"Sierra."

David and Brad shot each other a look, and David said, "What about Sierra?"

"I saw her."

And David felt icy cold right to his core. He almost shivered.

Randy frowned at Mark. "You mean you sort of crossed over for a few seconds, when all this happened? You saw her on the other side."

"No. Here. She's here. She's…coming for us."

Kevin's brows went up and he actually took a step away from the bed. "Mark, come on—"

"She's come back…for revenge."

The other three had been leaning closer and closer to better hear him, but now Brad straightened with a grunt. "You probably dreamed about her while you were unconscious, Mark. That's all. You're hurt pretty badly, you know."

"I know that," Mark said. "But it's not…a dream. I saw her—before…the accident. Waiting for me…outside the store. Just standing there in the snow, waiting. She came…for my soul…and she got it, guys. She got it."

Brad shot David a quick glance, then said, "Wait, wait, you're telling me this delusion started *before* you got hit by that truck?"

"No delusion!" He tried to sit up in the bed, but fell backward. The steady beeping of the machines increased in pace. A nurse came into the room, alarmed.

"She reached out…for me—might as well have… pushed me in front of…that truck." His brows crunched together. "Maybe—maybe she *did* push me. Without actually touching. 'Cause she's not…alive. She's a ghost… or something."

"He's too agitated, gentlemen," the nurse said. "You really have to leave." She shouldered her way in between them to the bedside. "Really—"

"No!" Mark shouted.

"Come on," Brad said. "This is ridiculous, Mark. You're hurt, your head's all messed up. Sierra's dead. We made a terrible mistake, but we told the truth, and we did the time." The nurse looked slightly alarmed at that. "It's over," Brad insisted.

"Really, sirs, you have to leave." The nurse was moving them bodily away from the bedside now.

And then Mark's hand flashed out suddenly, and closed around David's with a surprisingly strong grip. "I stayed alive…this long…so I could warn you…dammit. Listen to me. She's come back. She already had…her vengeance on me…but I'm telling you…you're next." His voice got suddenly louder, a final burst of strength empowering it. "She's come back! The girl we killed has come…and she's not going to rest until we're all dead just like she is."

And then his hand went slack, and his head sank heavily onto his pillows.

"I think he passed out," David said, leaning closer in alarm.

"I think it might be a bit more than that," the nurse said. "Get out. Stay with the wife until we call for you." Then she pushed a button on the wall and said, "I need Dr. Pollock, stat."

Brad was already heading for the door, and the others followed, just barely getting through it before three white-coated individuals came running down the hall and pushed past them to get inside.

"Man, Mark's messed up, isn't he?" Brad asked.

David nodded, knowing Brad needed some kind of re-assurance, because Mark's words had probably sent the same icy chills running up and down his spine as had brushed David's own. And with his physique, and the way he got out of breath just crossing a room, David didn't think Brad could handle too many shocks.

So he didn't say a word about what he thought he had seen outside that damned cursed house this very morning. "He's got a head injury, pal. That's all it is."

Brad seemed relieved, and then Janet was there, taking his arm. "They want me to stay out of the room while they examine him," she said. "What happened in there?"

Brad lowered his head, as did Randy and Kevin when she looked at each of them in turn. But when her eyes met David's, he said, "Why don't we find a place to sit and talk. You look like you could use something to eat. Is there a cafeteria or—?"

Janet sent a yearning look at Mark's closed door, but then nodded. "It's just down the hall."

David fell into step with her, and the others followed. He didn't feel like he could eat a bite, but once in the cafeteria he grabbed a plate and proceded to fill it all the same, hoping Janet would try to eat if the rest of them did.

He paid little attention to what he scooped onto his plate. There were fresh fruits, scrambled eggs, a stack of pancakes and piles of bacon and sausage. A typical breakfast buffet. He watched Janet as she put a minuscule amount of fruit and a pastry onto her own plate, then he led her to a table.

She sat beside him, and the other three men joined them. Kevin had to pull a chair from another table over to theirs.

David waited until she had taken a couple of bites, forcing himself to do likewise, and then finally he took a breath and looked her in the eye. "Do you know what Mark thinks, Janet?"

"No. But I know it has something to do with Sierra Terrence." She looked at each of the men. "I'm right, aren't I?"

They nodded, almost as one.

"He's been muttering her name in his sleep. Especially right after the accident, when he was unconscious. And when he woke up, he seemed scared to death and kept asking for you guys—just you guys. No one else."

David nodded. "He said he saw her—or her ghost, or something. That's what made him run out into the street like that. He thought she was after him. He thinks she's come back to get revenge on us, I guess."

"He hit his head," Randy told her, and he reached across the table to cover her hand with his own. "That's all it is. He's hurt and he doesn't know what's real and what's part of a dream or a hallucination or whatever this is. That's all."

Janet met his eyes. "I don't think so. Look, I don't want to scare him, or you guys either. But I know my husband. And I think he saw *something.*"

"No, Janet, no. He doesn't remember what happened," Kevin said. "He doesn't. This is all some kind of delusion."

She shook her head firmly, left, then right. "He saw something. I've never seen him that terrified. And he *got* terrified *before* the truck hit him. Something frightened him badly enough to send him running into its path." She looked directly at David then. "I want to know what."

David nodded. "I'll look into it, Jan."

"Will you?" She looked hopeful and surprised.

"You know how close we all are. I'm not gonna just let this go. He needs to know it's not real, and he won't accept anything less than proof. So yeah, you bet I'm gonna look into it. We all will."

She closed her eyes, released her breath all at once, and lowered her head. "Thank you, David," she whispered. "Thank you, all."

"Mrs. Potter?"

They all turned to see the doctor who'd rushed into Mark's room earlier approaching their table. They rose, all of them, and the fear that came into Janet's eyes tore at David's gut.

"It's all right," Janet said as the doctor—Dr. Pollock—looked at the men around her. "They're family. You can talk in front of them."

The doctor nodded. "Mrs. Potter, your husband has lapsed into a coma."

She faltered, her knees barely able to support her, and David quickly gripped her shoulders and eased her back into her chair. "Is he...is he brain-dead?" she whispered.

"No. But we have no way of predicting when or...or if he'll come out of this. We're going to have to wait and see."

"Oh, God, this isn't happening," she whispered. Tears pooled and then spilled onto her cheeks.

"I want you to keep talking to him, keep visiting him, keep encouraging him."

"He can still hear us?" David asked.

"That's the predominant wisdom, yes. And it could help." He put a hand on Janet's shoulder. "I'm sorry. I wish the news was better." With a final squeeze, he left the room.

"He waited for you," Janet told them. "It was so important to him that he managed to fend off a coma long enough to talk to you."

"He wanted to warn us that Sierra was coming after us next," David said, nodding. "And I know it's crazy, but to him, it's real."

"Yeah, and once we find out what he really saw," Randy said, "and we tell him, really convince him that it's all okay, he'll come out of this. I know he will, Janet."

"God," she whispered. "God, I hope so."

CHAPTER THREE

DAVID DIDN'T END UP GETTING his bag from the Jeep until much later that night. When they left the hospital, the four men drove down to Potter's Grocery, Mark's store, parked the SUV in front and looked sadly at the "Closed Until Further Notice" sign that had been taped to the front door.

"Look, let's talk to people, see if anyone saw anything that could give us a clue what really happened yesterday," Randy said.

Brad shook his head. "Don't you think the police have already done that?"

"Maybe we should talk to them, then," Kevin put in.

David nodded. "We'll do all of the above. Brad and Kevin, you stay here and talk to anyone who's willing. Randy, you can drive me to the police station. There's another grocery store out that way, so you can pick up supplies for the cottage while I talk to the cops. Okay?"

"I don't like the idea of splitting up," Brad said.

"Why not?" David was puzzled, but then he noticed that Brad's forehead seemed damp. "Brad, no one's after us, if that's what you're worried about."

"How can you be so sure?" Brad asked, casting a nervous look up and down the road. There were few people out, locals, moving in and out of the various shops along Main Street. "I mean, not a ghost, sure. But what if it's someone else? Some relative of hers out for revenge?"

"After twenty-two years?" David asked. "Come on, Brad."

"Is it so far-fetched? You heard Janet. He saw *something*."

"Yeah. Maybe someone who looked like Sierra. And he freaked out. Maybe this has been eating at him more than the rest of us, for some reason. Maybe his mind wasn't strong enough to deal with it, and seeing a girl with a resemblance to her was all it took to make him snap. Maybe a thousand other things, Brad, but it's not someone out to get us after all this time. It's not."

Brad held his eyes and shook his head. "Why would it bother him more than the rest of us, Dave? More than you, in particular? It couldn't have been worse on any of us than it was on you. God, you were in love with her."

"I was sixteen."

"You still are."

David had to lower his eyes. "Like I said, maybe his mind just wasn't able to handle it. Everyone's different. Mental health is…it's tricky."

"You being an expert and all," Brad said. But he opened the door and got out of the SUV, beer belly first. "Fine, Kev and I will walk around asking questions and hope to God she doesn't find us. Don't be long, okay?"

David nodded and sent a look toward Kevin, silently telling him to keep an eye on Brad. The guy was wavering on the edge of panic. Kevin acknowledged the unspoken message with a slight nod, and got out, as well.

Randy put the rental into gear and they pulled away. And then he turned to David and said, "So what do you *really* think?"

"Just what I said. I think there's probably a girl in town that looks a lot like Sierra. I think Mark saw her, and something broke inside his mind. And that's *all* I think."

"Just asking."

David sighed. Then he glanced sideways at Randy. "This is just between us, okay?"

Frowning, Randy nodded. "Okay."

"When I got into town this morning, I pulled over, in front of the house."

"The Muller House?"

He nodded. "Sierra House now."

"Yeah, I saw that. Kind of nice they did that for her, isn't it?"

"Nice, yeah," Dave said. "Anyway, I pulled over, just sat there looking at it. Remembering, you know?"

"I do know."

"And as I pulled away, or was about to, I saw this girl in my rearview. Just for a second."

Randy was dead silent, waiting.

David sighed. "For that instant, I could have sworn I was looking at Sierra. Not a lookalike, but *her.* You know? It *felt* like her. But when I turned around, she was gone."

He dared a look at Randy, who was driving with wide, unblinking eyes. "Do you think you imagined it? Because of all this, I mean?"

"It was before I knew Mark thought he'd seen her. So it wasn't instigated by that. But I suppose just being back here, being there at that place where it all happened—that could have triggered something. And I was running on empty. No sleep and all that. And worried about Mark and Jan and the boys."

"But…?"

He shrugged. "I've been dreaming about her." He sent Randy a serious look. "Don't repeat this, okay? But in the dreams, she says she's coming back."

"Holy shit, Dave. You think what you saw, what Mark saw, was *real?*"

"I don't know. It didn't feel like a hallucination or a memory. It felt like I glimpsed a real, flesh-and-blood young woman standing on the sidewalk across from the Muller place, staring at it just like I was. That's what it felt like."

"But when you turned around, she was gone."

"Right."

"Like, poof, vanished, in a way that couldn't happen? Or like she could have ducked around a corner or something?"

David frowned hard. "Let's find out."

"Huh?"

"Let's make a quick detour over there, pal. There's snow on the ground. Maybe she left a footprint or two."

"Now you're talking." Randy turned the car around and drove in the opposite direction, taking the turnoff onto Maple.

The only thing across the street from the house was a church, and today wasn't Sunday, so there was no one around. The sidewalk was snow-free, and there were no footprints in the snow on the far side of it.

"I guess she didn't step off the walk," David said softly.

"Either that, or she didn't leave footprints," Randy replied.

David sighed. "Let's get to the police station."

IT STORMED THAT NIGHT. The wind howled around the eaves of the cottage and snow slanted sideways through the night, tapping on the windows like a million tiny fingernails. The ocean slapped against the rocky shore below, frothing and foaming as if enraged.

Hell, maybe it was.

"So no one saw anything before Mark's accident?" David asked.

Kevin shook his head. "No. We talked to a couple dozen people, even found some who were fairly near him just before he lost it, but no one saw any dark-haired girl lurking around."

"Maybe they *couldn't* see her," Brad said softly. And then he crushed the beer can in his hand, dropped it onto the table and went to the fridge for another.

Randy picked up the discarded can and took it to the recycle bin. "You shouldn't be drinking so much, Brad."

"No? What *should* I be doing? An exorcism?"

"I'm just saying, you ate fried chicken and French fries and cheesecake for dinner, and you've been putting away beer and potato chips all night. A man your size—"

"That's how I got to *be* my size, pee-wee."

"No need to get nasty," Randy said, looking hurt.

Kevin sat looking uncomfortable, so David tried to change the subject. "The police are as baffled as we are. So they were no help, except to say that the driver wasn't at fault. The witnesses who saw it happen said Mark just ran into the street as if he were being chased, and right into the path of a delivery truck. But no one saw anything or anyone else near him."

"Sheee-it." Brad took a pull from the beer can that probably drained half of it as he crossed the room to part the curtains. He stood there, staring out at the storm for a moment. And then the can fell from his hand, the remaining beer spilling on the floor.

"Jeez, Brad, watch it, will you?" Randy snatched a dish towel that was hanging near the kitchen sink and hurried toward him.

David rose slowly. "Brad?"

"You know my father's really particular about this place," Randy said, kneeling near Brad and wiping up the beer. "I told him we'd—"

By then, David was across the room, a hand on Brad's shoulder. "Brad, hey, what's going on?"

Brad turned slowly. His mouth was agape, foamy spittle running from one corner, onto his chin. His eyes bulged, and he was as white as the snow outside.

"Brad! Hell, someone call nine-one-one! I think he's having a heart attack. Brad, talk to me, man."

But Brad didn't say a word. David tried to hold on to him, thinking he could maneuver him onto the sofa or something, but the man was just too big. His knees hit the floor, and then he toppled forward and didn't move.

The others gathered around him, Kevin already on the phone, giving the address, Randy kneeling beside Brad on the floor, loosening his clothing, feeling for a pulse.

"He's still breathing," he said, looking up. "His heart's beating—hard."

David looked out the window, sure Brad must have seen something that scared the hell out of him—and already knowing, deep down in his gut, what that something must have been.

And he was right.

She stood there on the cliffs, staring out over the storm-tossed water. Oh, he couldn't see her face clearly, given the darkness and the snow. But her dark hair blew in the wind, and she hugged her arms around her as if she were freezing.

"That's it. I've had enough of this bullshit." David turned, heading for the door.

"Dave, where the—?"

"Take care of him, guys. Randy, you know CPR as well as I do. If his heart stops, do it. Meanwhile, elevate his feet, keep him warm and make sure he keeps breathing and has a pulse. The paramedics will be here in no time—station's only a half mile away."

"But where are you going?"

"I'm gonna go deal with our *ghost*." He grabbed his Carhartt jacket off the hook near the door and was pulling it on even as he stomped outside.

The cold wind hit him in the face, sending a shiver up his spine as he moved around the corner of the house, over the frozen ground, heading toward the cliffs. Straining his eyes, shielding them from the falling snow with one hand, he caught sight of her standing there. At almost the same moment, he heard sirens in the distance—the ambulance coming for Brad. He was at once grateful for their speed and annoyed that the sound made her turn in his direction. Because the moment she spotted him, she ran.

Her trajectory was downward, angling away from him while heading toward the road. He quickly changed direction and began to run the same way, hoping to cut her off before she reached her car, or broomstick, or whatever the hell mode of transport she'd used to get here.

He pushed himself, and the snow wasn't deep enough to impede him much. Puffs of steamy breath emerged from his nose and mouth. The ambulance's flashing lights approached, and as it neared the driveway, it illuminated a vehicle parked along the roadside. It had to be hers.

He felt a rush of relief, the thought passing quickly through his mind that if she drove a car, she must not be a disembodied spirit. Banishing the notion as ridiculous, he headed for the car.

And he reached it, looked around, saw no one. Either he'd beaten her to the road or it wasn't her car, after all. He leaned his hands on his knees, gave himself a minute to catch his breath and glanced up toward the cabin where the ambulance was parked, its attendants presumably already inside tending to Brad. He'd better be all right.

A sound caught his attention, and he turned in the direction from which it came, watching through the darkness as footsteps, crunching rapidly through the snow, came closer.

And closer.

And then she emerged from beyond the overhanging limbs of a snowy spruce tree, looked up and straight into his eyes, and stopped dead in her tracks.

She wasn't a ghost. Puffs of steam emanated from her slightly parted lips.

She had straight, jet black hair and huge eyes of deepest brown, and skin that was coppery, like her mother's had been. She was beautiful, and she hadn't changed at all, that he could see. In twenty-two years, she'd aged only enough to appear more adult than teenager. She was the only girl he'd ever loved. And somehow he'd loved her more after her death than he had before.

Or maybe she was his obsession.

She was dead, and yet she was standing here looking at him.

Sierra Terrence.

CHAPTER FOUR

A Few Days Earlier
Denton, New Hampshire

HER EYES BURNED. HER lungs burned. Her *skin* was starting to burn. She struggled to breathe, but sucked only searing-hot smoke into her lungs. She couldn't see anymore, and her eyes stung as if they'd been irrigated with battery acid. She squeezed them tight as she staggered from the bedroom into the hallway, feeling her way, groping with her hands and moving forward even though everything she touched was hot, and hotter. Her only hope was to find the stairway. A way down. A way out.

Should have gone out the window. Should go back into the bedroom, make my way to the window. The boys might still be out there. Maybe...

She sank to her knees, suddenly unable to move another step. It must be due to the smoke, she realized, even as her consciousness slipped to blackness and back again, until it was impossible to tell which was which without the advantage of sight. It was pitch in the smoke. It was pitch in oblivion. One was the same as the other.

She moved her lips, because her arms and legs would no longer cooperate. She thought she could manage, perhaps, to scream for help—and she did, as loudly as she could with a voice gone hoarse. The sound was so loud and so real and so foreign to her own ears that it shocked her wide-awake.

Lifting her head, blinking the room into focus, Sara Jensen saw two sets of wide-eyes fixed on her. Her room-mates looked more than worried. They looked scared.

Nikki was closest, already coming closer, frowning, feeling for the pulse in her wrist.

"I'm fine," Sara said, and tried to pull her arm free.

"Yeah, and I'm an R.N., so shut up."

"It was just a bad dream."

"You were *screaming,* Sara." Nikki dropped her wrist and touched her forehead. She would be going for her bag next. "Not to mention you're soaked in sweat, shaking all over and your heart's running at about two-ten."

"It's the fifth time this week, Nikki," Cami said. "I've been worried sick about her."

"Fifth time?" Now Nikki really looked worried. She tilted her head, studied Sara in an intense way that made her want to squirm. "Why didn't one of you tell me? I mean, I only moved in yesterday, but still—"

"I was hoping it would go away," Cami said. "And…I didn't want you to change your mind about taking the room."

"You think I'm that hard-hearted?"

Cami shrugged.

"And you, Sara? Why didn't you say something?"

Sara shook her head. "I don't like discussing it. It's my problem, I'll deal with it."

Nikki sighed. "It's probably stress-induced. Stress will wreak havoc on your entire body, you know. And with stuff like that, not talking about it tends to just let it keep building."

Sara nodded as if in full agreement, but she didn't really think so. There wasn't any unusual amount of stress in her life. She was teaching art to elementary students and loved her job. She was painting—and even if the images were troubling, they were good. And yet she felt nervous, jumpy, as if something was wrong, but it was something too elusive to see or understand.

"So what's the dream about?" Nikki asked. "Is it the same one every time?"

Even as Sara began to nod, Cami jumped in. "She's trapped in a fire, unable to breathe or see or find her way out."

Nikki frowned. "And that's it?"

"That's it," Cami said. "Except that this time she screamed a name, instead of just a…well, a scream."

Sara looked at Cami, licked her lips. "I screamed a name?"

Cami nodded. "David." And she watched Sara's face. "That name mean anything to you?"

A chill moved through her, but she tried to ignore it. "Hell, I probably know a dozen Davids. None of them well enough to have me shouting their names in my sleep, though."

"So, tell me more," Nikki said. "What kind of place are you in? What do you see and hear—"

"Wait, wait, you can see for yourself." Cami bounced off the bed and crossed Sara's bedroom to where her paintings stood, covered in white sheets. One was on a tripod, and the others leaned up against the wall. Sara sighed and pushed her dark hair off her face. She had a headache.

One by one, and with great care, the petite redhead pulled the sheets off the canvases, revealing the paintings. One was of a big old house that appeared on the verge of falling down. It had rounded balconies outside several of the second-floor rooms, and a rounded front porch to match. There was a turret of sorts, with a cone-shaped peak on top.

The others in the series were the same, but each showed the house during a different season. The giant maple in the front lawn went from red buds and tiny leaves to full lush foliage to the scarlet and orange transformation of autumn.

"And then the new one. It's the worst," Cami said. Sara sent her a look and she returned a sheepish smile. "I mean, the scariest and most horrifying. They're good, they're all good. Just awful, you know?"

"I'm glad you're not an art critic, Cam. I don't think 'good but awful' would help me sell anything."

"Oh, Sara, you know I love your work."

Nikki was staring at the latest canvas as if mesmerized. The newest painting showed the house in flames, and a hazy face in an upstairs window. There were shadows on the snow-covered ground outside. As if people were standing out there, watching the place burn.

"Hey, Nurse Nikki," Sara said, trying to feign a casual tone, even though she was far from feeling okay. "You think you're going to come up with a diagnosis if you stare at that thing long enough?"

"It's the old Muller House," she said.

Sara felt her body shudder in involuntary reaction. The ripple of it rushed up her spine at the words, but she didn't know why. "It's not a real place, Nik. It's just made up."

Nikki turned to her. "You're kidding, right?"

"No."

"No, you had to have seen it. Maybe when you were a kid or something. It's a real place—hell, I used to walk past it every day on my way to school. It's all new and nice now, but it's really old. And you've captured it, right down to that big maple tree on the front lawn."

Sara got out of bed and moved toward the painting. "I'm sure I made it up. Maybe it's just similar."

"You're from Maine, right?" Cami asked Nikki. "Is that where it is?"

"Yeah. Port Lucinda. It's a small town on the coast." She looked at Sara. "Have you ever been there, Sara?"

"No. Never. It has to be a coincidence."

Nikki lowered her head, paced away from them. "Don't freak out on me, okay? But, um…that place is kind of famous in my hometown. They don't call it the old Muller House anymore. It's Sierra House now. A crisis center for teens."

Sara blinked and looked at her. "Sierra House."

Nikki put a hand on her shoulder. "There was a fire, I don't know, some twenty-odd years ago. A girl was killed. She was a runaway or something. The town restored the place and named it in her memory."

"Oh my God," Cami whispered.

But Sara was shaking her head. "It's not the same place. It's not, how could it be?"

"Sara," Nikki said, "I would tend to agree with you, but…there were five teenage boys sent to juvie for starting that fire. My mother grew up there. She knew them, used to talk about it all the time. How horrible it was that they did what they did, how no one knew the girl was inside and how those boys would have to live with that for the rest of their lives. Five boys, Sara. And look, look what you painted here."

Cami moved closer, tilting her head as she stared at the painting. Then she gasped, clapped a hand over her mouth.

Sara looked, too, at the shadows on the snowy ground. Five of them. Five shadows. She frowned, looked from Cami to Nikki and back again. And she knew she had to go to Port Lucinda. She had to see that place, uncover the story, for herself. She had to prove to herself that it wasn't the same house, that this was all just coincidence.

Because if it wasn't, then she didn't know what it was. She didn't know what it could mean. She didn't know why it gave her a sick feeling in the pit of her stomach.

SHE LEFT THAT VERY AFTERNOON—with a lot of help from Nikki, her brand new roommate and fast friend. Nikki had given her a set of keys to her mother's house in Port Lucinda, and told her to make herself at home there. Her parents were on vacation, and she'd phoned to ask if she could use the house for a few nights in their absence.

It wasn't entirely honest, Sara thought. Nikki didn't want to use the place herself—oh, she and Cami both would have come with her, if they could. But she was the only one with a pile of unused sick days at her disposal. Nikki's job as a nurse at the Trauma Center was as new as her room in their apartment, so she couldn't very well ask for time off. And Cami was in great demand, as well. She was one of three chefs at Denton, New Hampshire's classiest restaurant. One of the few female chefs they'd ever had, and the youngest of either gender. She had a lot to prove to the owners of Tastebud. And so far, she was knocking them dead.

Both of Sara's roommates wanted her to wait until they had time to come along. Both of them promised to join her in Port Lucinda if she hadn't returned by mid-week, when they both had days off. Both insisted she stay in near-constant contact by phone. And both were worried to death.

Those things they had in common. But they were on complete opposite sides in their opinions about Sara's *symptoms*. Nikki was convinced it was stress combined with having heard, and then buried deeply in her subconscious mind, the story about the Muller House tragedy. Maybe she identified with something about the victim, Sierra Terrence. It was certainly either that, Nikki opined, or a brain tumor.

Cami was convinced it was something far different. The ghost of Sierra, haunting Sara's dreams, trying to get a message through to the living, through her. When asked why a dead girl from Maine would choose Sara to dump her problems on, Cami hypothesized that maybe Sara was the only one the dead girl could reach. Maybe she'd tried with others. Maybe she even nudged Nikki to come live here, so that Sara would find out about the real location of the house. She had a mission to accomplish here, Cami insisted. And the ghost wouldn't leave her alone until it was done. Just like on *Ghost Whisperer,* or *Medium.*

Cami's theories made Nikki angry. Nikki's skepticism made Cami crazy. And all in all, Sara thought Port Lucinda, Maine, was going to be a peaceful haven from the friction at home, even if it were entirely populated by ghosts with unfinished business.

She drove her canary-yellow VW Bug to the address Nikki had supplied without a hint of trouble thanks to her handy little GPS system, its confident, computerized voice (she'd chosen the female version) guiding her right to the front door with a nearly cheerful-sounding, "You have reached your destination."

She reached up and shut it off. "Thanks, Jane-Jane." The house was gorgeous, a great big rectangle with a covered front porch, a wide, paved driveway and an attached two-car garage with room for an apartment above it. The lamps that flanked the entryway looked like a pair of old-fashioned carriage lamps, she thought.

She took out her key and opened the door, feeling as if she were intruding, and yet not. She hadn't driven into the village of Port Lucinda yet. This house was on the out-skirts, and she'd reached it first and felt inclined to estab-lish a home base before braving the next step on her journey of discovery, as she was calling this mad trip—even while knowing there was likely not going to be a damned thing to discover. She would feel silly for driving all the way up here by this time tomorrow. She would feel ridiculous.

But tonight, she felt afraid. And not quite ready.

And her cell phone was ringing already.

Thinning her lips, she toed off her shoes and left them near the front door, then answered the phone while walking slowly through the house and looking around.

"Are you there yet?" Nikki asked.

"I just walked in the front door. You're psychic."

"Don't talk like Cami. Listen, go into the living room."

"Nik, I'm tired. I'm hungry and I need to use the bathroom. Could you maybe chill, and let me call you back in a half hour?"

"No, but this will only take a minute. I've got some-thing for you."

Sara closed her eyes and sighed, but walked through a wide hall that emptied into a big living room with outdated, but spotless, furniture in powder blue.

"Go to the bookshelf," Nikki said. "See it?"

"Mmm-hmm." She crossed that plush cushy carpet to the bookshelf—built-in, floor to ceiling, five shelves and the length of the entire wall. There had to be a couple of hundred volumes there. "What am I looking for?"

"Mom's high school yearbooks. Should be on the bottom, toward the right."

Sara traced the spines with her eyes and spotted *Memories* on a handful of slender volumes, each one with a year after the word. "I see them," she said.

"Good, grab the one from 1988. The boys who set that fire are part of the sophomore class that year. Mom was a senior. She gave me their names, said everyone knew, even though they were too young for the press to make them public. It's a small town. And best of all, she said one of them still lives there."

Sara pulled the book from the shelf, then walked to an overstuffed blue chair. She leaned over to turn on a lamp before sinking nearly out of sight in the soft, snuggly seat. "So I'm looking for sophomores?" she asked as she opened the book. But she didn't hear the answer, because she'd frozen on the very first page. "Oh my God. Oh my God. Jesus, Nikki, what the hell?"

"What? Honey, what's wrong? What's going on?"

Sara could barely see now for the tears that had flooded her eyes. The very first leaf of the yearbook sported a full-page photo of a dark-haired teenage girl, obviously of mixed heritage, with bronze skin, like her own. She had very large, dark brown eyes that looked as if they were lined with kohl, and thick black lashes, just like her own. She had long, perfectly straight, perfectly black, shiny hair, just like her own.

In fact, she looked enough like Sara to have been her own sister. Maybe even a twin sister.

It took her several moments to realize that Nikki was shouting at her from the telephone, which had apparently fallen from her numb hands into her lap. Shaking herself, Sara picked it up. "First page of the yearbook, Nikki. It's a photo of…her. It reads, 'In Loving Memory of Sierra Terrence.'"

"Oh! Is that all? God, I was scared. So, what's she look like?"

Sara took a slow breath. "She looks like me. She looks…*just* like me." God, she didn't need this. Not now, when all she'd wanted was to rest, regroup, prepare. And now this? Hell.

"What am I supposed to think about all this, Nikki?"

"I don't know. I just… I don't know. Worse, I don't even want to think about what Cami's going to make of this latest revelation."

"Maybe…maybe she has a point."

"I never heard of a ghost that could make you look like an old photo of her," Nikki said. "Look, why don't you just lay low at my mom's for a few days. I'll come out Wednesday and we'll dig into this then."

Sara drew in another breath, closed her eyes slowly. "I'll think about it. But first, why don't you give me those boys' names so I can look at their photos. And then I promise, I'm going to get some food and some sleep before I do another thing."

"I have your word on it?"

"Yes, you do. I'm beat, and I can't take any more shocks tonight." She cast her eyes around the room in search of a pen, and not seeing one, opened the drawer in the end table and smiled at the accuracy of her guess. A pen and pad lay in wait. She took them out. "Go ahead with those names."

She proceeded to write them down as Nikki recited them to her.

CHAPTER FIVE

SARA DIDN'T KEEP THE PROMISE she'd made to her roommate.

She tried, she really did. She put her things in Nikki's old bedroom, which was right where Nikki had told her it would be. But not exactly the *way* Nikki had told her it would be. She'd said it would be exactly as she had left it. Purple paint on the walls. Cheerleading uniform hanging on the outside of the closet door, flanked by pompoms, boy band posters everywhere and her orange beanbag chair underneath the window.

It wasn't. It was a charming, neat-as-a-pin guest room. The walls were pale blue, to match the blue and yellow pattern of the curtains and bedspread. The colonial-style four-poster bed, matching dresser and nightstand all looked like a deep cherrywood, and all of the drawers were empty, as if awaiting guests.

She smiled and decided Nikki's parents were dealing far better with her being away from home than she thought they were. *Far* better.

She left her two bags, one big, one small, on the bed, and headed back downstairs to find something to eat. The fridge was fairly empty, as she'd expected. People didn't leave perishable stuff around when they went on vacation. But the freezer was well-stocked, and the cupboards were, too. She settled on a personal-size frozen pizza, popping it into the microwave. Some juice, with ice, because it hadn't been refrigerated, and she'd be good to go.

To sleep. She thought.

But she didn't go to sleep. She couldn't sleep. She tossed and turned in the quiet guest room. It drove her crazy, being so close to the town that held all the answers. Why sleep and wait? Why risk the repetitive dream of dying in a fire, returning to torment her yet again?

Or the other dream, the one she hadn't told her friends about.

The one where she was in the arms of a beautiful man— a man she'd never seen before. And loving him with everything in her. The emotion of it had come through her so powerfully that it felt as if it remained there, heavy on her chest, for the entire next day. And for a week now, she'd felt on the verge of weeping for a man who wasn't even real.

Indeed, why sleep and risk another dream?

Sitting up in the bed, she opened the yearbook, careful to avoid the page where her own face seemed to stare back at her. Instead, she flipped to the pages she'd marked, where the sophomore class were in a big group shot up top, and then in individual headshots below and on the facing page. For the tenth time that night, she skimmed those faces, dragging her forefinger over them and pausing on each of the ones whose names she'd written down.

She wondered if she would have been able to pick them out without the names. When she heard them, they hadn't seemed any more familiar than their faces. She'd felt that odd chill up her spine only once—and she felt it again now, when her finger and her gaze came to rest on David Nichols.

He was a gorgeous young man. His hair was unruly,

curling and light brown, blond bits here and there that probably got blonder in the summer and browner in the winter. Eyes all streaked with brown and green. When he smiled, there were dimples in his cheeks. Deep ones that were going to be there forever.

The image blurred and wavered before her eyes, and then as she blinked it clear again, she realized that the photo was in black and white. Not color. And yet, she'd been seeing it in color. Furthermore, he wasn't smiling in the photo. Only in her mind. At *her*. With some deep sort of emotion in his eyes. She'd been seeing him as if he were real—not a photograph. Something else. Something that felt an awful lot like…like a memory.

"David," she whispered, trying the name out on her lips, wondering if it would elicit anything more.

But there was something more. A very real resemblance between the boy in the photo and the man in her dream.

David Nichols wasn't in town anymore. According to Nikki, he'd moved away long ago. And besides, he was twenty-two years older now. Still, she couldn't quite explain the odd yearning in the pit of her stomach, the feeling that she had to meet him, to see him, to talk to him.

Maybe the one who was still in town could give her some answers. Maybe Mark Potter would even know where David Nichols was, how to reach him. Maybe. She would talk to Mr. Potter first thing in the morning, at his grocery store in town.

But in the meantime, she had to see that house—the old Muller place.

Giving up on sleep well past midnight, she decided there was no time like the present. She got out of bed, dressed warmly, donned her parka and walked into town. She didn't want to drive; it was too clear and crisp a night, and besides, she'd been driving all afternoon.

The village of Port Lucinda was less than a mile ahead, and as she moved through the silent, darkened streets, over well-maintained sidewalks, past shops that looked as if they were preserved from the previous century, she felt waves of déjà vu so many times that she stopped counting them. They came with every steamy puff of air she breathed.

Potter's Grocery was dark. Empty. She saw from the sign that they opened early, though, and she imagined Mark Potter would be there even earlier. So she would try to catch him on the way back.

But for now, her goal lay beyond the town of Port Lucinda. All the way on the other side, in fact. She walked on, leaving the village and its shops behind and following the winding road northward another half mile until, at last, she saw it.

The house rose up before her, the starry blackness of night its backdrop. There was no moon, and despite the stars, she thought it seemed the blackest night she had ever seen, anywhere. And there was that house, that very same house she had painted over and over again, standing in the midst of it.

There was no question it was the same building. Oh, it had been repainted, and it had been restored—but it was the same. Those round balconies, the turret, the scalloped siding that made the turret sort of birthday-cakelike. That had been clinging in bits and patches in her paintings of the place. The maple tree was the same—only it was bigger. Older than she'd depicted it.

The only difference she could see was the sign on the front lawn. *Sierra House—Teen Crisis Center.* The white wood sign hung from a post, suspended by iron S hooks that creaked as the wind blew.

She dragged her gaze away from the sign, and found

it riveted to a window on the second floor—and for the barest instant, she could have sworn she saw her own face staring back down at her from that window.

"So you've come back."

She gasped and turned to see an old woman, brown-skinned and mature, though beautiful. Her silver-streaked raven hair was wound into a tight bun and pinned to the back of her head, and she wore an ordinary sundress with a heavy peacoat over it, but she seemed as if she would be more at home in a brightly colored sari.

"Do you know me?" Sara asked.

"I know who you were. Perhaps not who you are. But you look the same."

"As…who?"

The older woman smiled. "Her," she said, and she pointed toward the exact window at which Sara had just been staring. "It happens that way sometimes. When there are things unsettled. But now you've come back. You'll work it all out."

Sara frowned even harder. "I don't know what you're talking about. Nothing's unsettled."

"Something is, or you wouldn't be here. I never did feel the entire story was known. Oh, Sierra, you'll work it out. You will."

"My name is Sara."

"It's all the same."

Sara was still shaking her head. "Who *are you?*"

The woman smiled mysteriously. "I'm an aunt. I saved my money. Came here to take care of you. But I was too late. You were already dead."

The woman's voice was warm, her face sincere, but Sara thought she was probably a little bit demented.

"Look, you might have been an aunt to Sierra, but I'm not her."

"You are," she said. "And you will be, until it's all worked out. You can't move on until it's settled. But you have to come to that in your own time." She patted Sara's shoulder and then stretched her arm, pointing a crooked finger up the road. "I live that way, near the trailer park where you grew up. Your father's still there, you know."

"No. No, I don't have a father. I was raised in foster care."

She smiled. "My house is yellow. It's the only yellow one on the block. When you are ready to know who you are, Sierra, you come to me. Okay?"

"Okay."

"My name is Pakita." Again the hand patted her shoulder. And then the woman turned and walked away, up the sidewalk, toward that yellow house that must not be too far.

So Sierra—the dead girl who looked like her, and who seemed to be haunting her dreams—still had family here. This slightly loopy aunt, and a father. Two things Sara had never had.

Shaking her head, she decided she'd had enough of this place—she didn't like it. She didn't know why anyone would. Turning, she headed back toward town, and when she made it there by five a.m., she figured Mr. Potter would show up to open his store in an hour, maybe an hour and a half. So she found a comfortable place to sit at the end of the alley between Potter's Grocery and the drug-store-slash-soda shoppe, where she was more or less out of sight. An upturned plastic milk crate made a great seat, and she took it, and she waited.

Mark Potter arrived about an hour later. He pulled his Cadillac into a spot along the roadside, and, taking his keys from a pocket, walked to the door to unlock it.

Delivery trucks had begun rumbling over Main Street, their noise signaling a firm end to the quiet of a Port Lucinda night.

She studied the man as he bent to the lock. He had changed quite a bit. He was bigger, of course, but he still had the same dark hair and striking, wide jawline that he'd had in the high school photo.

She said softly, "Excuse me. Are you Mark Potter?"

And the man turned his head slowly, a big smile on his face until his gaze fell on her. Frowning, he reached inside the now open shop door, and flipped a switch. The store's lights came on, and because she stood now right in front of the big window, they spilled on her. She shielded her eyes and backed up into the shadows again.

But he'd had a good look at her, and now his eyes widened.

"Are you?" she asked. "I think you are, but you're older now."

"I…I…" He held up a hand.

"I know, it's probably a shock to see me. I know I look like—wait!"

He didn't wait. Before she finished the sentence, he'd turned, his face having gone white, and just ran, just lunged really, headlong across the sidewalk and right into the road, even as yet another delivery truck rumbled by. It hit him instantly. He ran so directly into its path that given another microsecond, *he* would have hit *it*.

But it hit him instead. The impact was brutal, and she covered her mouth and averted her face, but her eyes couldn't turn away. She saw the man airborne, then crashing down onto the pavement. People came running, the truck driver, other shop owners, a jogger just passing by. They gathered around him, blocking her out, calling for help.

Sara thought she was going to vomit. She backed even farther into the alley, emerging into the wide paved areas behind the buildings, and walked toward the southern end of town, and Nikki's childhood home.

As she walked, she dialed the cellphone. And when Cami answered, her voice sleepy, she said, "I'm pretty sure I just killed a man."

CHAPTER SIX

"ALL RIGHT, ALL RIGHT," Nikki said. "You've had a day to recover while I found out what was what, and now you're showered, you're sitting, and you have some of that chamomile tea Mom keeps in the teddy bear cannister?"

"I'm clean, I'm sitting, I'm sipping. What have you found out, Nikki? Is that poor man dead?"

"I've talked to Mom, who phoned the town gossip, Nellie Camaroon, who is also the organist at the Methodist church."

"You didn't tell her why you wanted to know, did you?"

"And what would I have told her, Sara? That there's a ghost haunting my friend? Or possessing her, or... whatever the hell this is?"

"Past life."

"Huh?" Nikki asked, then she said, "Cami, come here. I'm putting her on speaker. Okay, Sara, say again?"

"Look, when I was out there—out at Sierra House—"

"When were you there?"

"About four in the morning yesterday, before I went to see Mark Potter and got him killed."

"He's not dead."

"Thank God."

"He's not far from it, though."

"Oh, hell."

"Get back on topic, Sara. You went to Sierra House in the dead of night. And what happened?"

Sara took a breath and sighed. "Most notably, an old Indian woman approached me. She called me Sierra, claimed to be my Aunt Pakita and said I had come back to work things out."

She heard Cami's swift intake of breath, and Nikki whispering the word, "Reincarnation?"

"I think that's what she was getting at. Turns out Sierra's father still lives here."

"You have to see him!" Cami shouted.

"Uh, don't think so. Look what happened to the last guy!"

"Maybe you could wear a disguise. Or even talk to him by phone."

"Maybe. But back to the subject, okay? What did you find out about Mark Potter, and the others?"

"Mark's injuries are pretty serious. Word is that he's been asking for the other guys—the other four guys. I know one of the nurses at Port Lucinda General, and she says they're all arriving this morning."

"They're coming here?" Sara swallowed hard. "All of them?" And in her mind's eye, she was seeing David Nichols. Those intense eyes, that warm smile. And her stomach was tying itself up in knots. She was feeling his powerful arms closing around her, and tasting his desperate kisses the way she'd been doing in dreams, night after night, since before she knew his name.

"Yeah. Randy Madison's family own a place out at The Heights. I can give you directions up there."

"I don't know."

"Look, you're there to find out what this is about. If you don't talk to them, don't talk to Sierra's father, don't even want to talk to this old woman who apparently wants to help, then what's the point? You might as well come home right now."

She drew a breath, sighed. "I know you're right."

But Cami jumped in. "No, she's not. Don't do one thing if you're scared. We'll be with you on Wednesday and we can be the ones to talk to all these people for you. Okay?"

"If I haven't managed it by then, sure," Sara said. "I'm gonna take a nap, I've been up all night for several nights in a row now. Maybe I'll know what to do when I wake up again."

"Keep us posted, hon," Nikki said.

"I will."

SARA TOOK THE NAP. And then she returned to Sierra House, by car this time, intending to look for the old woman, maybe talk to her, perhaps even get a phone number for Sierra's father. But the old woman wasn't at home, the trailer was in a park full of them and she didn't know which one to approach, and she found herself walking back up the road and staring at Sierra House again.

Until *he* came. His Jeep pulled to a stop alongside the road, and she knew him the minute she saw him. David Nichols. Older than the boy in the yearbook. Exactly like the man in her dreams. He sat there, staring at the house for a long moment, and she stood there, staring at him, with something happening inside of her that she had never felt before. God, she was so confused, so overwhelmed. She didn't even *believe* in reincarnation.

"He was your soul mate, Sierra."

She turned, expecting to see the old woman—but there was utterly no one there. And it shook her. The one thing she *hadn't* considered during all of this was that she might be losing her mind.

Now, though, hearing voices, seeing faces in windows when no one was there—now she had to consider it.

She dashed up the sidewalk to where she'd left her car, got in and drove as fast as she could back to the house, and then she shut herself inside, and paced, and wept, and racked her brain to think of an explanation. *Any* explanation. At length, she phoned Nikki, and without preamble said, "Phone your mom, right now. Ask her the name of the person who lives in the yellow house on Maple Street, a block up from Sierra House, near the trailer park."

"You don't sound right. Are you okay, Sara?"

"I'll tell you when you call me back with the answer. Please hurry."

"Okay. Sit tight. I should be able to reach her cell. I'll call you right back, either way."

Sara hung up the phone, and paced, and waited, and wondered if she needed to get herself into a hospital, or something. Her heart was racing. Her head was…it was just a mess. Jumbled, mixed-up notions and ideas. And an endless and ever-growing ache in her heart—a longing, yearning ache for a man she'd never even met.

The phone rang. Three minutes had passed, according to Sara's watch, but it felt more like thirty. She answered immediately. "Well?"

"Sammy and Lois Sheppard live there with their three dogs. No one else. He's a road crew guy for the county, and she works at the post office."

"You're sure it's the right house?" she asked.

"It's the only yellow house on Maple," Nikki said.

"And there are no elderly relatives living with them?"

"No. And if there were, they wouldn't be Indian women, Sara. That is why you're asking, isn't it? This woman you saw, this Pakita, she's messing with you for some reason."

Sara shook her head. "I don't think so. I think—I think she's not even real."

There was a long, long silence. Then, her voice taking on a new kind of tone, the kind she probably used for the most agitated patients in the E.R., Nikki said, "You know what? You shouldn't be out there alone. I really think maybe you need to just rest now, Sara. Just rest. I'm gonna come out there, okay?"

Sara wiped tears from her eyes, and shook her head as if Nikki could see her. "God, don't be so dramatic. I don't mean I think I'm imagining her," she lied. "I mean, I think she's not really some aunt of Sierra's. She's not really who she says she is, and she doesn't live where she says she lives. That's all. Not that she…you know, doesn't exist."

"Oh." She wasn't sure if Nikki was buying into her fabrication. But she wasn't ready to have her roommate cart her off to a mental ward for evaluation. She wished she'd never blurted her suspicion in the first place. But damn, she'd been stunned. Pakita was a figment of her imagination.

Or was she?

"I'm going to go out to Randy Madison's parents' house," she said. "I think my best bet is to talk to Dav—to talk to the four other men."

"Okay," Nikki said. "But just…be careful, okay?"

"Yeah. I will, I promise."

SARA DROVE OUT PAST TOWN, toward the ocean, angling her Bug up the hilly, narrow, snake track of a road that led into The Heights—the cliffs high above the Atlantic, where the wealthiest Port Lucindites lived.

The cottage where the men were staying was just as Nikki had described. Far more modern than Sierra House, and yet clearly mature, and solid. She didn't turn in to the driveway. She was afraid—so afraid. What would they say to her? Did they blame her for their friend's horrible accident? Would they think she was insane? *Was she?*

She pulled the car over along the side of the road, needing to work up her courage before she could face them—face *him*. David.

God, her heart beat faster at the thought of seeing him. Her blood heated and her skin warmed.

Getting out of the car, she followed a footpath that wound up a hill, through quiet pines part of the way and then covering a more barren, rocky terrain right up to the edge of the cliffs.

She stood there for a moment, staring out over the ocean. The wind blew inward, whipping her hair around her head. The air tasted like the sea. Below, the waves exploded in bursts of white foam as they crashed against the rocky shore. It was good here, she decided. Right here, right now, this was good. She would be okay if she could just spend a few more moments here, with the sea wind in her face.

Eventually, though, she felt eyes on her, and turned her head to the left. It startled her how close the winding path had taken her to the cottage occupied by David and the others. Far too close. She hadn't realized.

And, oh, God, there was someone looking right out the window at her, right now! Not David. One of the others, one who'd changed so much she couldn't tell which one he might be. He was pale, balding and overweight. And then he was staggering backward with his mouth gaping.

Sara frowned, straining her eyes, moving her body left and right to try to see what had happened to him. And moments later, she saw David's face in the window, staring out at her. And she saw raw anger in his eyes.

Turning away, she ran down the path, and she knew he was coming after her. She *knew* it.

But she ran. She ran, and the rocks were slippery and she had to take care not to fall. She ran, and the tree limbs tried to smack her, so she weaved and bobbed and avoided them with the skill of a boxer in the ring. She ran, and the road was nearly in sight, just around the next bend in the trail. She ran, and then she heard a siren.

And she stopped running.

Oh, God, what had she done? She'd thought the man in the window had glimpsed her and reacted in shock, alerting the others and sending David out to hunt her down. But now, she thought back on his pale skin, gaping mouth, staggering backward steps, and she wondered if she'd caused even more harm.

Please, she thought, no. *Don't let me have hurt another one.*

Swallowing hard, she pushed aside a low-hanging limb and stepped around it, expecting to see only her little Bug sitting on the other side awaiting her.

Instead, she saw *him.*

David.

Just as handsome as she had imagined he would be. Just as beautiful to her as he had ever been. As he had, it seemed in that moment, *always* been. Even though she'd never met the man before. Everything in her yearned to rush into his arms and whisper, "finally."

Again, she heard the heavily accented voice of the Indian woman, Pakita.

Your soul mate.

CHAPTER SEVEN

DAVID STARED AT HER as emotions he hadn't even known he could feel roiled inside him. Powerful as the waves crashing to the shore below the cliffs, they rocked him, and he couldn't even identify most of them.

He didn't know what to say to her. He just stood there, staring at her beautiful face and searching for words.

But she spoke before he could. She said, "I'm sorry."

He felt the shock rip through him anew, maybe because her speaking to him meant she was real. She was *real*.

"How…?" He lifted a hand with the unfinished question, and it was trembling when he moved it closer, the backs of his slightly bent fingers brushing over her cheek, making her eyes fall closed. "God, you're really here," he whispered.

"No," she said. "Not…not the way you think." She swung her head sideways, her dark eyes widening as she looked toward the house. "What happened?" she asked.

"I don't know."

"Yes, you do." She met David's eyes again, and he felt her willing him to be honest with her. "I saw him in the window—one of your friends. I couldn't tell which one. But I know he saw me, and something happened. Was it his heart?"

"It was Brad, and yes, I think so."

The paramedics loaded him into the back of the ambulance and it trundled away. Sara lowered her head, shaking it slowly. "I never meant to hurt any of them. I only wanted to talk to Mark Potter—he was the only one of you still in town, and I had so many questions—" She lowered her head as tears filled her eyes, and a sob choked off whatever remained of her words.

"I have questions, too," David said. "I don't—understand. Was it someone else who died in that fire, Sierra?"

"Oh, no, that's not—"

"And if it was, why did you wait so long to say anything? Why let us—especially me—go on believing—"

"It wasn't—"

"Do you know what that did to me? And God, why haven't you aged in all this time? I mean, you'd have to be—"

"I'm not Sierra."

He finally stopped speaking, and just stared at her, blinking in disbelief.

"My name is Sara Jensen. I'm twenty-two. I'm an art teacher from New Hampshire. I am *not* Sierra Terrence. I just…"

"If you're not her, what are you doing here?"

The ambulance pulled away, and he turned to watch it go, wondering how Brad was doing and feeling guilty for not being with him.

"This is a conversation that's going to take a while," she said. "And one we need to have—I mean, I need to have it. Sierra seems to be…all wrapped up in my life right now. And I don't think she's going away until I find out why. But…" Her eyes moved over his face, again and again, almost like a caress. She looked at him as if she were having trouble not touching him. And he got that, because he felt the same.

"Let's not do this standing on the side of the road," she said.

He nodded, and realized he was looking at her just as longingly as she was looking at him. "We'll go to the house." He reached for her as if to take her hand, as if it was the most natural thing in the world to do, but then he stopped himself, frowning.

She noticed, and for some reason, she closed the gap between his hand, hovering in the air, and her own. She slid her palm against his, and he felt a shower of sparks shooting outward from his chest into every other part of his body as he closed his hand around hers.

"I just don't want to…cause any more harm," she said. "When the others see me—"

"I'm pretty sure they all went to the hospital. They took the rental car."

"I don't want to be here when they get back," she said.

He nodded as they walked up the road, into the driveway and toward the front door. Once inside, he waved her toward the sofa and opened the fridge. "I can offer you hot coffee, cold beer or tap water."

"Nothing, thanks." She sat on the sofa, watching him. He didn't take anything either, and came to sit beside her.

"Do you want to call and check on him?"

"It's too soon," he said. "Besides, the guys will call me the minute they have anything to report. Why don't we get to you? Is there some reason you're avoiding the subject of what you're doing here?"

She nodded, to his surprise. "Because it's going to sound like I'm crazy." She lowered her eyes. "Maybe I am."

"Why don't you just start at the beginning?"

She tried to relax, he thought. At least she unclenched her fists and leaned back on the sofa. "Okay. Okay. I'm an artist. I paint when I'm not teaching. I've been painting several pieces where the focal point is a house. Always the same house."

"The Muller House?" he asked, knowing it without needing any confirmation.

She met his eyes and nodded. "Yes, although I'd never seen it before. Not until I came here the other day."

"Then how could you paint it?"

"I don't know. I've been having nightmares where I'm trapped inside that very house as it burns. I painted that scene, too, and there were five shadows on the snow outside, as if five people were standing there."

He said nothing for a long moment. And then, finally, his guilt burning in his belly, he said, "We did it. The five of us, Mark, Brad, Kevin, Randy and I. We set the fire that killed you. But I guess you already knew that, or you wouldn't be stalking us."

"Her."

"What?" He lifted his gaze to meet her eyes.

"You set the fire that killed *her*. I'm not Sierra, remember?"

He nodded slowly, but he couldn't take his eyes off her. "God, you look like her."

"I know. I saw her yearbook photo and thought I was going to pass out. But I'm telling you, I'm not her. I didn't even know that what I was painting was a real house—what I was dreaming about, a real event—until my new roommate, Nikki, moved in. She saw the paintings, and she's from here. She told me the story and I didn't really believe her. Not until I came here. Not until I saw that house, and…and you."

"Me?"

"The yearbook photo. It was so…I don't know. It shook me and touched me and jolted me all at once. The photos of the others didn't…it wasn't the same."

He nodded slowly. "That would make sense, I guess, if you were her. But you're not."

She slid a little closer to him on the sofa, and he noticed, reacted, deep down on a gut level, but held it inside.

"I've been having…other dreams, too. Dreams… Tell me, were you and Sierra…?"

"No." He said it too fast, still shaken by what she'd said. She'd been having other dreams. And then asking about sex. Hell, had she been dreaming the things he had? He cleared his throat, tried again. "I mean—hell, I don't know. We never dated. I wanted to and I think she did, too. We were friends, though. And I was working up the nerve to tell her I wanted more when she disappeared."

"Oh." She drew a breath. "I was out there, at the house."

"I thought I saw you there," he said.

She nodded. "I saw you, too. And then someone else. Only, I'm beginning to think I imagined her." She lowered her head into her hands. "God, I've cost two men their lives, and now I think my sanity is slipping, as well. I can't sleep for the dreams. Or barely function for the longing they leave behind. I can't—"

"Easy." He put his hands on her shoulders, amazed yet again that she was real. She lifted her head to blink into his eyes, and he saw that hers were brimming with tears and swirling with emotion. "You didn't cost anyone their life, at least not that we know of. In fact, we're the ones guilty of that."

"Then why were you the ones I wanted to cry out to for help?"

He blinked and stared harder at her, but this close, it was difficult to rein in the incredible urge to pull her closer, and to kiss her. "What do you mean?" he asked.

"In the dream—in the dream, I was trying to call out to

you for help. The last time, I did. I screamed your name, David, even though I didn't know who you were at the time."

He shook his head. "That doesn't make any sense."

"The Indian woman said you were my soul mate." She met his eyes, but then it seemed she had to look away. "But she thought I was Sierra. She said I had come back, because there was something that had to be made right. That I wouldn't know peace until I learned what it was, and fixed it."

"What Indian woman?" he asked.

"The one who seems to be a figment of my imagination."

"Come on, tell me about her."

She sighed, shaking her head. "She said she lived in the only yellow house on Maple Street. She told me my father was still alive, and in the trailer park further up. Only she was talking about Sierra's father, I think. She said her name was Pakita."

David sat there, gaping more with every word she spoke, and when she looked at him again she had to see it. But before he could speak, his phone started ringing. He yanked it out, barely able to tear his eyes from hers long enough to glance down at the screen. But then his attention was caught. "It's Randy."

"Go ahead, please. I'm as eager as you are." She lowered her head, whispering what sounded like a prayer as he answered.

"How is he?" he asked without preamble.

"Had a heart attack, but he's stable now. They say they won't know how much damage was done until all the tests are back, but he's probably going to need a catheterization. His arteries are plugged full of plaque."

"That's no surprise."

"So did you find the girl?" Randy asked.

"She's sitting here with me now, as a matter of fact."

"You…you're kidding, right?"

"No, and she's not a ghost. She's just an ordinary young woman who bears a striking resemblance to Sierra, and who wanted to know more about her. She never meant to hurt anyone. And we can hardly blame her for Mark freaking out and running into the path of a truck at the first glimpse of her, or Brad's poor, long-abused heart failing because she startled him. Hell, the way he was drinking, he might have collapsed before morning anyway."

"Oh, I'm with you there. Still…there's more to this than you're telling me, isn't there?"

David sighed. "We really haven't figured it out yet, Randy. But we're working on it."

"Good enough. Look, we're going to stay with Brad for a while. Then we'll head home. I'll fill Kevin in so he doesn't stroke out when he sees the Sierra look-alike, in case you guys are still there when we get back."

"Okay." David pocketed the phone, and lifted his head. "Brad's stable. His arteries were clogged, and you didn't have anything to do with that. The timing, maybe, but this was going to happen, and soon, with or without you."

She nodded. "Thanks for saying that."

"So what do you want to do, Si…Sara?"

She blinked slowly. "I want to find out whether I'm sane or not. Whether Pakita was real or a hallucination. That's first. And then, if I'm not crazy, then I need to find out what it is that needs to be made right—and—and fix it, I guess."

He nodded. "Pakita's real. I can take you to her, if you want."

She lifted her eyes to his, stunned beyond words. "What?"

"Will you come with me?" he asked.

Sara nodded hard. "Yes. God, yes, right now, if you can. I need to start finding some answers."

"And so do I," David said, unable to take his eyes from her face. Her beautiful, beloved face.

CHAPTER EIGHT

IT WAS, SARA THOUGHT, utterly ridiculous that, with her life falling apart at the seams and her very sanity in question, she couldn't seem to think about anything else but David. David's hands. David's mouth. David's eyes.

She'd only just met the man, but it felt to her very core as if she would *die* if he didn't touch her. Kiss her. Soon.

She stood beside him at the headstone of Pakita Kasir, chilled to the marrow to realize the woman she'd seen and spoken to was not a hallucination. She had been real, once. And she had been related to Sierra Terrence, who was buried right beside her. It almost would have been easier to believe she'd imagined the woman than to believe she had seen a ghost.

"She was real," she whispered. "But I couldn't have seen her. I couldn't have talked to her."

"How else would you have known where she lived twenty-some years ago? In the only yellow house on the street?" David asked. "Or even that she was Sierra's aunt?"

"I don't know." Sara had turned her eyes away from the grave of Pakita, and was staring now at the headstone beside it. Sierra's grave.

"It must be hard for you to be here," David said softly.

She lifted her eyes quickly. "Why would it be? It's not my grave. I'm not her." The wind blew. She shivered and hugged her arms around her.

"I know, I know. I just… You're connected to her somehow. I mean, you must be."

"Apparently."

"But how?" he asked.

"I don't know."

"No, really." David touched her shoulder, turning her so that she faced him instead of the cold gray stone. And she wanted nothing more in that moment than to be folded up in his arms, held against his broad chest. She felt as if she'd been waiting forever for him to find her, and now that he was here, she didn't have the guts to tell him so. "Really," he went on. "You must have some gut feeling about all of this. What is it?"

She lowered her head. "Did you love her?" she asked.

"Nice way to change the subject." David sighed. "You're freezing. Let's get you inside." He took her arm and started to lead her back to his car. Hers was still parked along the roadside in The Heights.

But after only three steps, she planted her feet in the snow, and he was forced to stop. He frowned at her, puzzled. "What's wrong?"

"I want you to tell me. Did you love her?"

His lips thinned, he blinked slowly. "I was sixteen."

"That's not an answer."

"I know. I know it's not. To be honest, Sara, I've been asking myself the same thing for the past twenty-two years. At the time, I thought I loved her, but I thought I loved the three girls who'd captured my attention before her, too. The thing is…I never stopped thinking about Sierra. I never stopped aching, hurting, regretting, wishing it had been different. I've never thought about any of the other girls I dated the way I keep thinking about her."

"But you didn't set a fire that killed any of them, either," she said.

Her words hurt him. Hurt him badly, she saw that in his face. "No," he said softly. "No, I didn't."

"So maybe that's why you've been obsessed with her."

"Maybe. But over the past couple of weeks, it's been—"

"It's been what?"

He blinked, searching for words. "Worse, I guess. I've been dreaming about her—or you—I'm not even sure which."

"What happens in the dreams?" she asked.

He parted his lips, then closed them again, and shook his head. "Let's get in the car where it's warm."

"Because I've been dreaming about you, too," Sara said, still not budging. "I've been dreaming about making love to you." She blurted it quickly, forcing the words out before she lost her nerve. "Is that what happens in your dreams, too?"

He held her steady gaze, his eyes showing surprise, and then gradually softening into something else. "Yeah. That's what happens."

"Did you ever—make love with her, in real life?"

"I never even kissed her."

"If you kissed me, right now, do you think you'd be kissing her, in your mind?"

He lifted a hand to her face, his fingertips gently pushing the hair off her cheek, and sliding slowly down it. She let her eyes fall closed, and felt his breath on her lips as he moved closer. And then, suddenly, only cold.

"I'm not going to kiss you, Sara."

Her eyes flew open, and then burned, though it was ridiculous to feel this much disappointment over a man she'd just met. Even if it did feel as if they'd been together for lifetimes.

"Why not?" she whispered.

"Because—because you're sixteen years younger than me."

"That's not a reason, and I think you know it." Her eyes were wide now, and focused on his.

He nodded. "Maybe not. Then let's go with this one. I don't know the answer to the question you asked me. I don't know if I'd be kissing you, Sara, or if I'd be kissing a memory that has built up in my mind until it's more than it ever was, or probably ever would have been. And that wouldn't be fair to you." He turned then, started walking. "I'm going to the car."

She stood where she was. "Pakita said you were my soul mate. Do you feel that's true?"

He stopped walking, but said nothing.

"She spoke to me as if I *was* Sierra. She kept saying that I had come back, to make things right. I think…I think she was talking about reincarnation, David."

Turning slowly, he faced her.

"I'm very scared right now. Because the next thing I need to do is talk to Frank Terrence, and for some reason I'm petrified of doing that. If you leave me now, I don't think I can do it. And I feel like I have to. I need you, David."

His face seemed so incredibly sad. "This is tearing me apart, you know that, right? To go back over all of this, to open it all up again—it's killing me."

Sara lowered her head, closed her eyes and felt tears burning to escape. And she didn't look up, not even when she heard his footsteps coming closer, hurrying through the snow. And then he was clasping her face between his palms, tilting her head back and lowering his mouth to hers. The instant his lips touched hers, she twisted her arms around his neck, and the sound emanating from her chest was one of mingled longing and relief. She opened to him, pressed tighter, kissed more deeply. He hugged her waist and bent over her, and it was as if they were sucked into the spinning spiral rotation of a whirlpool, where nothing else existed beyond this. This point of contact. This kiss. It was everything in that moment. It was *everything*.

When he lifted his head away at last, his eyes were tumultuous. There was desire there, yes, but there was also confusion. And above all else, this overwhelming sense of relief. It was an exact mirror of what she was feeling.

"That didn't feel like a first kiss," she whispered.

He nodded in agreement. "Maybe it would be better not to…try to analyze it right now."

"I don't know that I could if I tried."

"No. No, neither do I," David said. "So let's leave it for now. I'll go with you to see Frank Terrence. But if we don't want the man to keel over dead, maybe we should do something about your…appearance?"

"How? You have a suitcase full of disguises in your Jeep?"

He shrugged. "No, but I have a baseball cap and sunglasses."

"Not very creative, but I suppose it'll do."

He took her hand and started toward the Jeep. She went a few steps, but then stopped him and when he turned, she leaned up and kissed him again.

He stared down at her. "I don't know what this is, Sara."

"Don't you want to find out?"

His eyes were pained, but sincere, too. "I don't know. Honestly, I don't know if I can handle it."

She felt her brows push against each other, but then nodded as she tried to understand. Every time he looked at her, he must be reminded of his crime—the mistake that had resulted in a young woman's death. Horrible death, at that.

And that might very well be too much for anyone to bear.

"I guess I get that," she told him. "Try to hang in with me, though, would you? Just until I figure out what the hell I'm supposed to be doing here?"

"I don't think I have a choice."

"I'd never try to push you into—"

"No, that's not what I meant." He hooked an arm around her waist, pulled her closer, held her in a tight, warm embrace, and his face was in her hair, and she knew he was feeling, smelling, relishing her, just the way she was relishing him. "I meant, I don't think I could stay away from you if I tried. At least, not now. Not yet."

"But maybe…later?"

"Sara," he whispered, dropping his forehead against hers. "We just met. Why don't we try to take it moment by moment here? Just for now? Think you can do that?"

"I feel like I've been waiting my whole life to find you," she whispered. "I feel like we've always been together. And I don't know anything about you. And that makes no sense whatsoever, David, but that's what it feels like."

"I know."

She held his gaze for a long moment, then nodded. "Okay. As long as you know."

"I do." With a deep sigh that sounded like one of regret, he looked at his watch. "It's after nine. He might be in bed if we wait much longer."

"Let's go, then."

CHAPTER NINE

SARA WASN'T SURPRISED that David knew which trailer lot belonged to Sierra's father, Frank Terrence. Even though the trailer, he said, had changed. She stood slightly behind him, hunching into her jacket, wearing a Red Sox cap with her long hair pulled through the opening in the back, ponytail style, and a pair of sporty sunglasses, both borrowed from his car.

And yet when the man opened the door, she recoiled, and wasn't sure why. She'd expected—well, not this. He was tall and lean, wearing a pair of olive-green work pants and a matching shirt with his name on the pocket patch. There were pens and a tire pressure gauge in that pocket. His hair was neat, and short, and shock white, but thick. And his face was clean-shaven.

"Yes?" He looked at David, almost glanced at Sara, but then refocused on David again. "You...you're the kid who killed my daughter."

"I'm hardly a kid anymore, Mr. Terrence."

He narrowed his eyes in anger. "That doesn't change history, does it? What the hell are you doing here?"

"I...wanted to ask you...a couple of questions about Sierra. If you're willing."

"Well, I'm not. And what the hell good do you think it's going to do you anyway? After all this time?"

"Please, Mr. Terrence," Sara said, and finally, for the first time, the man focused on her. *Really* focused.

His expression changed from one of anger to one that seemed curious or perplexed. "Who are you?" he asked.

"Sara Jensen. I'm an art teacher from out of town. I was visiting friends, and I…well, I was touched by the Teen Center and how it was named after your daughter, and I just…wanted to know more about her." She shrugged, and noted that he still looked doubtful. "I want to tell my school board and community about it, see if they'd consider setting up something similar in my town. It's just…such a great…resource. For kids."

After a moment's consideration, he nodded slowly. "All right," he said. "You can come in. But I can only give you five minutes. I have things to do."

"That's fine," she said. "And thank you, Mr. Terrence. I'm so sorry about what happened to your daughter."

"Sure you are." The man stepped aside and held the door open. David went in first, and Sara followed close behind.

The trailer was nice. A high-end double-wide, with peaked ceilings, hardwood floors and gleaming countertops. You wouldn't know, from the inside, that it wasn't a one-story house.

"This is nice," David said softly. "It's different from the one you had before—"

"There was a significant settlement," Frank Terrence said. "The town owned the house. It should have been locked up, so kids couldn't get in there."

He shrugged. "Not that any of that brings my girl back, now, does it?"

David lowered his head. "I'll never, ever forgive myself for that night, Mr. Terrence. It haunts me to this day."

He grunted, but turned his focus to Sara. "What are your questions?"

"Do you know why Sierra ran away?"

"She was upset about her mother leaving," he said. "Tammy up and moved back to India, to be with her family. Said we were incompatible."

"Tammy?" Sara tipped her head to one side. "The name doesn't sound Indian."

"Tamara," he said. "But I never went in for that Hindu nonsense."

"I see."

He squinted at her, tipping his head to one side.

"Did Sierra's mother come to her funeral? Or her Aunt Pakita?" At his surprised look, she added, "David told me about her. Your wife's sister, right?"

He shook his head. "Her mother left me no contact information. I couldn't even tell her her little girl was dead. Not that she deserved that consideration. She walked out on us, after all."

She nodded. "Surely Pakita told her."

"I wouldn't know. I didn't have much cause to interact with Patti."

"Patti." She repeated it deadpan. "You don't have much respect for your daughter's cultural heritage, do you, Mr. Terrence?"

He tipped his head to one side, and quick as a cobra, he reached out and snatched the hat and glasses from her in one swift move.

Sara jumped, and tried to smooth her hair.

Frank Terrence stared at her, rising slowly to his feet. "Jesus H. Christ," he muttered. "Who the hell *are you?*"

"I told you who I am. I'm Sara Jensen from New Hampshire. I'm an art teacher." As she spoke, David rose, and planted himself squarely between her and the agitated man.

"But you look...you look just like..." Frank Terrence

pushed a hand through his thick white hair, and shook his head. Tearing his gaze from Sara, he speared David with his eyes. "What is this really about?"

David said something, but Sara didn't hear him. There was a loud buzzing in her ears, and her vision went black, as if she were a television set whose power cord had been yanked from the wall. She just sort of…tuned out.

"LOOK, MAYBE SARA HERE feels more connected to Sierra because of the resemblance, but it's really not as strong as it seems at first," David said. He thought if he could ease the man's mind, he might defuse his anger and mistrust.

But the man was staring at Sara, and David found himself compelled to turn and stare at her, too.

Only, the woman looking back at him didn't feel like Sara. Particularly when she began to speak. Her voice was higher pitched, and had an entirely different inflection to it. And her words were haunting.

Staring at Frank, her eyes blazing, she said, "I want to know what you did with my mother, you son of a dog!"

The man stood up so fast the chair in which he'd been sitting tipped over and hit the floor. He raised a trembling arm, long forefinger pointing at the door. "Get out."

Sara blinked, and rubbed her eyes.

"Get the fuck out of my house, *now!* And don't you dare ever darken my door again. Do you hear me? Never!"

Sara frowned at him, then at David. "What happened?"

"Never mind. Come on." He took her arm, tugging her to her feet and then hustling her out the door, which slammed the minute they were through it.

They were almost to the car when she asked him again, "David, tell me what happened?"

"What do you remember?"

"I don't know. I was sitting there, and asking him questions, and then I had this moment of…I don't know, lapse. Almost like I blacked out, only I didn't fall over or anything."

He opened her door, helped her in, then went to his side and got behind the wheel. He had the Jeep underway a few seconds later, and he knew she was waiting, none too patiently, for an answer.

Choosing his words with care, he told her, "You said, and I quote, 'I want to know what you did with my mother, you son of a dog.'"

He glanced her way as he drove.

She was frowning hard. "No, I didn't."

"Yeah, you did. And it wasn't in your voice. You sounded…you sounded like Sierra."

"Oh, come on, David—"

"I'm not making this up. Hell, Sara, why would I?" He sighed even harder, shaking his head. "Where are you staying?"

"We can't go where I'm staying. We haven't solved anything yet."

"I think it's time to call it a night, hon. Where are you staying?"

Frowning, but capitulating, Sara told him the address on Oak Street, and he knew right where it was.

"I don't understand any of this," Sara said. "Why would I ask him something like that? Sierra's mother went back to India."

"Did she?" David shook his head. "I don't know. You know, I only met the woman a few times, but she seemed totally devoted to Sierra. Seems odd a woman would leave her teenage daughter behind. Maybe we need to look into that. Maybe Frank Terrence abused the woman, giving her no choice but to leave. Or something."

Sara looked at him, and he saw so much in her eyes,

so much he wanted to explore, to know. But he had to avert his own, to focus on his driving.

"He wasn't…what I expected," Sara said at length.

"No?" Curious, he looked at her as he drove. "What did you expect?"

She shrugged. "I don't know. I guess I thought he'd be overweight, unkempt, unshaven, dirty, with a beer in his hand."

He nodded. "That's exactly how I remember him. He's pulled himself together, apparently. But yeah, you just described him to a T, the way he was when Sierra was still alive. It's uncanny how well you nailed him."

She frowned in thought.

"It's like I have some of her memories," she said softly. "God, maybe this reincarnation stuff is…real."

He looked at her. "Maybe it is."

They didn't speak again for the remainder of the drive. Not until he pulled the Jeep into the driveway of the attractive house where she was staying.

"Friends of yours live here?" he asked her.

"My roommate Nikki's parents live here. But they're on vacation."

"So it's just you and Nikki." Why was he doing this, he asked himself? Was he an idiot?

"Nikki's still in New Hampshire. She'll be here tomorrow night."

"Oh." He shut the engine off.

"I want you to come in, David."

He turned, looked into her eyes and nodded, because he was helpless to do anything else. Her lips pulled very slightly at the corners. Not a smile, but as close to one as she could probably manage tonight.

Then she opened her door and got out, and he opened his and followed her.

Unlocking the house, she went inside without looking back. David went in, as well, and tried to feign interest in the house's decor, looking around as if it mattered to him, seeing nothing but Sara.

"This way," she told him, and she started up the stairs.

Frowning, he remained at the bottom, looking up at her as she ascended. "Sara, I don't know if—"

She turned quickly, looking down at him. "You said you'd been dreaming, too."

"I have." God, she was beautiful.

"If you've been having the same dreams I have..." She let her voice trail off.

"Similar dreams, maybe—"

"But not the same ones?"

He tipped his head to one side. "How could they be?"

"How could any of this be?" she asked. And she came down a step. "I'm wearing gauzy white. You're not wearing anything at all. It's outside, and it's raining. The ground is wet, but we don't seem to notice. We just sort of tangle ourselves up in each other, and we're kissing like there's no tomorrow, and—"

"Okay, okay." He felt everything she described as if it were happening then. And he felt more than that. He felt stunned, because she was describing the exact dream he'd been having, night after lonely night.

She came down another step. "If you've been dreaming it, too, then it must mean—"

"It could mean anything, Sara."

"Pakita says we're soul mates. What if she's right?"

"What if she's not?"

She shrugged, coming down one more step, standing now just one step above him, putting them at eye level. "What if it doesn't matter?" she asked. She slid her hands over his shoulders, interlocking her fingers behind his neck. "Right now, David, I need someone's arms around me. I don't think I've ever really needed that before, but I need it now. It may not be very politically correct or logical. But I need it, and you're here, and I think you need it, too. Can we just leave it at that, and not worry about the rest? Just for tonight?"

He didn't answer, because she pressed her lips to his. The kiss caught fire, and he felt himself nodding, wrapping his arms around her. He slid his palms down her back, over her hips and thighs, and then pulled her legs up around his waist and climbed the stairs. She wrapped her body around his like a spider monkey, clinging as they made out in motion. At the top of the stairs, he muttered, "Which way?" against her lips, his entire body ablaze.

She wriggled her hips against his, tightening the grip of her legs around his waist, and tipped her head slightly. He moved in that direction, up to the first door. She took one arm from around his neck to reach behind her, twisting the doorknob and pushing it open. David carried her inside, and they collapsed onto the bed.

He no longer thought about what he was doing. They'd taken this beyond thought. There was only feeling now. Desire, passion, longing. It felt, for all the world, like a longing that had been with him his entire life. And it felt far above and beyond his teenage crush on Sierra, or the regret he'd felt about her death all this time. This felt like more.

It felt, he thought, though it scared the hell out of him to think it, like destiny.

CHAPTER TEN

SARA HAD NEVER FELT anything like what she was feeling with every touch of this man's hands, and mouth. The bedroom was dim, but not pitch-dark. Still, they were enfolded in soft shadow as they tumbled to the bed, tugging at each other's clothes until they were both naked, their limbs entangled, their lips questing, asking and receiving, offering and giving.

She felt things in disjointed bursts of sensation. His hairy calf brushing over her smooth one. His fingers sliding over her arm, and then her belly. The hardness of him pressing against her thigh.

And then pressing inside her. Just that naturally, just that easily. They moved as if there were one mind operating both of their bodies, coming together, pulling apart, but not too far, and coming together again. They clung and moved and strained, and their sounds were soft and desperately hungry.

She couldn't believe the feelings, the passion, and then the utter bliss as sensation exploded in every part of her. She cried out his name, sinking her fingers into his shoulders as her entire body trembled in release.

He held her to him, rolling onto his side, pulling her against his chest, wrapping his arms around her, kissing her hair. As her senses began to operate normally again, she heard wind moaning in the night beyond the house's walls, and wet snow falling gently against the windows.

She closed her eyes, and thought about saying something. But there were no words that could have told him what she was feeling just then, and she was afraid that to speak at all would break the spell.

So she didn't. She just lay there, falling asleep in his arms.

But her dreams were far from the peaceful bliss she'd felt with David. In her dream, she was a young girl, cowering in her room as she heard the sounds of raised voices, and then of hands striking flesh. Her parents, fighting. He was hitting her again.

It was nothing she wasn't used to. It was nothing she hadn't been through a hundred times. She knew to stay put when it happened. She knew to stay quiet, to wait until her father left in a rage before she went out to tend to her mother's cuts and bruises. She knew not to tell.

But this time when the blows stopped and the house went silent, and her father's pickup roared away, she slid from her bedroom to find that she was alone. Her mother was nowhere to be found.

DAVID SPENT AN HOUR trying to make some kind of sense out of all that was happening, or even any of it, but there didn't seem to be any rhyme or reason that he could find. And the sex between him and the beautiful young woman in his arms was more confusing than anything else.

She wasn't Sierra. Even if her whole reincarnation theory were true, she wasn't Sierra. He knew that. He wasn't confused about that.

This pull she exerted on him wasn't his old high school crush resurfacing. But it didn't feel like something new, either. It felt old. Older than either of them.

And he didn't understand that.

Eventually, realizing Sara was sound asleep, David slid out of the bed, moving carefully and trying not to wake her. He felt around the floor, locating his clothes, pulled on his jeans and then padded barefoot into the hallway and down the stairs, extracting his cell phone from his pocket on the way.

He wandered to the kitchen while dialing, opened the cupboards in search of a snack. Randy answered on the third ring.

"Hey, pal, it's me."

"Dave? Where the hell are you, we've been worried sick!"

"I'm still with her."

"Her?" And then, "Oh."

"Look, how is Brad?"

"He's going to be okay. So who is she, Dave? What does she have to do with Sierra?"

"She looks like her."

There was a long pause, as if Randy was waiting for more, and when only silence ensued, he said, "And?"

"I don't know. I...I don't know." He heard Sara moving around, coming down the stairs. She was wearing a filmy white nightgown and robe when she reached the bottom. He recalled seeing them hanging from the bedpost like ghosts, and he shivered. "Sara?" he called.

But she didn't respond. And Randy was talking again. "The doc said Brad's arteries were so clogged, this could have happened at any time. And the longer it took to happen, the worse it would have been."

"Yeah?" He'd returned to his hunt for a snack. "Cindy get here yet?"

"She'll be here in the morning."

"Great." David heard the wind get suddenly louder, and felt a wet breeze sweeping through the house. "I've gotta go, buddy. I'll talk to you tomorrow."

"But...what did she say? Why is she here?"

"I'll fill you in tomorrow." He disconnected as he stepped into the doorway, giving him a view of the foyer and the front door standing wide open, rain spattering inside. "Sara?"

He pocketed the phone, pulling on his shirt, rushing to the open doorway. A warm front had moved in, turning the snow to rain. Sara was walking down the road, her feet dragging in the slushy rainwater. "Sara!"

But she didn't respond. David quickly stuffed his feet into his shoes, and, wishing for a jacket, he ran out after her. But she'd vanished. He couldn't see her anywhere. Frantic, he rushed to his Jeep, opened the back, and retrieved a flashlight. Then he got into the front and started it up, driving up the road in the direction he'd last seen her. He put the window down and aimed the flashlight out into the rain-soaked night, calling her name. "Sara! Where are you?"

Eventually, he caught a glimpse of something white, far in the distance. Disappearing into the town's densely wooded area far from the road.

He pulled the Jeep over and got out, taking the light with him and racing through the woods. "Sara, please wait!"

But she didn't. Still, a glimpse of her told him which way to go, and he was moving a lot faster than she was. So he caught up to her soon enough.

She was kneeling on the wet ground, pawing through the snow to the dirt beneath.

"Sara!"

But she didn't respond. Not until he went up to her and put a hand on her shoulder. Then she sucked in a loud gasp, and her head shot up fast, eyes wide and terrified. She stared up at him, blinking through the raindrops. "David? What—what are we doing out in the rain?"

He crouched down in front of her, clasping her shoulders. "I don't know. You led me out here. You were digging in the dirt." He nodded at her hands.

She looked down at them, at the icy, wet earth coating them, shaking her head slowly. But then she stopped, and looked at the ground again. "I think…I think someone's buried here."

"What?"

"I think it's my…Sierra's mother. Tamara."

"Jesus. Sara, what makes you think—"

"I dreamed…but I wasn't me, in the dream, I was her. I was in my room, listening to them fight. To him beating her. And after he left, I went out to see if she was okay, but she was gone. She was just gone. The next day he told me she'd gone back to India. But I knew he'd killed her. I *knew*."

David swore under his breath.

"It took me a while to figure out where he would have put her body. But then my cat got sick, and I wondered if she might die, and I remember thinking about the place in the woods where we always buried our pets." She looked around. "This place," she said. "I came out here with a shovel—I was determined to find my mother, to find the proof. But he saw me leave, and he followed me. And I knew I was right when I found a spot of freshly turned dirt. But he saw me digging, and he starting yelling, and he sounded like I'd never heard him sound before. I thought he was going to kill me, too. So I ran."

David nodded slowly. "You ran. You hid out in the old Muller House."

"Yes." She looked at the ground. "But I never found my mother."

Lifting his head, he said, "I have a shovel in the Jeep."

"Get it, would you?"

He reached out for her hand, and she took it, and let him lead her back to the Jeep for the shovel. Then, in the rain, she held the flashlight while he dug in the spot she indicated, the spot where Sierra had been digging sixteen years ago because the earth had been freshly turned there.

It didn't take long. The first bone gave itself up easily, only about six inches down. It was white, with bits of pink satin clinging to it.

Sara dropped the flashlight. "Mommy," she whispered.

And then there was a horrible sound, a wet smack, and David was falling facedown in the dirt.

"David!" she shrieked, lunging toward him, but then freezing in place when she saw Frank Terrence standing there, a shovel in his own hands. She shook her head as she backed away. "You killed your wife," she said softly. "That's why Sierra ran away."

He held her eyes. "How did you know to come here? To this spot?"

She stared straight back at him. "I remembered we used to bury pets here."

"Remembered?"

"Buttons, that odd little dog with the watch-eye. Gretta, the beagle. That ugly old stray cat we called Bob."

"How do you—"

"Why did you kill her? Why?"

Frank shook his head, then suddenly lunged at her, shovel flying. It connected with the side of her head, though she tried to duck the blow, and Sara saw stars. And then she sank into blackness and more.

She was back there. She was back in the past on the last night of her life. Hiding from her father inside Muller House. She'd been there for a week, and so far no one had found her. But it was only a matter of time. She knew that.

But that night, she'd been distracted. That night, David

had come, along with his four best friends. They'd been moping, and drinking on the front lawn, and she'd been watching them surreptitiously, wishing she had the nerve to go out and speak to David. She'd been drawn to him for the longest time.

And yet, she didn't. She just remained inside and watched him, yearning and wishing and dreaming.

When the boys tossed the homemade firebomb through a window, it frightened her. She'd jumped, and panicked, rushing to put it out. But the thing had flickered and died all on its own. She'd seen it happen, and then she'd laughed to herself at the ineffectiveness of their brilliant, drunken notion. Thank God it hadn't worked, she'd thought.

And then she'd heard her father's voice behind her, saying, "This couldn't be more perfect, could it?" He was pouring gasoline from a can, and when she saw him, he tossed some of the fluid in her direction. Then he hurled the empty can at her and it hit her in the head, sending her to her knees.

"I didn't mean to kill her." The man's voice was almost a whine. "She hit her head on that damned Kwin Yon statue she was always—"

"Kwan Yin," she whispered, seeing it in her mind's eye, porcelain white and beautiful.

But Frank didn't seem to hear her. "It was an accident. I'm not going to prison for an accident. But I will, if I let you live. I will."

She was vaguely aware of him striking matches and tossing them into the pools on the floor. The gas caught and blazed up with a powerful *whoosh!* And Sierra shielded her eyes and backed away. Her father ran for the back door, and she saw his foot go through a weak spot in the floorboards. Flames rose between her and escape, and she cried out for help.

Frank jerked his leg out of the hole in the floor. It came out shoeless, with a bleeding cut in his calf. And yet he turned, and limped away, not even looking back. Leaving her surrounded by fire. Leaving her to die.

Sierra retreated up the stairs and headed to the window, but the boys, seeing the flames, had turned tail and run. It was too far to jump. She ran back into the hallway, choking now on the smoke. But the stairs were engulfed, and there was no way out. And then the smoke overcame her, and she fell to the floor, David's name on her lips.

As it was again now. She moaned David's name and opened her eyes, waking from the nightmare only to find there was no waking from it.

She was no longer in the past. This was no longer a memory or a dream. She was in the old Muller House— Sierra House—*now*. And it was burning, just like before. She was on the second floor, lying in the hall, choking on smoke. And David was lying close beside her.

She crawled over to him, shook him to try to wake him up, gasped for air and tried not to feel the cloying heat as the flames rose from the ground floor and began creeping up the stairs toward them.

"David! David, please wake up!"

He didn't. But as she shook him, she felt the hard lump of his cell phone in his pocket, and quickly, she yanked it out and hit the dial button without even inputting a number in her panic.

To her surprise, she heard ringing on the other end, and pulled the phone close, looking at the screen, which told her she was "Calling Randy…"

A man's voice answered. "Dave?"

"Help!" Sara cried.

"What…who is thi—"

"Help us, please! We're in the house. It's burning. We're trapped. Please—"

"Sierra?"

"David's unconscious. It wasn't him. It wasn't you, any of you, it was my father. Oh, please, please—" She choked on the smoke, but heard Randy shouting orders to someone before she keeled over and passed out cold.

WHEN SHE WOKE, TWO VAGUELY familiar men were leaning over her.

"Come on, come on!" they shouted. One of them already was helping David to his feet, shaking him awake. And the other was scooping Sara up into his arms. Together the group headed for the stairway, but she heard David say, "We can't get out that way. The entire ground floor is engulfed."

Lifting her head, she choked out the words, "Just like last time." She shook her head. "What are you guys doing here?"

"We got here before the firefighters—what were we gonna do, stand out there and wait?" Kevin said. "If we go down, we go down together."

"Over my dead body," David said. "Hand her over, Kevin, and then follow me." He took Sara from Kevin's arms, and the three of them headed down the second floor hallway to the farthest end, then entered a room there and closed the door behind them.

It appeared to be a library. Randy raced to the windows, flinging them open wide. The rush of fresh air was almost too good to believe. Sara sucked in breath after breath of it as David carried her close to the window and set her down on the floor.

"The floor's hot!" she cried, hissing air through her teeth and pulling herself to her feet. But her feet were bare, and burning.

"Just breathe. Breathe as much as you can." David ripped the drapes from the windows, rushing to stuff them against the bottom of the closed door, even as Sara yanked a chair closer to the window and knelt upon it to get her feet up off the scorching hot floor.

"Sirens!" Randy said. "I hear sirens!"

"Good." David returned to the window, putting his face to the outside air. "They'd better hurry. It's too far to jump."

Kevin said, "We're going to *have to* jump. I don't think we have a choice. And while dying with her this time around might be poetic irony, maybe even justice, I'd prefer not to."

"It wasn't you," Sara said, but her throat was raw with smoke. "The firebomb you threw went out. I saw it. It was my father. Her father. It was Frank. He was here, too, with gasoline. He set the fire. He killed me—her—because she knew he'd murdered her mother."

"What?" Kevin and Randy said it almost as one.

The three men looked at each other, and then at her. David said, "We have to get out of here, or it's not going to make a difference. It's only the second floor. We can lower you half the distance, Sara. Come on, climb over."

"But—"

"Do it," Randy ordered. And there wasn't time to argue. Sara set her rear end on the windowsill, and swung her legs around. David gripped her forearm, and she locked her hand around his. Randy did the same with her other arm, and the two men leaned over as far as they could, until she dangled so low, her feet were touching the top of the window below.

"On three, let go," David said. And she heard the roar of flames beyond him, and knew the fire had somehow breached the room where they'd taken refuge. "One, two…"

She released her hold on *three* and plummeted ground-ward, hitting far faster than she had thought possible. The impact knocked the wind out of her, but she scrambled to her feet again, casting her eyes up toward that window.

But this time, she saw only flames on the other side. "David!" she cried.

And then sirens and lights, heavy hands moving her away, water blasting the cursed house. But no sign of David.

She sobbed as she told the firefighters where the three men had been, and pushed against the oxygen mask they kept pressing to her face.

And finally, she saw them. All three, stumbling around from behind the house, their faces sooty, their backs bent. Arm in arm, they came, and when they looked up and saw her, white smiles appeared in their sooty faces and they shuffled closer.

When they finally reached her, all three men wrapped her in a group hug. They were all sobbing. She sobbed, too. Something powerful was happening here. Eventually, Randy and Kevin backed off a little, but David kept holding her, and she didn't think he had any intention of letting go anytime soon.

As she looked at the faces of the men, she saw the wonder in their eyes, and she understood it. This was no ordinary night, she thought as the firefighters did their work, trying to save the old Muller place yet again. This night, history had repeated itself. Men who'd lived with misplaced guilt had the chance to relive the worst night of their lives, and make it come out right this time. She hadn't died in the fire this time. She'd lived.

And she knew why. She had to live to tell the tale. To tell the truth.

David stared down into her eyes. She blinked through tears as she met his. "It's over, isn't it?" she asked him.

He smoothed a thumb over her cheek, catching the tear and probably some soot along with it. "No, Sara, I hope not. I hope it's just getting started."

And then he bent and he kissed her, and she relaxed against his strong chest, nestled in the embrace of his powerful arms and felt as if she were right where she belonged.

EPILOGUE

SARA STOOD WITH A SMALL group at the cemetery, where the body of Sierra's mother, Tamara, was being given a proper burial, right beside her daughter and her sister, Pakita.

Tamara had been killed by a blow to the head, the autopsy had determined. And when he'd been picked up for questioning, Frank Terrence had confessed to every-thing…murdering his wife, setting the fire that had killed his daughter twenty-two years ago and setting the more recent one intended to kill a young woman who bore a striking resemblance to her. He claimed she'd come back to make him pay for what he'd done. But most people thought the years of guilt had finally driven him insane.

Nikki and Cami were there, as were all five of the men who'd spent the past two decades blaming themselves for the young girl's death. Mark was in a wheelchair being manned by his wife, Janet. But he looked good, and was expected to make a full recovery. Brad was walking under his own steam, and already ten pounds lighter since the heart attack. All five men looked years younger, just by the removal of the burden they'd been carrying from their souls.

David and Sara stood arm in arm, and they remained at the grave after the others had all gone. Sara said, "It's odd. I grew up in foster care. I don't even remember having a mother of my own. But I feel like maybe I do now."

David nodded, holding her more closely. "What are you going to do now, Sara?"

"That kind of depends on you," she said softly. Turning, she gazed up into his eyes. "I could go back to New Hampshire and pick up my life where I left off. Or…I could start looking for openings for an art teacher in Boston."

The tension that had been in his face vanished, replaced by a warm, real smile. "You'd do that?"

"Yeah, I would. I mean, maybe we just met—"

"Or maybe we didn't," he said.

"But either way, I want to see where this goes. It's…it's powerful, what's between us. It could be…it could be the real thing. I want to find out."

"I do, too, Sara. I do, too." He held her even closer. "You gave my life back to me."

"Well, you returned the favor." She smiled up at him. "So what are you doing for the rest of it?"

"If I have my way, a lot more of this," he said, and he bent over her and kissed her as if there were no tomorrow. But for the first time, it really felt like there was.

* * * * *

Don't miss the SECRETS OF SHADOW FALLS,
*an all-new romantic suspense trilogy
from Maggie Shayne
and MIRA Books:*

*KILLING ME SOFTLY, July 2010
KILL ME AGAIN, August 2010
KISS ME, KILL ME, September 2010*

LADY OF THE NILE
Susan Krinard

CHAPTER ONE

London, 1890

"YOU ARE QUITE INCORRECT."

Leo Erskine heard the voice, ringing as clear as the bells at Winchester Cathedral, but he didn't register the flustered response of the learned gentleman at the podium. He was too thoroughly occupied with examining the lady who had spoken out so boldly.

She was lovely, of course. One could hardly be a duchess and fail to be lovely, could one? The fact that she was only the dowager duchess at a very young age could scarcely be held against her.

He noted the other faces turned toward her, some quizzical, others admonishing, and a few—belonging to those gentlemen with minds liberal enough to appreciate intelligence in a woman, or simply engaged by her beauty—openly admiring.

The lady finished her brief argument with the distinguished Egyptian scholar, looked down her nose at him—an impressive feat, given her position below the dais—and swept from the lecture hall. Her skirts, draped with pleated linen and cinched with a gold sash in the ancient style, rustled furiously, and her long earrings tinkled with every long stride. If she had been a royal princess, she could not have been more regal.

Of course, that was exactly what she claimed to be.

Leo excused himself to his astonished companions and followed the dowager from the room. He knew very well that his fascination with her was not due to her beauty, remarkable as it was. Nor was it because of her influence in Society, whose members were not prepared to forgo her elaborate parties and elegant balls because of a little old-fashioned British eccentricity.

No, it was not such shallow motives that brought him to observe her so closely whenever they met. Since the marriage of his friend the Earl of Donnington to one of the dowager's select friends—Nuala, the former Lady Charles Parkhill—he had been thrown more often into the dowager's company. And he had begun to think that she actually did believe that she was an Egyptian princess come back to life.

That was the problem. She believed it. Just as his own father had believed. And died for it.

"Good afternoon, Mr. Erskine."

He came to a sudden halt, moments from colliding with the woman in question. She stood before him, chin lifted, cool green eyes appraising. "You wished to speak to me?" she asked.

Unaccountably flustered, Leo bowed. "I fear I have disturbed you, Your Grace."

"You fear no such thing. You have been following me. Have you something to say?"

Her frankness must have discomposed most English gentlemen. Leo had seen far too much of the world to take it amiss. "You have made no friends in the Museum today," he said with equal candor.

She laughed, a warm, rich sound that Leo felt down to his toes. "I have never desired the friendship of men who are prone to such egregious errors," she said.

"Are you so certain of your facts, Your Grace?"

The humor vanished from her face, and those remarkable eyes, made even more striking by the careful application of kohl, regarded him steadily. "I was *there* when the events in question occurred," she said.

Events that had taken place three thousand years ago.

Delusion. Yes, that was the source of her certainty, not a deliberate desire for attention. "If so," he said, "your knowledge would surely be invaluable to historians all over the world."

THERE WAS NO MOCKERY in his voice. If there had been, she would have turned on her heel and walked away.

But Tameri remained where she was. She might have ignored such a comment from any other man. Indeed, she had never been troubled by Leo Erskine in the past. Of late, however, she had been seeing more of him at social events she had attended, even the most exclusive. It was a development no one who knew him could account for. Studious, solitary, ever courteous but generally aloof… those were words to describe the second son of the Earl of Elston.

And attractive. Not handsome, not precisely. But he was tall, leanly muscular, and possessed a sort of calm authority that Tameri could only wish she truly felt.

"You know your own sex and avocation, Mr. Erskine," she said at last. "The so-called expert's reaction to my correction would be a typical response, would it not?"

"And yet you continue to try."

"I cannot allow such misinformation to be disseminated."

"Perhaps you might have approached the matter more delicately."

Now he *was* mocking her. "In former days," she said,

"men such as Dr. Elgabri would have been put in their place."

"In what manner would you prefer to go about it, madam? By decapitation, drowning or impalement?"

Her throat closed, and she almost looked away. *The dark. The dreadful dark.*

No. She would not let him claim victory in this engagement. She would not allow him to sense the doubts within herself.

"I have never sought to execute anyone, Mr. Erskine," she said, fighting the tremor in her voice.

"I beg your pardon, Your Grace. Of course you have not."

She considered that he might actually be sincere in his apology. He almost looked contrite, his light brown eyes earnest behind their spectacles.

But I see it, she thought. *You do not believe me. You think, like the rest, that I am a fraud.*

They were wrong, all of them. For she remembered. Only bits and pieces, seen through a heavy mist, but she *remembered.* If she could convince but one man, a learned and thoroughly practical man like Mr. Leopold Erskine…

A man who would certainly deem her truly mad should she make any such attempt and fail.

Why should I care for his good opinion? Why—

Someone jostled past them, a young man who apologized profusely and stared at Tameri a moment too long. Erskine smoothly drew him away, exchanged a few pleasant words with the youth and returned to Tameri's side.

"Newly come to London," he said. "Naturally he would find you intriguing, Your Grace. As one might expect."

"You need have no concern for me, Mr. Erskine. I am accustomed to such behavior from those unacquainted with Society."

"Of course." He took her arm, an impertinence she was too startled to correct, and led her away from the flow of pedestrians on Great Russell Street. When he stopped at the corner of Bloomsbury Street, he did not release her.

"I have enjoyed our conversation, Your Grace," he said. "Perhaps we might continue the discussion another time."

Tameri freed her arm. "What would you propose we discuss? Perhaps you find my way of life a source of amusement. Perhaps you intend to make a study of me."

He flushed, a most subtle change of color under his surprisingly sunbrowned skin, and she knew she had caught him out. Other scholars and skeptics might speak critically of her among themselves, women might gossip and twitter, but few would dare to confront her directly. Leo Erskine was prepared to provoke the displeasure of one of the most wealthy and, yes, influential leaders of Society for the sake of his scientific curiosity.

That was why he had appeared at so many functions at which she had been present. That was why he had followed her today.

"I am not an exotic bird, Mr. Erskine, to be cataloged and dissected," she said coldly. "I may be compelled to live in a world not my own, but I do not bestow my confidences on common soldiers."

"Soldiers?"

Tameri clutched at her skirts, striving to keep her feet. What had she said? What had she just remembered?

The amorphous image flew from her mind, and she found Erskine staring at her with real concern.

With pity.

She straightened and pushed past him. "Good afternoon, Mr. Erskine," she said.

"Wait." He caught her up, slowing his stride to match hers. "At least permit me to escort you to your carriage."

"That will not be necessary."

"Lady Tameri."

She could not have taken another step even had she wished to do so. He knew the name she had chosen for herself, the name she preferred over the title her husband had given her. The power of that name on his lips—the name of her other self—held her like the net of a bird-catcher hunting on the Nile.

"Convince me," Erskine said. He removed his spectacles as if he were deliberately setting aside any barrier that might stand between them. "Convince me that what you believe is true, and I will find a way to convince the world."

She met his gaze. Once again she was challenged to accept his sincerity, and she began to wonder if she had judged him too harshly.

Yet how could it be? Was it even remotely possible that he *wished* to be convinced, that his keen intellect might be fit to grasp the secrets of the ages?

Could he, believing, help her uncover all that had been forgotten?

"I have told you that I will not be an object of study," she said, deliberately scathing. "Surely you do not intend to 'help' me out of the goodness of your heart. There must be something more you want of me."

He withdrew a pace as if she had affronted him. "Madam," he said with cool formality, "I am neither in need of your wealth or your patronage, nor do I wish to impose upon you. You may trust me or not, as you prefer." He bowed stiffly and turned to go.

"Wait!"

Erskine stopped without turning. "Your Grace?"

She threw caution to the fresh late spring breeze. "I am having an intimate gathering of friends at Maye House on the twelfth. I would be pleased if you would join us."

"Even though I am not an intimate friend?"

Something in his words struck a deep and terrifying chord, but she forged ahead. "You will know most of the others in attendance," she said. "You shall not be a stranger."

His shoulders relaxed, and he turned again. "Then I shall be honored, Your Grace."

Steadying her hand, she extended it toward him. "Lady Tameri, Mr. Erskine. As my friends call me."

His grasp was warm and dry and firm, his fingers surprisingly calloused for a gentleman scholar. "Lady Tameri," he said, holding her hand far longer than was proper.

A shock of familiarity passed through her. She had held this hand before, in just this way. Before the darkness. Before...

She broke free before she could utterly humiliate herself and rushed away to find her carriage.

CHAPTER TWO

LIAR.

Leo stood in the drawing room beside Lady John Pickering, listening with only half an ear to the woman's pleasant conversation.

He had known the moment he had offered to aid the dowager duchess that he had made a mistake. He had made a promise he could not possibly keep, based upon an impossible premise.

Convince me. He had set Lady Tameri a challenge that she had not been able to resist. A challenge given under false pretenses.

For he knew she would never be able to convince him. No detail of her supposed "past life" could shake his conviction that she was in the grip of a powerful delusion, no plea for understanding could move his resolution.

She *was* in need of a different sort of help. As his father, the Earl of Elston, had once needed help he had not received. No one outside the family had known of his profound belief that he was the modern incarnation of Leonardo da Vinci. He'd had the sense to hide his particular form of madness, as Tameri did not.

But he had paid for it, nevertheless. Leo had been home from school when the earl had taken his own life, despondent over his inability to convince even those closest to him that he was the great artist and inventor reborn.

Leo's elder brother Harry had succeeded to the title, but Leo had carried the guilt of their father's death long after he had left England on his first sojourn to North Africa.

He had failed the earl. Now he had the opportunity to see that such a tragedy never happened again.

But he must move with extreme caution lest he drive Tameri still deeper into her fantasies.

Leo was distracted from his troubling thoughts by the remarkable room. He had attended a few of the dowager's social events in the past, but on each occasion they had been held in larger, far grander rooms or in the unusually extensive gardens at the rear of the house.

This room, though much smaller, was scarcely less impressive than the ones he had seen before. Statues of archaic Egyptian gods gazed with varying degrees of gravity and benevolence at the mere humans among them. The walls were painted with bright murals depicting daily Egyptian life, and the mantelpiece was virtually covered in dense rows of hieroglyphs. Leo excused himself to Lady John and approached the fireplace. The hieroglyphs were not random scratches inscribed for purely ornamental purposes, but words he might have translated had he been given more time.

An expert advised her, he thought. An expert who was fluent in the old Egyptian writing. Leo knew each and every such specialist in England. Had the dowager's wealth tempted one of them? Had she employed a linguist from another country?

"Quite extraordinary, are they not?"

Leo straightened in surprise. "Boyd?"

The lean, dark-haired man bowed and smiled. "Erskine. It has been a long time."

An understatement of monumental proportions. "A

very long time," Leo said. "I had no idea that you had returned to London."

"I have not chosen to advertise the fact."

Indeed. And why should he? Lost in the bloody aftermath of the siege of Khartoum, Alastair Boyd had emerged from the desert three years later a broken man, muttering in a language no one understood. He had not spoken of his experiences, and after a few months in civilization he had vanished again, apparently unable to endure a world no longer his own.

That broken man was no longer in evidence. Boyd was vibrantly healthy, confident, smiling. Except for his tan and the almost burnt-red look to his hair, he was once again the perfect English gentleman.

And he was a guest in Lady Tameri's house. An "intimate" guest.

"I am glad to see you returned," Leo said, aware that the silence had gone on too long.

"I see the questions in your eyes," Boyd said with a wry smile. "I have aspirations to write a book about my experiences. You shall have to wait until it is complete to satisfy your curiosity."

"I beg your pardon."

Boyd waved the apology away. "It's only natural."

His careless demeanor seemed somewhat less than convincing to Leo. "Have you known the dowager long?" he asked.

"Our families were acquainted before my recent sojourn in Egypt and the Sudan."

In which case he must have known Lady Tameri before she had become duchess, when she was still little more than a girl. She had been much younger than the duke, and had not been seen frequently in Society after their marriage. When she had appeared at the duke's side during formal functions, she had dressed like any other woman, and had occasioned no gossip of any kind. It was only after the duke's death, and the inheritance of the title by the duke's younger brother, that she had appeared in her Egyptian garb and begun to remodel Maye House.

Do you know what changed her? Leo wanted to ask. But it wasn't the time or the place. "You are fortunate," he said.

"Indeed. We have become very…good friends since my return."

Leo felt himself bristling at the smug tone of Boyd's voice. "The *friendship* of an intelligent, independent and wealthy woman committed to remaining a widow must be a valuable commodity."

Boyd's lip curled. "You surprise me, Erskine. You were never known for such scurrilous innuendo before I left England."

The innuendo had been Boyd's, but Leo knew he *had* changed. He hardly knew what devil had taken hold of him.

"I am not good company tonight," he said.

"Then you ought to excuse yourself rather than ruin the lady's entertainment."

"Perhaps you're right."

"I would advise it." Boyd leaned closer. "As much as I value the dowager's friendship, I am under no illusion as to her state of mind. She is quite mad."

Leo started. "And you call yourself her friend?"

"Is it not what everyone believes, even yourself?" Boyd favored Leo with a condescending smile. "Such eccentricity is not without its own merits." He sighed. "Let me be frank, Erskine, for your own sake. I fear that you have *too* keen a regard for the lovely lady. Enjoy her company, if it suits you, but do not become involved."

Momentarily speechless, Leo clenched his fist and gave serious thought to the prospect of felling Boyd where he stood. But he mastered his irrational impulses and walked away before he could change his mind.

Become involved. He was certainly not involved in the way Boyd suggested. But what of Boyd? He was charming, handsome, sophisticated in manner and dress. Was he taking advantage of Tameri, relying upon her "madness" to ease his way into her confidence…and her bed?

Such unworthy thoughts were entirely baseless, at least as they pertained to Tameri herself. Leo scarcely knew either Boyd or the lady in question. He had jumped to ridiculous conclusions for inexplicable reasons.

He had no further time to consider the source of his wild speculation. The call to dinner came, and he was compelled to offer his arm to the elderly Mrs. Poole and proceed into the dining room.

The dinner was pleasant enough. The dowager's servants were graceful and efficient, each one dressed in spotless white linen. Conversation was light, presided over by Lady Tameri in her usual Egyptian-style gown. Her inlaid collar glittered in the candlelight, and her black hair glistened.

Whatever uncertainty she might have displayed during their meeting at the British Museum, it was nowhere in evidence now. She was not merely a princess but a queen, secure and unassailable in her majesty. She showed no particular attention to Boyd, who sat several seats away. Once or twice her gaze found Leo, but there was nothing "intimate" about it. He had been granted the favor of attending upon her, and that was sufficient honor.

No one protested when Tameri failed to follow the usual custom of leading the ladies from the dining room, leaving the men to their cigars and brandy. She continued to preside over the table, drank with her guests, including the women, and only after a leisurely period rose to usher everyone into the Gold drawing room.

To Leo's surprise, Boyd disappeared before the guests had gathered again. Lost in his own thoughts, Leo wandered out of the room and along the landing. Deeply preoccupied, he had paused before a closed door when Lady Tameri found him.

"Mr. Erskine?"

He turned quickly. "Lady Tameri. I apologize—"

She lifted an elegant hand. "My guests are departing. Perhaps you would enjoy a tour of the house?"

Leo parsed her question for sarcasm and found none. He almost asked if Boyd had left with the others, but thought better of it.

"It is late," he said. "I ought to return another time."

"I seldom retire before three. Early morning was always my favorite time in the palace, when the heat of one day was over and the new had yet to begin."

"What palace might that have been, Lady Tameri?"

Her smile was an enigma. "There will be time for such discussions, Mr. Erskine. Shall we proceed?" She swept ahead of him, her long golden sash trailing behind her. Effectively silenced, Leo followed, breathing in the delicate scent of her unfamiliar perfume.

There was much to see. Her home was a virtual museum, and every chamber she showed him on the first and second floors was as lavishly decorated as the drawing and dining rooms, featuring magnificent reproductions of Egyptian sculptures from the Middle and New Kingdoms, beautifully rendered murals and fine, intricately carved wooden furniture. The walls of the ballroom bore a stylized depiction of the Nile, complete with hip-

popotami, crocodiles and fishing boats, and the floor was
inlaid with the cartouches of great pharaohs.

One small chamber was entirely devoted to perfect
scale models of palaces and temples, complete with
pillars, obelisks and columns adorned in brilliant blues,
greens, reds and ochers.

But it was the final room that outshone all the others.
Tameri led him through a smaller drawing room and
paused at a pair of locked doors, plain and unadorned. She
produced a key and opened the doors.

The antechamber was dark and silent. Tameri lit a small
lamp beside the door, and the cabinets and figurines
leaped into sharp relief.

It was a collection of treasures such as Leo had never
seen. Glass cases housed remarkable artifacts, clearly of
ancient provenance. An elaborately ornamented sarcopha-
gus of the late Middle Kingdom lay on a dais on the far
side of the room. A remarkable basalt sphinx, man-
headed, perched on a table beside it. An exquisite canopic
jar with a lid in the shape of a woman's head looked out
from a niche in the wall behind. Above all else had been
placed a faience sculpture of Isis and her son, Horus.

Speechless, Leo made a slow circuit of the room.
The first case held splendid examples of fine Egyptian
jewelry: a golden collar adorned with rows of beads
carved of lapis lazuli and carnelian; a simple diadem of
solid gold; an openwork pectoral decorated with lotus
flowers and griffins; a flawless scarab amulet of glass
and wood. Each piece was an original, each preserved
in all its antique glory. Beside it, great irregular blocks
of stone with relief images of a victorious pharaoh and
his humble captives had been fitted together to form part
of a wall. Leo knelt to examine it. There was no doubt
as to its authenticity.

Leo rose to face her. "How did you come by these?" he demanded.

"I have contacts in Egypt," she said coolly.

"You mean tomb-robbers," he said. "Men who deal in stolen artifacts."

"And are your kind any better? You, who have no right, have desecrated tombs meant to shield the remains of their owners for all time, fouled the resting places of the mightiest pharaohs. At least I—" She broke off, breathed deeply, and regained her composure. "These were made for my family."

"Your family?"

"My *true* family. These things belong to no one else."

Leo met her gaze, struggling against a strange tightness in his chest and the fierce pounding of his heart. "They belong in a museum, where everyone can enjoy them, not merely a privileged, spoiled woman who believes herself superior to every man, woman and child in England."

Her skin, already pale, grew whiter still. "If you are an example of such a man, then I have good reason to feel so. *You* were born a peasant, and yet Osiris—" Bewilderment crossed her face, and she reached for the case behind her. "Asar, my love, my king…"

Leo caught her before she slid to the floor. She began to shake violently. The skin of her wrist was cold, her breathing shallow.

All anger forgotten, he half carried her back into the drawing room and to the nearest chair.

"Tameri!" he cried, gripping her shoulders.

She stirred, catching her breath. Her green eyes opened, half-lidded, dreamy, seductive. Her lips parted.

"Asar?"

What happened then was completely beyond Leo's control. He pulled her against his chest and kissed her. Her

mouth opened, permitting his seeking
with hers. He could feel every contour o
that she wore no stays and very few ur
speared her fingers through his hair,
urgency that brought Leo's body to pai

Leo had sought to be a gentleman al
roared inside him now was anything but
than the fire of lust. More than any em
experienced.

"Aset," he murmured. "My love, my

Her lips lost their pliancy. She pushed
face flooding with hot color. She sprang
aside, and resumed her icy dignity as in it were a royal
cloak of jewels and spun gold. Without a word she strode
to the bell pull and summoned one of her white-clad
servants.

"Shenti," she said, "please summon Mr. Erskine's
carriage."

The footman glanced at Leo and bowed. "Sir, if you
will…"

Leo found his voice again, remembering what had
happened just before his unforgivable indiscretion. "Your
mistress is not well," he said. "A doctor—"

"I am very well, Mr. Erskine." She looked again at Shenti,
who made it clear that he would not leave until Leo did.

She's afraid. Afraid of him, but not because of the kiss.
If she were as horrified by her behavior as he was by his,
that was not what concerned her now.

As he followed Shenti to the entrance hall, Leo considered the situation with as much detached rationality as
he could muster. Tameri was plainly ill, perhaps danger-
ously so, not merely delusional. If he had not caught her,
she might have fallen on the display case and injured
herself. Such seizures seldom occurred in isolation.

Twice he had seen her enter an altered state of consciousness, a disconnection from the real world. He was certain that she had not "performed" for him in an effort to convince him of her sincerity. She had truly lost control.

Just as he had.

It was obvious that she would not consult a doctor on her own, yet Leo couldn't see how he might convince her. When had her physical illness started? Was it directly tied to her delusions?

Someone must look after her. Certainly not "friends" like Boyd. It was clear that she had no particular regard for him, in spite of *his* insinuations, and Leo didn't trust him, though he couldn't have said precisely why. The so-called Widow's Club, of which she was the most prominent member, must surely have some influence over her.

Lady John Pickering would certainly be receptive to his concerns, as would Lady Selfridge. They knew he was not apt to consider women delicate flowers in need of constant male protection. They need never know what had just transpired between him and the dowager.

Every instinct urged him to protect Tameri. But how could he protect her from himself, when even he didn't understand his own bizarre lapse? What had driven him to take advantage of her at her moment of greatest vulnerability? He was no rake, as Sinjin had been before his marriage. He could certainly master his desires.

Until that reckless moment in the drawing room, he had not desired Tameri at all. Had he?

Leo shook his head and climbed into his carriage. He *would* find answers, whether Tameri chose to cooperate or not. It was no longer simply a matter of helping her overcome her self-deception. Not when her very life might be at stake.

Her life, and his sanity.

Sinking into the seat, Leo closed his eyes and remembered the feel of her small hand in his. The dim interior of the carriage filled with hot, white light, and his own voice whispered words not his own.

"Aset. My love. My queen."

"Sir?"

He started awake. The coachman stood at the open carriage door, his face creased with worry.

Leo nodded brusquely, descended and walked a little unsteadily to the door of his townhouse. The busts of Aristotle and Archimedes, Copernicus and Galileo greeted him in the entrance hall, their sightless stares disapproving. He went immediately to his library and selected the most tedious archaeological volume he could find.

His efforts were to no avail. He roamed the house like an unquiet spirit until dawn, counting the hours until he could reasonably call on the ladies of the Widow's Club.

When he saw Tameri again, he, at least, would be in perfect control.

CHAPTER THREE

IT WAS QUITE IMPOSSIBLE for Tameri to avoid him.

Wherever Tameri went—everywhere she looked—he was there. Though she gave no dinners or parties or musical entertainments during the first few days following their disturbing encounter, Leo appeared at each and every one of the half-dozen functions she attended, always hovering somewhere in the background. Watching. Waiting.

Tameri did her best to forget what he…what *they* had done at Maye House. She tried to go about her usual routine, but found her thoughts constantly drifting to Leo's lean, passionate face, the insistent warmth of his lips. She was constantly distracted by questions: what had happened just before the kiss? What had she said or done to provoke Leo to such an action? Why had it seemed so important to show him her beloved collections, all in hopes of convincing him that her beliefs were real?

Why was she so terribly drawn to him when she knew her destiny, as yet unrevealed though it was, demanded that she remain pure and committed to the cause?

Alastair had warned her, in the vaguest terms, not to have anything more to do with Leo Erskine, though he had avoided telling her why he offered such advice. Perhaps he knew something she did not. Perhaps he had been right.

Troubled and bewildered, she failed to respond to invitations or answer calls. The housekeeper and maids and footmen flitted about like shadows. Her chef, an Egyptian trained in both European and Asian cuisine, attempted to consult her in vain.

Three days after the incident, Clara Pickering, Frances, Lady Selfridge and Lillian, Lady Meadows, called upon her. Their grave faces almost convinced her that they had guessed exactly what had happened.

"How are you?" Clara asked, searching Tameri's eyes. "We did not see you at Lady Loving's ball."

"Lady Loving was quite disappointed," Frances said dryly, smoothing her tailor-made jacket. "You have seldom been known to pass by an invitation."

"I think she was relieved," Lillian said. "She can be quite pleasant, but she is also very envious of your beauty." Her round face wore an uncharacteristic frown. "Why *didn't* you come, Tameri?"

"We heard that you were a little out of sorts," Clara said.

Tameri sat quietly in her high-backed chair, meeting each inquisitive gaze in turn. Since she had founded the Widow's Club, she had been the nominal leader of the group, though it was otherwise an entirely egalitarian organization. None of her fellow members had ever had cause to worry about her before; *they* had never questioned her past or her way of living.

"You need not be concerned," she said as the tea was brought in. "The Season seems very tedious this year, and I merely wished more time to myself."

The women exchanged glances. Tameri poured the tea and, in a moment of inattention, spilled a scalding drop on her hand. Lillian was quick to produce a handkerchief to dab at the burn.

"It is nothing," Tameri said, continuing to pour. "Tell me, what is the real reason you have come?"

"Are you quite sure you aren't ill?" Lillian burst out.

"I cannot imagine where you might have heard such a rumor," Tameri said, "but it is quite false."

"Of course," Clara murmured. They let their tea cool a little and sipped in silence. After the requisite time for the call had passed, the three ladies rose and made their farewells.

Tameri retreated to her bedroom and tore off her diadem. Who could have made such a ridiculous claim and worried her friends?

The answer was plain enough: Leo Erskine. Yet she was not in the least bit ill. She might not be able to account for her behavior with him—and the humiliation had been acute—but surely *he* would not broadcast his unseemly conduct to Society. Why should he approach members of the Club and suggest that her health was a matter for concern?

She set about reassuring her fellow widows by attending a number of social events, playing her usual role without difficulty. But *he* continued to watch her as if he felt no shame whatsoever. And she could not bring herself to confront him.

Even more disturbing was the unusual attention of the Widows, especially Clara and Lillian. Their keen eyes seemed to mark out her deliberate evasion of Mr. Leopold Erskine, and she became certain that he had approached them with some tale she could not openly refute.

He is still attempting to label me an impostor. He had never intended to let her convince him. He had named her a spoiled woman who hired grave-robbers to please her own vanity. A woman of precarious morals, who would give herself to a man so evidently her inferior.

The first fortnight passed without another disturbing incident between them. The Season went on as it always did: young girls desperately seeking eligible husbands, young men reluctantly recognizing their own duty to wed, all whirling about in a froth of balls and operas and visits to the theater. Tameri had always stood above the marital fray. No man would ever own her again.

At the beginning of the third week, a new antiquities collection was acquired by the British Museum. Two dozen fine Egyptian artifacts had recently been donated by a prominent collector, and his generosity was to be celebrated with an exclusive reception.

There was never any question that the dowager Duchess of Vardon would be invited. She knew the likely consequence of her attendance would be another meeting with Leo Erskine, in much closer quarters than she would prefer, but as long as he was content to observe her from a safe distance, she had no reason for concern. And she would by no means surrender any of her usual pleasures because of him, or what he thought of her.

The reception was crowded, replete with ladies of the highest fashion and their gentleman escorts. Most of the attendees were mere dilettantes who were interested in any new fad. They would look their fill, make the usual appreciative noises and move on to the next diversion. They were quick to acknowledge Tameri with smiles, simpers and bows.

The men who had acquired the new collection, the fine and learned scholars who considered Tameri such a nuisance, were far less effusive in their welcome. They knew better than to offend her, but their air was patronizing when they answered her inquiries or attempted to counter her arguments pointing out the many errors in their assumptions and conclusions about the past.

Erskine was not among them. Perhaps he had finally grown weary of studying her. She searched the crowd surreptitiously, but found no tall, long-legged gentleman with an affable smile and the marks of spectacles on the bridge of his nose.

She should have felt relief. She could now put him from her mind entirely. But an implacable inner voice insisted that he was not through with her, nor she with him.

My love.

Tameri started from her reverie, excused herself to the enthusiastic young gentleman who fancied himself such an expert in matters he knew nothing about, and made a quick circuit of the main exhibition room. The objects were well-preserved and respectfully displayed, but they had nevertheless been stolen from those for whom they had held a far deeper meaning.

A single extraordinary sculpture had been given pride of place: a woman's elegant head, long-necked, serene and beautiful. The limestone still held traces of the original color in the lips and eyes. Her crown marked her as royalty. She might almost have been a mirror-image of Tameri herself.

"It *is* rather uncanny."

Tameri turned sharply. Leo Erskine stood at her shoulder, examining the sculpture through his unfashionable spectacles.

"I beg your pardon?" she said stiffly.

"The resemblance. Quite remarkable."

Tameri twitched her skirts aside and began to walk away.

"Lady Tameri."

She stopped, shivering at the gentle insistence of his voice. "Mr. Erskine."

"There is no need for us to go on this way. We are not children."

A pair of elderly women, leaning on one another's arms, nodded to Tameri and passed on. The crowd had thinned as the hour grew later, and there was a pocket of stillness around her and Erskine that seemed to suspend the moment out of time.

She turned again. "No," she said. "We are not children. Neither are we friends, Mr. Erskine, despite the mistakes we have made."

"Was it a mistake, Tameri?"

His use of her name without the usual title steeled her resolve. "Even a princess is not perfect, Mr. Erskine. Good day."

"Have you had another seizure?"

The room gave an uneasy turn. "I do not know to what you are referring. But if you have approached my friends and given them to understand that I am ill, I demand that you cease."

"You *are* unwell."

A tremor started in her legs and worked its way up her spine. "Good day."

She walked away, hardly knowing where she went, and found herself in front of a closed door. She plunged through it without thinking and entered a tiny, dark room, scarcely more then a closet, that had clearly not been intended to welcome the general public. There was but one object in the room: a painted cedar chest, perched on legs carved in the shape of strange animals, displayed on a raised platform. As if in a dream, Tameri moved to the chest and laid her hand on its smooth, cool surface.

"It has a secret chamber," Erskine said, entering behind her. "No one has been able to determine how to open it."

Only half-aware of Erskine's presence, Tameri ran her

fingers over the engraved hieroglyphs and the painted figures at the center of the chest's lid. She knew the goddess who posed with hands raised against her enemies: Isis, Aset, Lady of Heaven, Great of Magic. Before her stood Osiris, Asar, bound in his funeral wrappings. And across from both the good gods stood the one who hated them above all others: Set, Sutekh, brother of Asar. God of chaos, god of storms. His head was that of a strange beast, flat-topped ears upright, curving snout like that of no other creature.

"He lusted after the Lord Asar's throne," she murmured. "He desired to rule all the Black Land, and killed the Good God. He cast his coffin into the Nile."

"When Aset found it," Erskine continued softly, "and Sutekh learned that she might restore Asar to life, he tore his brother's body into fourteen pieces."

"But Aset found the pieces and put them back together. For a little time she restored him from death. Before he returned to the Underworld, he gave her a son."

"Horus. Heru of the Horizon, who battled Sutekh and won."

But Asar and Aset were never reunited. Asar remained in the Underworld, Aset in the land of life and fertility. Always to remain apart…

Tameri pressed her hand to her forehead. Warm, strong hands caught hers.

"Come," Asar said. "Come away from this place."

She looked up into his face. How beautiful it was. Just as it had been before Sutekh had wreaked his havoc. She smiled, touched his cheek and looked again at the chest. With a pass of her fingers she found the hidden catch and lifted the top.

Within lay the sacred scroll, just as she had remembered. She heard a low sound as if of astonishment, but it held no meaning. The scroll was light and fragile in her hand. She unrolled it carefully.

The answer was here. The answer she had forgotten.

She raised her eyes to her husband. "The time has come," she said. "The waiting has ended at last."

CHAPTER FOUR

LEO SAW THE UNFAMILIAR light in her eyes and knew it was happening again. The very fact that she had been able to open the chest was proof enough. He moved closer, casting his consternation aside, and made ready to catch her should she begin to fall.

"The waiting?" he repeated.

Her gaze was clear, certain and bright with love. He had no other word to describe the way she gazed at him.

Yet it really wasn't *him* she was looking at, but someone else. Someone who wore the face and name of a god.

"Show me," he said gently.

She gave the papyrus to him with a formal bow, palms flat. The ancient paper, remarkably preserved, creaked as he unrolled it and began to read.

The text was crisp and clean, as if it had been set down yesterday. Each glyph seemed to stand above the surface of the papyrus, imbued with an almost magical luminescence.

It was a prophecy. Couched in the ritual language of the ancients, it revealed the story of Isis and Osiris and Set. It described a world in which the gods were very real, their pain as genuine as that of any mortal.

Leo read, unrolling the scroll a little at a time until he reached a section set apart from the rest. The hieratic writing was utterly different than any he had seen. He looked into Tameri's face. Her eyes were still dreamy, still fixed on him as if she saw in him her only salvation. A shiver of entirely irrational excitement—or fear—left him paralyzed.

Osiris and Isis reborn. Reunited in this world, in this plane, through the willing sacrifice of two chosen believers. Two who would give up their own bodies and souls to the god and goddess, so that the realm of mortals would be safe from Set for all time.

She thinks she is one of them.

He had no time to grasp the enormity of the implications. Nausea clenched his stomach, and the room went black...

Maahes stood beneath an awning, feeling the hot desert wind on the bare skin of his legs and chest. This was a quiet place, a private place, forbidden to all but the most devoted followers of those who knew the true purpose of the ceremony. Who knew how vital was the outcome of the mating and transformation to come.

Before him lay the mouth of the tomb, the place readied for him and his bride. It was a portal, not to death, but to joy. As the priests chanted and rattled their sistra, calling upon the Great Ones, waking them from their long sleep, the only coolness came from the lady beside him.

She, who was so far above him in every way. She, who had accepted the call to become Aset-in-Breath. When first they had met, she had looked upon him as if he were no more than the cattle in the fields or one of the slaves who carried her litter. He was a common soldier in service to Pharaoh, chosen for reasons he could not guess to become her husband for this one night.

Lady Tameri's eyes found his. They were as green as the Nile in flood, like the eyes of the palace cats. They had not lost their haughtiness, nor did they find favor with him, though he had been told he was not uncomely. Once again he resisted the urge to fall at her feet. Once again he reminded himself that he, in this place and time, was her equal.

And he pitied her. He, born in a mud hut in the poorest quarter of the city, pitied this beautiful woman because beneath her contempt lay fear. Fear of losing herself. Fear of becoming a goddess.

He, too, was afraid. But he held out his hand to clasp hers, finding it cold despite the heat, and her fingers stiffened. Still she did not withdraw. She gazed ahead at the portal, her profile flawless and still.

You will not despise me when we are together again, he thought. There would be only eternal union, and a long battle against the Evil One. A battle they would share in hope.

The priests finished their invocations. Two of the highest among them, one vowed to Asar and one to Aset, took their places at either side of Maahes and the Lady. No words were spoken. All had been explained. Defying her fear, Tameri entered the long passageway. Maahes joined her, gripping her hand the more tightly. At the entrance of the tomb, the gods, illuminated in bright hues by the finest artisans, opened their arms in welcome.

Only a single lamp brightened the interior. The surface of every wall was covered with writings describing the story of Aset, Asar and Sutekh, and the tale of Heru's defeat of his murderous uncle. It spoke of Sutekh's desire to regain mastery of the world, to leave his exile in the desert and reclaim the kingdom he had lost.

A couch had been laid for Maahes and Tameri, the finest furnishings arranged for their comfort. Bread and honey, beer and fruit, fresh and plentiful, had been provided to break their long fast. Tameri removed her hand from his and watched as the priests set the door in place.

They had done their part. The rest was up to the chosen ones.

Tameri sat on a cedar chair inlaid with ebony and ivory, her gaze still fixed on the black square of the door. Though her posture was that of the princess she was, she did not deceive him.

"My lady," he said, kneeling beside her. "It will pass."

She looked at him, her face an elegant sculpture in the lamplight. "Yes," she said in a flat voice. "Soon we shall be no more."

"It is not an ending, but a beginning."

She laughed as if she had heard a trained monkey speak. "You have great faith, peasant."

"I believe that Sutekh will rise again. He must be stopped."

"Spoken as a good soldier." Her fists clenched in the folds of her fine pleated apron. "You have little to lose."

"You regret your choosing."

"I do my duty for love of my goddess. But I…" She closed her eyes.

"Was there one you favored, Lady?" he asked softly. "One with whom you would have shared your life?"

She turned and struck him. It was not by any means the worst pain he had felt, but his temper rose.

"We are here together," he said. "Let us enjoy what time is left."

Her green eyes were dark as ebony. "Do you desire me, peasant?" She stood, displaying the supple curves of her body beneath the sheerest linen of her sheath and apron. Her nipples had been rouged with henna, rising to peaks under the wide straps of her dress. The secret shadow between her thighs made him harden.

Maahes rose. "How could any man not desire you?"

She trembled, crossed her arms over her breast and walked to the murals on the nearest wall. One wide panel dominated the rest: surrounded by flowering lotuses and still waters, Asar and Aset lay together, the goddess impaled upon the god's erect member.

Maahes came up behind Tameri and laid his hands on her shoulders. "You are beautiful," he whispered. "More beautiful than the lotus flower."

"Such speech from a soldier," she said, attempting to mock him. But her breath caught as he ran his palms over her arms and cupped her elbows.

"Your skin is bathed in honey," he said, touching her neck with his lips. "New wine it is, to hear your voice."

She turned in his arms, her gaze bent from his. "I am afraid."

He lifted her chin and stroked her cheek. "All of life is within us now," he said. "It cannot be stolen from us."

Resting her palms on his chest, she let him embrace her. And as her body pressed against his, he knew she had at last let fall the final barrier between them.

Tameri was a feather in his arms. He carried her to the couch and laid her upon it. Her eyes did not flinch from his as he knelt beside the bed, slid the straps of her dress from her arms and touched her breast.

"How can this be?" she murmured. "How can I feel so—"

She spoke no more as he took her brown nipple between his lips. Her back arched high. He stroked her thigh through the fine linen as he suckled, and her breath came fast.

"Maahes," she cried. He raised her again, untied her sash and removed her sheath. Her nakedness was as sleek as a leopard's pelt. He worshiped her, paid tribute to her breasts and belly and thighs and what lay between them.

"Like wine," he whispered, drinking deeply. She parted her thighs with soft whimpers of excitement. He removed his kilt with a sweep of his hand and lay beside her. She touched his cheek with little words of endearment and locked her legs about his waist.

One thrust, and they would be joined. Once he entered her and she took his seed into herself, all that they knew would change. But first there would be pleasure, the clenching of her body around him, the flight of the hawk at twilight.

He slid deeper inside her. She cried his name again and again. He moved, felt the wall that had never been breached, closed his eyes.

Now.

"Leo!"

He opened his eyes. Tameri lay beneath him, her skirts and petticoats rucked to her waist and her drawers torn as if by impatient hands. His trousers were unbuttoned, and his cock...

Leo lunged up and away, fumbling for the buttons. Tameri lay still a moment longer, her eyes no longer green but black.

"Where are we?" she said. She turned her head, seeking him in the darkness. The door was closed, and there was no other light save the faintest luminescence emanating from the chest.

Half-afraid to touch her, Leo reached for her hand to help her up. With a sharp motion she pulled down her skirts and scrambled out of his reach to sit against the wall.

"Tameri," he said hoarsely. "I don't know... I didn't mean—"

But she didn't seem to hear him. "Where are we?" she repeated. "It is so dark. So dark."

"It's only a room in the Museum," he said, keeping his distance. "If you will wait here, I'll make certain—"

That no one saw us, he thought. He could only pray that it was so. Part of him was still in that other place, unfulfilled, aching with need. But none of that mattered now.

He found his way to the door. It wouldn't open.

"We cannot get out," Tameri said, panic rising in her voice. Her shoes scuffled on the floor. "They have sealed us in!"

Leo made one more effort and then accepted the fact that they had somehow got themselves locked into the room. "No one has sealed us in," he said. "The door has accidentally been locked. Someone will find us soon."

"No. No one will come."

The words were no longer fearful, but dull with despair. Erskine could just make her out where she stood against the wall, her arms tightly clasped across her chest. Just as she had stood in that other place and time.

"There is nothing to fear," he said. He reached for her, stopped, let his arms fall. He dared not touch her again.

But she came into his arms, letting him hold her as he so desperately wished to do, though his common sense told him that this was as much a dream as that other vision. He stroked her hair, black as that *other* Tameri's had been, fallen loose about her shoulders.

"More beautiful than the lotus flower," he murmured.

She raised her eyes to his. "You were there," she said haltingly. "You were…"

The door creaked open. Leo let Tameri go, tucked the scroll in his coat and stepped away. Light spilled into the room.

"Who's there?" a man's voice demanded.

Leo went to meet him. "Leo Erskine," he said. "And Her Grace the dowager Duchess of Vardon. We took a wrong turn, I fear."

The man, one of the Museum attendants, glanced from

Leo to Tameri. He stared an instant too long at Tameri's loosened hair.

"I...see," he said, remembering the wisdom of diplomacy. He moved from the doorway. "Your Grace?"

Whatever her previous fears, Tameri seemed to have regained her usual aplomb. Leo watched anxiously as she left the room, praying that the young man would continue to be prudent. He paused just outside the door and gave the attendant a long, meaningful look.

"Her Grace has always been a generous patroness," he said casually. "It would be a pity if she were to lose interest in the Museum."

The young man's gaze flickered downward. "I quite understand, Mr. Erskine."

Leo clapped his shoulder companionably and followed Tameri, but his legs were not quite steady. It was all bluff. As it was surely bluff on Tameri's part, as well, though she moved with her accustomed assurance.

The assurance of a true princess. A princess afraid of the dark.

Giving his head a quick shake, Leo let Tameri get well ahead and paused before the Egyptian bust he had examined earlier, waiting until he was certain that he could face the world with composure.

A world that no longer seemed entirely his own.

He smiled and nodded to a few acquaintances, paused to exchange a few words with one of the Museum's directors and left the building. He knew he ought to go after Tameri, make sure she was well, but he also knew she would only rebuff any offer of aid. The papyrus rattled with each beat of his heart. He was, as Tameri had said, no better than a thief.

But he must understand. The scroll held the answers he had been seeking. He had meant to save Tameri from herself, but he had begun to wonder if he must save himself, as well.

CHAPTER FIVE

TAMERI'S FIRST THOUGHT was to go directly to her friends in the Widow's Club. It was an instinct she followed as far as Wilton Crescent, where her mind cleared and she remembered how Frances, Lillian and Clara had badgered her about her supposed "illness." She had never fully confided in any of the widows where her dreams and visions were concerned; they knew and accepted her assumption of a past life, but if she were to attempt to explain the rest, they were likely to feel even more justified in their fears for her. Far less would they comprehend how she had come to find herself lying on the floor, legs exposed, with Leo nearly ready to…

Tameri bit her lip with such force that she drew blood. She had always been one of the most adamantly dedicated of the Widows, refusing to consider either marriage or a less formal liaison with the many men who would have been happy to share her bed, "eccentricities" or no. How astonished the others would be if they knew.

The vision had been so real. So true. Leo would never have acted in such a way had he not been caught up in it with her.

It cannot be.

She refused to consider the matter further—or to allow her body to feel again what she had felt in that ancient time. The wetness of his tongue on her nipple.

The glide of his hands on her naked flesh. The nearly unbearable sensation of his thick, hard member between her thighs.

Help me, Aset. Help me.

Perhaps the goddess heard her, for she was able to return to Maye House without her coachmen or the other servants recognizing her distress. She attempted to answer letters and invitations without success, then retreated to the conservatory, where she sat amongst the potted palms and exotic flowers of tropic climes she had never seen.

How often she had thought of visiting Egypt. Egypt, her Mother, the very breath of her life. Of that other life.

Where the tomb waited, its mouth gaping to receive its sacrifice….

A distorted memory, no more. Her destiny did not, could not, end in such a terrible fate. And Leo had *not* been in that tomb with her. He was *not* Maahes, beloved of Asar.

Leo. A lion's name. And Maahes was the Egyptian lion god, who stood beside the sun god as he battled the evil serpent god Apep.

Only coincidence. Her imagination.

I could not love him.

But was that part of the destiny she refused to acknowledge? Was it the tomb she feared most, or Leo himself? And what had become of the scroll they had found? She had never seen its contents. Had Leo taken it?

Tameri brooded until nightfall, pacing the garden, the corridors and her private suite. The inscriptions of peace and joy and love painted on her walls gave her no comfort, nor did the images of benevolent gods and their good works on behalf of mankind.

She was almost relieved when Bab announced the arrival of a visitor. It was well past the hour for calling, but Tameri could not bar him from her door. Especially when she so badly needed the understanding of one like herself. Even if she could not tell him the full truth.

Alastair Boyd entered the drawing room, bringing with him the scent of a scalding desert wind. His dark, intense eyes sought hers as she rose to meet him.

"Something has happened," he said without preamble.

She sent Bab for tea and settled herself again, making certain that her skirt fell in perfect pleats over her knees. "I have remembered more," she said.

"Indeed?" He sat in the chair opposite hers and leaned forward, his brown hands clasped. "What have you remembered?"

The desire came over her to tell him all, to confide in this one man who knew better than any other how high were the stakes.

"A ceremony," she began cautiously.

"What sort of ceremony?"

"An invocation of Aset and Asar. Priests were leading me to…" She was unable to finish.

"Were you alone?"

It was a disturbing question, when she had just told him that there had been priests present. He couldn't know what she had discovered in the dream, or its terrible implications.

"Yes," she said, lying without understanding why she did so. "I understood very little, only that I was a part of the rite. That it was a part of the Great Battle."

"Ah." He leaned back, satisfaction in his sun-bronzed face. "Perhaps this is the sign that the time has almost come for you to reclaim all you have lost."

Lost—over the millennia, the long miles, the years in England when she had been unaware of the Battle and her role in it. A role of leadership that would end in triumph, not a slow, suffocating death.

"It is too soon," she said. "I will know when Aset chooses to tell me."

"Of course." He frowned, studying her face. "Yet there is more, is there not?"

Her wayward, common flesh betrayed her with a blush. "Nothing."

"You have seen *him* again."

How did he know? Had he seen her and Leo at the Museum? "I have not," she said coldly. "But if I had, it would be no concern of yours."

"But I warned you. He is not to be trusted."

"Trusted with what? You never bothered to explain."

"He is a distraction, not worthy of your majesty. You can afford no such diversions now, when we are so close."

"You speak as if you fear that he has designs upon me. Such is hardly the case. He has no interest in me except as a…a curiosity."

"You underestimate yourself, Tameri." He rose and came toward her. "Any man would desire you."

She started. Maahes had spoken nearly the same words.

Boyd was not Maahes. He was, like her, a reincarnation, but of a priest named Sinuhé. Her loyal and devoted servant, bound to the same cause.

"I assure you that he does not, nor I him." She moved to get up, but Boyd blocked her way.

"Prove it," he whispered. "Prove that he is nothing to you."

The scent of his body, redolent of unfamiliar spices, washed over her. She felt his lust, as shocking as anything she had experienced since Leo Erskine had first come into her home. He had never behaved so. It was as if he had forgotten who she was.

"Move aside," she commanded.

"I was a high priest of Aset," he whispered, running his

fingertips along the line of her jaw. "I am worthy of you as is no other."

She was almost afraid of him. Almost. "Save your devotion for the goddess."

He caught her up in his arms. He was strong, like a force of nature, like a gathering storm. "Can't you see? We were meant to be together, to fight the evil side by side."

But it was not you *I saw. Not Sinuhé to whom I gave my body.*

And if it were not? How better to remove Leo and the vision from her thoughts than to accept Boyd's advances? If she must give way to passion over which she had no control, why not let it be to the man who could truly share all that lay ahead?

"Yes," he murmured, his breath caressing her mouth. "Together, Tameri."

The resistance went out of her body, and she lifted her lips to his.

LEO LET THE BOOK FALL with uncharacteristic violence, raising a cloud of dust. His housekeeper knew better than to intrude upon his library, and he had let it become little better than a rat's nest.

A nest of utterly useless volumes, not one of which could shed the slightest illumination upon the indecipherable contents of the papyrus spread beneath a pane of glass on his desk.

He spiked his hands through his hair, carefully gathered up the precious scroll and strode for the door. Whatever venerable scribe had written these words, he had not meant them to be read by any but one familiar with a dialect unknown to modern scholarship.

The door slammed much too loudly as he closed it. His

expression had the unwelcome effect of alarming his few servants, who were not accustomed to encountering anything but a most amiable and liberal master. He might have done a better job of calming himself had he believed it was only frustration that fed his foul mood.

But it wasn't. Since he'd left the Museum, every minute had been consumed with thoughts of Tameri and the softness of her skin, the taste of her breast, her little gasps of pleasure.

It wasn't real. There was not, had never been a man named Maahes, nor another Tameri. No chanting priests, no tomb, no sacrifice.

Except that the hallucination had been real enough that he had nearly taken her like some rutting beast.

In a fine froth of bewildered anger, Leo visited several scholars who had more than a passing familiarity with hieratic writing. As he had expected, not one had anything useful to contribute, though all three revealed keen interest in the document and eyed Leo with speculation and, in one case, suspicion.

When there was nowhere else for Leo to go and nothing for him to do, he went to Maye House.

The hour was very late, but even had Tameri not told him that she never retired early, he would have made the attempt. He waited a good ten minutes before a servant answered the door, just a few seconds before Leo had determined to break it down.

The man was clearly flustered, high color in his normally impassive face.

"The dowager is not at home," he said.

"I must speak with her at once."

"I am sorry, Mr. Erskine." He attempted to close the door. Leo wedged his foot between door and doorjamb.

"Kindly tell your mistress that I am here."

Something in his voice or face must have warned the servant that Leo was in no mood to be trifled with. He invited Leo into the entrance hall, asked him to be seated and walked quickly away.

Leo didn't wait. He followed the footman upstairs to the door of the Gold drawing room and strode in, barely avoiding the servant as he walked through the door.

And stopped. Tameri was in Alastair Boyd's arms, and he was kissing her.

The words Leo shouted were in a language he had heard only in a dream. Boyd leaped away from Tameri with a roar no human voice could make. Heat blasted Leo's face. The footman fled the room.

A deep, unfathomable hatred expanded in Leo's chest, crowding the air from his lungs. "Boyd!" he snarled.

Ignoring Tameri, Boyd came to meet him. "Is it to be here, then?"

"Get out."

Boyd smiled, showing far too many teeth. "You have made a mistake, Erskine."

"If you think… If you believe for one moment…" The fearful energy coursing through Leo's body began to dissipate. "Leave, or I'll drop you where you stand."

"Of course." Boyd was an ordinary man again, but Leo had no doubt that he was dangerous still. "You are not only a man of books, are you, Erskine? So few know how many years you spent wandering parts of the world into which no sane Englishman would venture, battling the elements, savage beasts and even more savage men with your wits, a Webley British Bulldog and your fists. Only it appears that you have no pistol, and your wits have deserted you."

Leo raised a fist. "I haven't forgotten how to use these."

Boyd stepped back. "I have more regard for the lady's sensibilities. You shall have what you wish, but not now."

"You're a coward, Boyd. Whatever happened to you in that desert—"

"Silence!"

Both men turned to Tameri. She was nearly trembling with rage, her pupils so wide that they dominated the verdant green of her eyes.

"Enough!" she cried. "I will have no men brawling in my chambers like rutting bulls!"

"I was not doing the rutting," Leo snapped.

"Leave this house!" she commanded, leaving no doubt as to whom she spoke. "I do not wish to see you again!"

Leo searched her face for some sense behind her furious words, but it was hard and unforgiving. *She does not recognize me,* he thought wildly.

"You heard the lady," Boyd said.

"You've done something to her!" Leo snarled.

"I've evidently done what you could not," Boyd said with a mocking grin.

Leo shook with rage. But there was no profit in remaining, not while Tameri gazed at him with such loathing. Somehow Boyd had poisoned her mind against him, though he didn't know how or why. Common jealousy was the simplest explanation.

But Leo did not believe it.

"You shall have what you wish, but not now." Boyd was just as eager to make mincemeat of Leo as Leo was to disassemble his rival piece by piece. But their antipathy went beyond whatever each of them might feel for Tameri.

What do *I feel?*

Recognizing the necessity for a temporary retreat, Leo left. There was nothing Boyd could really do to harm

Tameri; he might seduce her, but she was a grown woman who had the right to make her own choices.

Does she? Do I?

He ignored his carriage, walked as far as the nearest pub and gave himself to oblivion.

CHAPTER SIX

TAMERI STOOD BEFORE the warehouse door, enveloped in the dark, hooded cloak that protected her identity from the common folk who wandered these mean, comfortless streets. She had grown to know this place well, but the poor neighborhood seemed more and more a ghost of itself, shrinking and fading, as she herself had begun to fade.

Her feet carried her down the hidden staircase, but she was scarcely aware of her progress. She had felt strangely detached ever since the night Alastair Boyd and Leo Erskine had quarreled, and she had driven Leo away.

It was for the best. But when it had happened, when she had told Leo she never wanted to see him again, she had not realized what she was saying. Only after Alastair had gone had she remembered, and understood. She still could not quite recall what Alastair and Leo had said to one another, but it scarcely mattered. The deed was done.

All for the best, though her heart had shriveled and her body felt like that of an old woman, functioning only because necessity demanded it.

The others were waiting for her when she reached the doors to the basement. She knocked twice. The doors opened, and the woman within bowed deeply, her linen sheath pressed to her body by a gust of wind trailing in Tameri's wake.

The votaries had already gathered and stood before the dais, where the priest waited to begin. They turned and bowed, some sinking to the floor as Tameri walked past them.

They knew her. Over the past months they had gathered here as if urged by some voiceless summons…only a few at first, then more, until there were two score followers, all committed to the Great Battle. Their cloaks lay draped across the chairs set out for them; there was no need for secrecy here.

The goddess stood on the dais, her limestone figure benevolent and smiling, bearing a crook in one hand and an ankh in the other, the sun disk and horns of Hathor upon her head. The priest, draped in leopard skin, smiled and bowed to Tameri as if nothing at all had occurred in her drawing room two days before.

"Lady," he said. "It is a blessed day."

She studied his face, its harsh planes framed by his black wig. There was more in his eyes than respect or even satisfaction. He believed what had passed between them held greater significance than what she ascribed to it. A kiss was not necessarily a promise of something more. And he knew better than anyone why she must remain free to follow where Aset led her.

But he was as necessary to the cause as she, though they both waited for the sign, the dream, the vision that would make all plain and set them on their proper paths.

"The time is coming, my lady," Sinuhé said, touching the sleeve of her cloak.

She inclined her head, preparing to move past him to the dais. He stopped her.

"You are still troubled," he said. "Has Erskine sought you out again?"

"No. I am well."

"Yet your visions remain clouded. The goddess has said that Sutekh has risen. We must know how to proceed."

She pulled her sleeve from his grasp. "As you said, the time is coming."

"I know a woman," he said, "who might help us."

"A woman?"

"A mystic who sees into the past and the future. If anyone can find the true meaning behind what you have experienced, it is she."

"Do you think it wise to trust an outsider?"

"As I said, I know her well. Her path is not ours, but she, too, will be needed when the Battle begins."

Tameri could summon up no argument against Alastair's proposal. Once she had been content to wait for answers, but now she understood the true peril of such delays. Was it not worth trying anything in order to find the next step, the path that would set the Great Battle in motion and clarify her position in it? She was still only mortal, and mortals could so easily fall.

"Very well," she said. "I shall meet her and determine if she is worthy. Where is this 'mystic' to be found?"

"Not far from here," he said, the warmth of approval in his voice. "I will take you after the ceremony." He accepted her cloak, bowing, and she moved to stand before Aset, lifting her hands as she began the chant. The others took it up, their voices lapping at the walls like gentle waves.

"Praise to you, Aset, the Great One, Lady of Heaven, Mistress and Queen of the gods.
You are the First Royal Spouse of Osiris,
The Bull, The Lion who overthrows all his enemies, The Lord and ruler of eternity."

No fear, no anger. Only peace in this place, where the

offerings of flowers gave off their sweet scent and the forthcoming conflict seemed very far away. As far away as the voices of the priests who had led her into the tomb, pronouncing their last blessings as she plunged into darkness, the soldier at her side.

Her voice faltered. The acolytes fell silent. The air grew thick, as if someone had sealed all the windows and filled the room with noxious smoke.

Gasping, Tameri backed away from the smiling goddess. Her sandal slipped on the edge of the dais. Sinuhé caught her as she fell and eased her to the floor.

"Mhotep!" he cried.

Tameri coughed and opened her eyes. "There is…no need for a doctor."

But her protests were ignored. Mhotep, known to the world outside these walls as Dr. Thomas Newton, knelt to examine Tameri while the anxious congregation looked on. He asked her a series of questions, felt her pulse and said that he could find nothing wrong.

"There *is* nothing wrong," Tameri said, sitting up. She took several slow, careful breaths and smiled. "I am only a little tired."

"She must get more rest," Mhotep said firmly.

"I agree," Sinuhé said. "I shall see to it."

Mhotep nodded, bowed to Tameri and left them alone.

"I see how much you wish to deny it," Sinuhé said, "but you must think not only of yourself, but of everyone in this room and our larger purpose. You will lead us in Aset's name. She can act only through you."

Tameri pulled free of his supporting arms. "Perhaps I am not the one."

"You are. But the stress of your burden has taken its toll. We must seek aid wherever we can find it." He helped her to stand. "We will go to my friend at once."

Yes. Anything, anything at all that might put an end to this limbo. She turned to address the congregation with words of reassurance. Sinuhé reminded them that the Lady Tameri had many heavy burdens and duties to attend to.

"Come," he said, taking her arm again. She could smell the scent of his skin, the odor of burning sand and relentless heat. Not like Leo, who smelled of sandalwood, rich earth and growing things.

You will never see him again.

LEO CROUCHED AT THE DIRTY window, watching the ceremony as his legs cramped and his fingers grew numb.

He felt for the papyrus as he had done so many times during the past few days, as if it might yet divulge its secrets. But the words he could not read remained unintelligible, their meaning beyond his reach.

As Tameri was. Three nights ago, she had made her distaste for him—and her preference for Boyd—quite clear. *He* had made a few bold promises to himself: that he'd sincerely and humbly apologize for the advantage he'd taken of her in the Museum; that he'd admit how far his skepticism had fallen, and how much he needed her help to unlock the secrets of the papyrus she had found; and, above all, to make her see that Boyd was a villain, though he had absolutely no proof that such was the case.

Instead here he was, creeping after her like a jackal. Observing rites not meant for his eyes.

I witnessed them once before. I was a part of them.

But he still didn't believe it. Not yet. Not until he looked into Tameri's eyes and saw again what he had seen then.

He shifted, attempting to stretch his legs, and leaned closer to the window. Tameri was stepping back from the dais. Falling. The man who caught her, bewigged and draped with a leopard's pelt, murmured in her ear. Leo stiffened. He could not see the man's face, but there was an intimacy in their posture, in the priest's touch.

A dozen seconds passed before Leo felt himself under control again. Control to which he clung by the merest thread.

She is mine.

Bright light swallowed by darkness. The honeyed scent of her skin. Her moans as he parted her thighs…

The roaring in his ears deafened him, and for a moment he saw nothing. His forehead bumped the glass. He opened his eyes.

Tameri was gone, and so was the priest.

Leo sprang to his feet. Nothing resembling rationality moved him; it was all emotion and instinct and fear. He ran to the front of the building, pulled open the door and found a narrow corridor leading to a staircase. The door at the bottom was locked. He pounded on it repeatedly until someone came to answer.

The man was dressed in a light linen tunic, barelegged and wearing a wide golden collar. He gave Leo a startled glance and hesitated just long enough for Leo to push past him.

The echoing room had been decorated with Egyptian wall paintings and false columns, all dominated by the large stone goddess on the dais. A dozen faces turned toward Leo; the man who had come to the door ran after him, his sandals slapping on the cold cement floor.

"Sir!" he cried.

Leo ignored him. "Where is she?" he demanded of the next man he met.

The fellow gaped. "Who are—"

"Tameri! Where has she gone?"

A woman with serene, pretty features, her eyes rimmed with kohl, approached Leo cautiously. "Why do you seek her?"

"She's in danger."

Uncertain glances were exchanged, and several other devotees gathered around Leo. "She is in no danger," the doorman said. "She is with our—"

Leo saw several men and women disappearing behind the statue and ran after them. A small door led directly outside. Leo caught up with the group ahead of him and grabbed one of the men by the arm.

"Where did they go? Tameri and Boyd?"

"I don't know," the man stammered.

Cursing under his breath, Leo closed his eyes. It was impossible that he should know what direction Tameri and Boyd had taken, but his feelings continued to circumvent his usually reliable brain. He set out east, passing streets that became more and more disreputable as he proceeded. Buildings long left untended crumbled into the rubbish-filled alleys, and men with shadowed eyes stared after him as he passed.

Chance alone brought him to a corner just in time to see a cloaked figure enter a doorway at the end of a narrow alley. He slowed as he approached the decrepit building, which was hung with a nearly unreadable sign advertising the skills of a fortune-teller.

Leo pushed at the creaking door and ducked under a ragged curtain. The smell of incense washed over him. A woman stood in the dark, close room, facing the door as if she had expected a visitor.

"Welcome," she said in a smooth, deep voice bearing the accents of the East. "You have come to know your future."

Dressed in a gown of ebony silk that matched her hair,

the woman might have stopped any man in his tracks. She was not as beautiful as Tameri, but even Leo was not entirely immune to her sensual allure.

"A man and a woman entered here," he said.

She arched her perfectly shaped brows. "You are the first I have seen since sunset," she said. "Will you not be seated?"

"I haven't time," he said sharply. He moved for the back of the room, draped like the other walls in a red paisley brocade.

"Stop. You have no right." She moved closer and laid her hand on his arm.

"I know she's here."

She captured his eyes with her own. "Perhaps I can tell you what you need to know."

He seized her wrist. "Tell me now."

Her body tensed. "You are not what you seem."

"I am a man who can make a great deal of trouble for you if you do not tell me the truth."

The woman sucked in her breath. "He does not know," she whispered, as if to herself. "I must—"

"He? Boyd?"

Flinching, she tried to break free of his grip. "I know only what *he* has told me. By Sekhmet I swear this."

Leo's incoherent fears took frightening shape. *"Where is she?"*

She sank to her knees. "*He* told her that I could look into her soul and lift the veil that bars her from the truth. I failed, and they left."

"What does Boyd want with her?"

The fortune-teller's dark eyes lost their focus. "It is the ancient war," she said. "The battle that never ends."

In that other place, in the blackness of a tomb, the one called Maahes had thought of eternal unions, of the long battle against the Evil One. Leo cast the thought aside.

"No more riddles!" he snapped. "Where has he taken her?"

"I do not know."

"By God, if she comes to any harm…" He twisted the woman's arm, and she gasped.

"He will kill me!" she cried.

Some unnameable power within him transformed his last shreds of patience into ruthlessness. "Choose," he said.

She met his eyes, and what she saw in them broke the last of her resistance. "He said he would take her by train to Marseilles, and from there by ship to Egypt."

Egypt.

"She did not go willingly," he said harshly.

"He told her that she must go to the Black Land at once. She refused him." The woman shuddered. "One does not refuse *him.*"

"Not even a goddess?"

The words made no sense even to him, and yet they rang with truth. Aset had ever stood proud and brave against the God of Chaos. As she must do so now….

Leo's brief distraction gave the woman the chance she'd been waiting for. She twisted free and lunged for the front door. He moved with inhuman speed and barred the way.

"Fear *me,*" he said.

"I do," she whispered, falling to her knees again. "I do, Oh Lord of Eternity."

He gazed down upon this mortal woman with contempt for her pathetic devotion to the evil one she served. "You shall go with me to the train. You shall help me find them."

"Yes."

"Prepare yourself."

She rose, a wash of black hair falling across her face

as she backed through the curtained rear doorway. He didn't bother to follow. She would not dare defy him now.

The scent of incense grew cloying in his nostrils. He returned to the front door and leaned against the jamb, his mind suddenly clouded and thick with confusion.

Air. He stumbled out the door and into the fetid street. A shadow moved away from the wall, and pain exploded in his skull.

And then he knew no more.

CHAPTER SEVEN

THE WORLD SWAM BACK INTO FOCUS.

Tameri stared up at the ceiling, bewildered by the movement she sensed beneath her body. The surface she lay upon was solid enough, padded but firm. She tried to raise her arms and found them tied with silken cord.

She tried to remember. The woman's hovel. Her catlike stare as Boyd introduced her to Tameri. The strange perfume that had made her feel so dizzy. Hands supporting her, voices...

A painful cramp seized at her stomach. She rolled to the side, leaning her head over the edge of the couch. Bile rose sour in her throat.

"Have no fear, my lady. It will pass."

She forced herself to breathe and straightened. Boyd sat on a velvet-covered bench, regarding her with a faint smile and no concern at all. Her heart contracted into a small, icy pebble.

"Where are we?" she asked.

"Haven't you been on a train before?" He crossed his legs and reached into his jacket for a cigarette case. "You seem put out, Tameri. You should know that I've done everything to insure your comfort...the most private of private cars, complete with every luxury a lady might desire."

She struggled to sit. "Comfort?" she repeated, raising her bound hands.

"Ah, yes." He considered his unlit cigarette with a slight frown. "Perhaps that wasn't necessary. But you are apt to be unpredictable, my lady. You might suddenly develop certain…abilities that might surprise us both."

The car gave a jolt as the train bounced over an uneven stretch of track. Tameri tasted something other than sickness on the back of her tongue.

She'd been drugged. Boyd had drugged her. She was being kidnapped.

"What do you want?" she asked, striving to maintain her composure. "Why are you doing this?"

"You know part of the story already," he said, releasing a plume of smoke into the stuffy car. "It was ever your desire to go to Egypt. Now you will get your wish."

"You are taking me against my will!"

"Had I thought you more malleable, I would have used mere persuasion. But your acquaintance with Leo Erskine has aroused unfortunate doubts in your mind. It was very foolish for you to become involved with an outsider, Tameri."

"I am not involved with him!" She tested her bonds and found them unyielding. "Is this jealousy, Alastair? Can you have gone so far, simply to—"

"Jealousy? Of a mere mortal?"

Her hands began to go numb. She spoke with great care. "We who obey Aset know that we are destined to aid the Good Gods in fighting the god of storms, but surely you don't believe that we are other than mortal ourselves."

"Don't I?" He finished his cigarette and tossed it to the carpet. "You yourself have been possessed by Aset on more than one occasion."

And she had. Only here, in this moment of extremity, did she fully remember the time in Maye House, and again in the Museum, when she had seen in Leo not merely a soldier named Maahes but also a god. When she had become the goddess herself.

"How would you know such a thing?" she demanded.

He sighed like a schoolmaster burdened with a particularly dull pupil. "I saw Aset stand before me in your drawing room, casting Erskine from her presence."

"That was not—"

"I recognized it because it happened to me, my dear. Only I have left my mortal self behind forever."

"You are Sinuhé, a priest of Aset!"

"Long ago. Long before this incarnation. Before he found me wandering in the desert and preserved my body for his use."

The numbness had spread throughout Tameri's entire body. "Who are you?"

He smiled, and there were too many teeth, too wide a mouth, too much red in the eyes. "Don't you know, Princess? I am your enemy."

Sutekh.

There was no use in further struggle, but Tameri fought until Boyd—the god of chaos—brought forth a cup and forced the stinking contents into her mouth. Her final thoughts were of Leo, and what an utter fool she had been to send him away.

IT WAS THE NOISE THAT woke Leo, the scuffle of boots and bodies around him. He tried to sit, but the dizziness and nausea forced him down again. His uncertain vision picked out perhaps a half-dozen men, four of whom seemed vaguely familiar to his aching eyes. The other two were thickset and armed with knives and cudgels, which they were attempting to use on their opponents.

For a moment Leo was lost in confusion. He remembered speaking to the fortune-teller, and hearing her confession about the kidnapping. *"The ancient war,"* she had said.

That was the last thing he recalled with any clarity. The rest had been like a dream, as if he had not been in control of his own body. Something had been said of a train to Marseilles, with Egypt the ultimate destination. He had threatened the woman. And then…

Leo reached within himself, clutching at the core of determination and strength upon which he had relied in many a sticky situation. He got more than he bargained for. A rush of pure, hot energy surged through his body, pulling him to his feet. He charged the nearest knife-wielder, knocking away the man's weapon with a slice of his hand. The man grunted in startlement as he fell. Someone shouted; the other ruffian flew past Leo, followed by three of the half-familiar men.

The fellow at Leo's feet tried to rise, and Leo stamped down on his wrist, almost taking pleasure in the man's howl of pain. The unnameable power coursed through his veins, alight with the joy of triumph over his enemies.

"Mr. Erskine?"

He turned to the owner of the hesitant voice, whom he knew at once to be one of the worshippers in the warehouse temple. The gray-haired gentleman had thrown a cloak over his Egyptian costume, but it was evident that he and his companions had come directly from the warehouse.

"They were trying to kill you," the man said, still panting from his exertions. "We arrived just in time."

Leo's head began to clear again. "You followed me?"

The man glanced at his companions, who had gathered around him. "We knew you were following the princess. It was necessary that we learn your purpose in pursuing her."

Both anger and triumph deserted Leo in an instant. "She did something to me," he said. "The woman in the shop."

Another exchange of glances. "I am Dr. Thomas Newton," the gray-haired gentleman said. "Who was this woman you speak of?"

Leo shook his head, doing his best to disregard the savage pain inside his skull. "There's no time to explain. Tameri has been kidnapped."

"Kidnapped?" Newton echoed. "What do you mean?"

"By Boyd," Leo said. "He's taking her to Egypt."

All four of the men exclaimed at once. "But surely…" Newton stammered. "Sinuhé would have no reason—"

"'The ancient battle,'" Leo quoted. "'The war that never ends.'"

"Eye of Re," Newton said in a choked voice. "Is it possible?"

"I don't know what's possible," Leo said, "but I'm going after her." He heard the ruffian stir and nudged the man with his boot. "Secure these men, and see that they do not follow me."

Newton stared into Leo's eyes. "Sinuhé is not what he claimed to be," he said slowly. "But neither are you."

"I don't know what you're talking about."

"Don't you?"

"I've no time!" Leo snapped. "It's nearly dawn. I must find the fortune-teller."

He stepped over the groaning thug's body and broke into a run, searching for some familiar landmark. But if the fortune-teller's shop was anywhere in the vicinity, the woman had surely removed any sign or marker that would identify it. He stopped in a street that looked like any other in the rookeries, breathing hard.

A train bound for Marseilles. That was all he knew. It would have to be enough.

Two of Aset's followers caught him up, breathing as raggedly as he. "The ruffians have been secured," Newton said, bracing his hands on his knees. "What do you want us to do?"

"Nothing." Leo hesitated. "If you've any money, give it to me. I'll need it for fare."

"We've none with us," Newton said. "If you'll return with me to my home—"

"I've a little cash. Go at once to St. John, the Earl of Donnington, and request on my behalf that he immediately wire five hundred pounds to my account at the Banque de France in Paris."

"Surely, if Boyd is what you claim, you should not go alone."

"I must." Leo gauged the direction of the rising sun and turned west, readying himself for another hard run.

"Great Asar!" Newton called after him.

The word was like a silken noose around Leo's neck, jerking him to a halt. "I have nothing to do with your gods," he said. "Pray that they have more ability to protect their own than they've shown thus far."

Newton made no further attempt to stop him, and he ran until he was well out of the rookeries and could hail a hackney cab to take him to Victoria Station.

No one there could remember a beautiful, dark-haired lady accompanied by a handsome man with a tanned complexion, and Leo found no further help in Dover. He crossed the Channel, collected his money in Paris and bought tickets for the next train leaving the city for Marseilles. Just before his departure, he found a clerk at the station who responded to his description of the people he was seeking.

At least he was not too far behind them. But once Boyd and Tameri reached Marseilles, the trail could rapidly grow cold.

The journey all but drove Leo mad. He could not sit for more than a few minutes at a time, and haunted the corridor outside his private car both day and night. Once in Marseilles, Leo looked up an old acquaintance, one Bébert, who had on occasion provided Leo with certain unusual items a British agent, archaeologist and adventurer might require in his work. Bébert sent his own agents scurrying throughout the city, inquiring at hotels, ticket offices and wharves, but it was as if Boyd had never been there at all. Only when Leo was about to board a steamer bound across the Mediterranean did Bébert himself come to meet him with word that several Turkish *vilains* attempting to steal a beautiful green-eyed woman from the *monsieur* with the dark red hair had met with an ugly end in the Vieux Port.

No one else had caught a glimpse of either Boyd or Tameri. Leo knew that he couldn't afford to linger in Marseilles. He would have to assume that Boyd had boarded a ship for Egypt.

The voyage to Egypt was without incident, and Leo disembarked in Alexandria, breathing in the thick, fertile scents of the delta. After questioning the dock workers at the quay, he caught a train to Cairo and went directly to Shepheard's Hotel, where he inquired of the clerks on the off-chance that Boyd had taken Tameri there. No such person had checked in. The other hotels popular with European tourists were equally barren of clues.

But Leo was not without resources. He had made many reliable contacts in Cairo over the years, and he called upon them now. Men who knew every back street and alley in the city were eager to take his money. Shopkeepers and merchants were recruited to watch for the couple, and Leo continued to search himself.

Two days after his arrival, his efforts finally bore fruit.

A man of dubious reputation, who had on more than one occasion directed Leo to smugglers attempting to sell Egyptian antiquities on the black market, had heard that the two Europeans had been seen boarding a boat bound up the Nile.

"I was told that the dark Inglizi and the beautiful *sayyida* were bound for Luxor," Abbas said, casting a nervous glance over his shoulder. "But the man with whom I spoke would say no more. He was very much afraid."

"Why afraid?" Leo asked.

"He would not say."

Nor would Abbas elaborate. Leo sensed that he, too, was afraid.

But of what? Boyd was only one man, and though he, like Leo, had experience in Egypt, he had no real power to threaten anyone.

And yet...

"He will kill me," the fortune-teller had said, just before Leo had fallen into the waking dream. *"One does not refuse him."*

Who in hell was he?

Leo pressed a wad of bills into Abbas's hand. "Arrange passage for me on the next train and report back to me at the hotel. You shall have twice as much as I've already given you."

Abbas wavered, but in the end he agreed. Leo made his own arrangements, outfitting himself for every eventuality he could imagine. He bought a good pistol and a selection of knives which he could carry hidden in his clothing and boots.

Abbas returned by nightfall, informing Leo that the train—bound for Asyut, 234 miles south of Cairo—would leave early the next morning. Once in Asyut, Leo would hire a boat to take him the rest of the way to Luxor. It was a trip with which Leo was very familiar. And when he got to Luxor…

One way or another, Boyd was not likely to survive their next meeting.

CHAPTER EIGHT

CONSCIOUSNESS CAME AND WENT, flickering like a candle in flashes of light and darkness. Tameri had fleeting visions of trains and busy streets, ships and tossing waves, a teeming throng of humanity crowding about her in a strange city. She felt burning heat on her face, and the coolness of deep shadow.

And always she was moving, carried or forced along by merciless hands. Sometimes other voices spoke, often in foreign tongues, words tinged with fear. Tameri had no chance to cry out for help; as soon as the thought came into her head, it faded again.

At last there came a time when the constant motion stopped. Tameri drifted for a while on the edge of waking, aware that something had changed, something her bewildered mind was unable to grasp.

Wake up.

She opened her eyes to utter blackness. A scream built in her throat, as instinctive as the wail of an abandoned child.

No one came for her. She lay rigid on an ungiving surface and tried to hear past the roar of her heartbeat. Voices, droning in a continuous swell of sound. Chanting. Words that were half-familiar.

Because she had heard them before.

Slowly her eyes adjusted, and she realized that the

blackness had been within her own mind. The chamber was lit by a pair of lamps that caused the shadows to leap and dance. She pulled at her bonds…soft and silken, as if the one who had imprisoned her wished to preserve her delicate flesh. Her dress was little more than a wisp of the finest, sheerest linen, her collar a tracery of gold wire and beads.

A tomb. She was in a tomb. But there was no feast here, no furniture inlaid with ebony and ivory and gold.

And no Maahes to hold her hand, to give her courage in the face of oblivion.

Oh, my love…

She forced herself to examine the chamber more closely. She lay on a couch that was little more than a wooden bench. The walls were painted just as she remembered…but there was something wrong. Some of the frescoes had been damaged. No, deliberately defaced. And over them had been laid pictures of a god—a god with a drooping snout and long, squared ears.

This is not possible. It could not be happening again. Aset would have shown her the truth long before this.

But it was not Aset who had told her. It was Boyd, whose eyes glowed crimson and whose teeth gleamed like an animal's.

"Have you accepted at last, Tameri?" Boyd said, strolling into the chamber as if it were his private domain. "Do you know who I am?"

She looked at him with new eyes…at his dark hair streaked bloodred—Sutekh's color—and his bronzed skin that had never grown paler in spite of England's often dreary weather. In defiance of every natural feeling, Tameri's courage returned. This was her enemy. The enemy she had known she must eventually face.

Now the time had come.

"When did it happen?" she asked calmly. "When did Sutekh take you?"

"He saved me," Boyd said, leaning casually against the wall beside the heavy stone door. "I was lost in the desert, and he gave me a choice. To die slowly and terribly, or to live as a god."

"A god of Evil."

"Am I?" He sighed and shook his head. "Mortals so often confuse chaos with evil."

"You desire more than chaos, Sutekh. You desire to rule the world and cast it in your image."

He cocked his head. "Ah. The *goddess* speaks."

Tameri felt a shifting, as if her body had moved without really moving at all. *Aset.* She remembered so many things, now that it was too late.

"So you remember at last?" Sutekh purred. "How you gave yourself to the priests so that Aset could be born into this world anew?"

Oh, yes. It had all been true, every last part of that last and most terrible vision.

"The common soldier, Maahes, stood beside you, though he could never be your equal," Sutekh continued. "*He,* to become Asar. Your mate. Perhaps it was his very unworthiness that ended your pitiful attempt to stop me."

"We *did* stop you," Tameri said, meeting his burning gaze. "You have been powerless these thousands of years."

"Powerless?" Sutekh bared his teeth. "Think again, Great of Magic. Who was it that killed Maahes with a scorpion's venom? Who sealed you into the tomb to be buried alive?"

Tameri plunged into the past. She was with Maahes again, and he was about to enter her, to claim her for himself and for his god. But a shadow had come into the tomb. Maahes had cried out and fallen from the couch. Tameri had knelt beside him and watched him die.

"Did you guess then that you would die even more slowly?" Sutekh asked. "That the door would close, never to open again, and that Aset would abandon you to suffocation?"

Tameri felt herself beginning to gasp for breath, as if the walls were collapsing around her. "Aset…she did not—"

"She left you because she had no power to save you. As she has none now." His teeth glinted. "I knew that she had chosen you again, Tameri. I knew the time was coming when she would summon you to sacrifice yourself as you did before."

"Because Sutekh had reentered the world."

"And this time I shall work my will with none to stop me." He raised his arms. "When I killed your mortal avatars, my ancient enemy, I destroyed your hope of reunion. Now I shall do so again!"

Tameri's laugh was little more than a wheeze, but it wiped the triumphant expression from Sutekh's face. "You have forgotten one thing," she said. "There is another you must have to complete your design. He who would be Asar. Where is he?"

"You know, do you not?" Sutekh hissed. "You know who he is. As I have suspected since first he came to your house."

Like a vast khamseen blowing scorching sand across the desert, despair swept through Tameri's soul.

"The soldier named after the Lion god has been reborn in another lion," Sutekh said, his voice thick with satisfaction.

"But he did not *remember*, did he? Instinct alone guided him in your defense. A pity he will never fulfill the great part he was to play."

At first Tameri scarcely heard him. She was thinking of Leo...of that strange attraction she had felt on the day of their meeting at the Museum after the lecture. Of how much deeper those feelings had grown. And of the dream they had shared in the museum vault.

She and Leo had come together there, just as their former selves had done in this very tomb. They had nearly completed the bond that would have brought Aset and Asar back into the world to fight the god of chaos.

If only Leo had acknowledged the truth. If only she had been less afraid. If only she had *seen.*

A pity he will never fulfill the great part he was to play....

Tameri sat upright on the couch, straining against her bonds with such force that the cords groaned. *"Where is he?"*

"Alas," Sutekh said, regarding her as one might a dung beetle busy with its labors. "He met with an unfortunate accident when he attempted to follow us after the ceremony."

Tameri muffled a cry of anguish. "You lie!" she shouted, struggling to rise from the couch.

"I lie when it suits my purpose," Sutekh said. "But I have nothing to gain by doing so now. He is dead, and you shall serve me by dying the ultimate death and closing the gate to Aset forever."

THE DAY WAS BRUTALLY HOT, and the wind cast grit and sand into Leo's eyes with every step he took.

The Nile was far behind them now, him and his unwilling companion. The sun had not yet reached its peak, and yet it seemed as if there had never been any water within a thousand miles of this remote valley with its many excavations, abandoned to the relentless summer sun.

Here lay hundreds of tombs, the final resting places of kings and queens, princes and courtiers. Once the chambers, cut deep into the hills, had been repositories of treasures almost beyond modern conception. But there had been thieves even in the time of the pharaohs, men who had been willing to risk the curse of the gods by stealing what belonged to the gods' children.

Since then, adventurers had regularly raided the tombs, leaving rubble and silence in their wake. Only in the past fifty years had the true archaeologists arrived, scholars more interested in learning the secrets of the past than in the wealth they might obtain.

Some said that all the tombs had been discovered, all the riches taken, all the secrets revealed.

Leo didn't believe it. He knew these barren hills and cliffs contained so much more than even the most dedicated scientist could imagine.

When he had arrived in Luxor, he had found the city empty of tourists. None of the natives admitted to having seen the Inglizi. Every instinct told Leo that Boyd had come to Luxor for one reason: he was taking Tameri to the Valley of the Kings.

Leo had nothing more to go on. He still had no idea what Boyd wanted with her. He had only the waking dreams he had tried to deny, the alien words that had come out of his mouth, the scroll. But he could still not decipher the last part. The part he so desperately needed to understand.

On his first night in Luxor, after he'd found a ferry to cross the Nile and a donkey boy to accompany him into the Valley, he lay on his bed at the Luxor Hotel and drifted into the dream. The dream of himself and Tameri in a tomb as yet unraided, arrayed with golden statues and furnishings fit for Pharaoh himself.

There, on the walls, the story of Aset, Asar and Sutekh played out as if it were happening all over again. Sutekh had been defeated. For a time.

But he would rise again. And only the two who had fought him before could stop him when he returned.

Leo wiped grit from his lips with the back of his hand. The scroll still nestled inside his jacket, against his heart. He looked up into the searing blue sky.

He had been in that tomb. He knew it existed, untouched even now, hidden behind another cut into the face of the cliffs. *That* was where Boyd had taken Tameri. He knew because his heart spoke of truths his mind as yet refused to accept.

Boyd had warned him away from Tameri the first time they had met in her drawing room. The second time he had challenged Leo as if they were enemies, not rivals vying for the same beautiful woman.

"Is it to be here, then?" When Boyd had spoken those words, Leo had thought he meant a simple fight. But there had been more behind the question, more behind his eyes. Something more than human.

Perhaps the late Earl of Elston had been mad when he had claimed a previous existence. Perhaps *his* visions hadn't been real. But Tameri wasn't mad or delusional. She never had been.

Leo urged his donkey into a faster trot. The Valley split into two branches, and Leo entered the eastern wadi. The red cliffs rose high to either side. After a short while Leo realized that the boy and the other two donkeys, along with the supplies they carried, were no longer with him.

It didn't matter now. Leo knew where he was going. He could only pray that Tameri would survive long enough for him to reach her.

CHAPTER NINE

THE CHANTING WAS DEEP and familiar, echoing from another chamber beyond Tameri's sight. She knew the words, though they were of a language she had not spoken in thousands of years. They called upon Sutekh, invoked his power and cursed the names of the Good Gods.

And they told of a great sacrifice. A sacrifice that would end only in eternal death.

Sutekh himself had been gone for hours, leaving Tameri to remember his threats and feel the depth of her aloneness.

Leo is not dead. Only that thought kept her from sinking deep into a despair from which she could never emerge. As long as Leo was alive, Sutekh could not succeed.

Tameri pulled at her bonds for the hundredth time, but Sutekh had bespelled them to hold above and beyond any mortal's striving. If she alone could have stopped Sutekh, she would gladly have given up her body and soul to Aset. If her ending could save Leo, she would die with gratitude.

But she had grasped Sutekh's purpose. He had spoken of barring Aset from returning to the mortal realm to fight against him. But Tameri believed that he meant to lure Aset into this chamber with tricks and stratagems, bind her to Tameri and destroy both of them.

Was such a thing possible? Could a god be destroyed? Tameri dared not take the risk. Aset might save her if she chose, but Tameri would do everything within her power to keep the goddess from joining with her.

The chanting grew more distinct as the priests drew near the chamber entrance. How long had such men kept reverence for the god of chaos alive? Where had they hidden to work their foul schemes and pray for Sutekh's return?

I curse you, she told them, though she knew that her curses were useless. Even as she finished the thought, the chanting ceased, and Sutekh returned.

"All is finished," he said, "except for the summoning."

"I will not let you," Tameri said, meeting his gaze with all the ferocity she could muster.

He laughed with those gleaming, serrated teeth. "You have no power, Princess. You never did." He gestured to someone behind him, and two shaven-headed priests in leopard-skin capes and broad collars positioned themselves to either side of him. They raised their arms as Sutekh began to speak.

Nausea coiled in Tameri's throat. She fought. She filled her mind with her own chant of defiance. The smell of incense choked her. The voices boomed in her ears.

And Aset came. Perhaps she had been taken unaware. Perhaps Sutekh had managed to shield his presence. But the goddess came, and filled Tameri with her joyful spirit.

Do not fear what is to come, child, she whispered. *Your long journey is ended. All is as it should—*

"No!" Tameri screamed. And she pushed with all her might, casting the goddess from her mind.

Agony beyond anything Tameri had ever known gripped her body. She arched up from the couch with a hoarse cry, and Aset cried out with her. Tameri's bonds snapped like tissue, yet she lay still.

Aset was gone, driven away by one who should have welcomed her. But the goddess was safe. She would escape the trap.

Sutekh and the priests approached the couch, unaware that their summoning had failed. One of the priests pushed her back down, while the other produced a wickedly curving knife with a bejeweled hilt carved in the shape of the Sutekh beast twined about by bare-fanged serpents.

"You shall never destroy me, brother of my husband," Tameri said, praying that she spoke convincingly. "You shall fail."

"Your time is done, Aset," Sutekh said. His face distorted, lengthened, grew a downwardly curved snout and tall, squared ears. "Now it is *my* world."

The priest raised the knife.

Frantic cries and shouts of alarm stopped him in his strike. Gunshots silenced them. Sutekh spun toward the chamber door.

Leo plunged through it, a gun in each hand. He shot the priests before they could take a single step in his direction and aimed both weapons at Sutekh.

"Tameri," he said, never taking his eyes from the monster. "Are you all right?"

"Run, Leo!" she cried.

He ignored her and advanced on Sutekh. "He's gone, isn't he?" he said to the god. "Boyd no longer exists."

Sutekh bared his sharklike teeth. "He was of some use for a time."

Leo edged toward the body of the priest with the knife and kicked the blade away. "Tameri, can you get up?"

"Yes. But—"

"Go, quickly. I'll hold him."

"I will not leave you!"

"She is wise," Sutekh said. "You may have killed my

priests, but you will not find it such a simple matter to eliminate me." He lifted a languid hand, and a spiral of cutting sand rushed through the doorway to encircle Leo and rip the guns from his grip.

"I could flay you alive if I wished," Sutekh said. "But since you have survived, you also will serve me before you die."

With startling speed, Leo flung himself through the spinning curtain and hurled himself at Sutekh. Tameri caught the flash of a blade just before it struck Sutekh full in the chest.

Sutekh howled. The whirlwind collapsed. Tameri leaped up and attacked the god from behind, clawing at his ears and the coarse red fur of his head. His arm swept back and flung her against the wall.

"Tameri!"

The voice was one she knew, but she could no longer remember to whom it belonged. Two men converged in her mind. Two men and yet a third, who was not a man at all.

Strong hands clutched her shoulders, lifted her, pulled her to her feet. "He has gone, Tameri. We must—"

Crimson heat exploded through her closed eyelids. She heard the thump of Leo's body as it hit the wall. She fell beside him and opened her eyes.

Sutekh had grown to such a height that the tips of his ears brushed the chamber's ceiling. He wore a kilt woven of golden thread, armbands of precious platinum and a collar of ebony beads over his broad, naked chest. He raised one long-nailed hand, and Leo was propelled into the air by some invisible and irresistible force. He dangled there like an insect at the end of a fisherman's hook.

"You see?" Sutekh said. "You cannot wound me. You cannot kill me." He clenched his hand into a fist, and Leo's breathing grew strangled and hoarse. "I could crush you with a thought. But you may still save yourself, and your bitch."

"Let…her go," Leo croaked. "Do what you want with me, but let her—"

"Let us ask the princess," Sutekh said. "Your lover will surrender his life for yours. Would you do the same?"

Tameri braced herself against the wall and inched her way up until she was on her feet again.

"I would," she said, finding that she still had strength and courage enough to hold the evil one's gaze.

"Such devotion is admirable. But neither of you need die." He grinned at Leo, whose face had begun to go white. "You need only call upon him to whom you have already offered your life."

"No!" Tameri cried. "It's a trick—"

Scorching wind caught her, seized her limbs and lifted her just as Sutekh let Leo fall. Unseen fingers squeezed her throat.

"It is no trick that you shall die unless your lover chooses to save you."

"No," Tameri whispered. But Leo was already up, catching his breath, facing Sutekh like a warrior born.

"What must I do?" he demanded.

Tiny starbursts sizzled inside Tameri's head. The tomb and the figures in it wavered like an illusion of water in the desert.

And then it was all changed. All but Sutekh, who gazed upon the young Egyptian soldier with open glee.

"Think, Maahes," he said. "You died once in this place, for nothing. You cannot be victorious. Save yourself. Save your lady. Call upon the gods who have left you to your fates. Let *them* bear the punishment!"

Maahes clenched his fists. Perspiration sheened his

chest and arms, the rigid tendon and muscle of his well-honed body. *How could I ever have found him less than beautiful?* Tameri thought. *We were always meant for one another. The gods themselves declared it.*

And I declare it, my love. We shall be one, even if we die.

"Do not, Maahes," she said. "I am not afraid."

But Maahes looked up at her, a terrible resolve in his clear brown eyes. "What must I do?" he asked again.

"You have the knowledge, and the power," Sutekh said. "It was granted to you by those who now betray you. Summon them!"

Maahes closed his eyes and raised his head. His chant rose to pervade the tomb, reaching out beyond the door and through the long, dark passageway to the desert beyond. Clouds of dust rained from the roof, and the great stone blocks groaned.

The invisible fist clutching Tameri's neck released, and she plunged down to sprawl at Sutekh's feet. She pushed to her hands and knees and began to crawl toward Maahes, reaching for his sandaled feet.

It was too late. A breath of cool, fresh air drove out the fetid heat, and Tameri felt his coming: Asar, deceived as Aset had been deceived, coming at the invitation of his most loyal servant.

"Ah," Sutekh said. "At last it will end."

Helpless, Tameri watched as Maahes began to tremble. Spasms wracked his body, and his jaw clenched with such force that she feared it might break. For a moment he went limp. And then it was as if the very sun had come up in his face, and he opened his eyes.

Even a god could feel shock, and Asar stared at Sutekh in bewilderment.

"You," he said. "What are you—"

A deadly lance of sand shot from Sutekh's outthrust hand. It struck Maahes-Asar full in the chest. He staggered but did not fall. He extended his arm, palm out. Sutekh snarled.

But even Tameri knew it was not a real contest. Asar had been taken unaware, trusting in his avatar to act only for the greater good. And Maahes held him back. Maahes would not give himself completely.

He will not leave me.

Neither Asar nor Sutekh once glanced at Tameri as each struggled for dominance. But they had also forgotten Aset.

There was no choice. Only in concert with her husband could the goddess hope to defeat the god of storms. Tameri spoke silently, recalling the words with ease, twining them about with a warning.

When Aset came, *she* was not deceived. She encircled Tameri with fierce gentleness, the heart of a warrioress and mother protecting her child.

Yet she did not take Tameri's mind. She hid herself, burrowing deep inside Tameri's soul, allowing Tameri the final decision.

Tameri rose, her limbs strong and sure. She stepped between Asar and Sutekh, facing Maahes as if the god of chaos were no more than a fangless snake to be ignored as vermin. Before Sutekh could react, she stepped toward Maahes and kissed him on the lips.

Radiant illumination, as cool and blue as clear water, splashed outward from their brief joining, encircling them both in a shield of light Sutekh could not penetrate. Maahes was stiff for a few seconds, and then gathered her into his arms.

"My lady," he murmured. "My love."

Sutekh roared behind them, but his voice was as thin

as a wailing babe's. Tameri took Maahes's lean, bronzed face between her hands.

"There is but one chance," she said, speaking with Aset's voice. "But one power that can overcome our enemy."

He traced her back with his fingertips. "We will be vulnerable. We may fail."

"This is our final opportunity, My Lord Asar. There will be no other."

"We may yet escape."

"And leave these mortals to their deaths? Leave Sutekh to make of the world a desert where hope withers like reeds in the drought?"

Asar was silent, searching her eyes, her heart. "Are they willing?" he asked.

"Let them speak."

Tameri felt Aset retreat again, restoring voice and body to her control. She could feel Sutekh at her back, but for a moment—this fragile moment—the blue light protected her and Maahes.

Maahes. And Leo. Nothing separated them now; they were one and the same, joined across millennia.

"Do you understand?" she whispered.

Her love—scholar and soldier, gentleman and peasant—pulled her close and pressed his face into her hair.

"Asar was right," he said. "There is only the merest chance. They will end with us if we fail."

"It is worth the risk." She drew back to look into his eyes. "Once we were willing to sacrifice ourselves for the sake of the good. Asar and Aset are prepared to gamble their immortality on the chance that we *will* succeed."

He tucked her head under his chin, and she could feel the shudder of his breath. "I would not lose you again."

"If we are victorious, nothing will be lost." She kissed the hollow beneath his collarbone. "And we will have *this,* my love. Let us make these minutes an eternity."

She felt him turn away, his rough black hair sliding beneath her fingers. But then he tilted her face and bent to kiss her again.

CHAPTER TEN

THERE WAS NO TIME FOR gentle loving, tender caresses or whispered promises of eternal love. The protection that permitted them this time together would not last; Asar and Aset, powerful as they were, could stretch themselves so far and no farther.

Leo no longer doubted. He no longer feared his other self, the man he had been when he had first loved Tameri. He *was* Maahes.

And he was Asar as he gathered Tameri up and carried her to the couch, kicking aside her broken bonds as he knelt to lay her down. Asar waited within him, waited for him to finish what Maahes and Tameri had begun so long ago.

Tameri was ready. Love shone bright as lapis lazuli in her eyes. No fear troubled the smooth and gentle planes of her face. She lifted her arms to him. He rested one knee on the couch and removed her transparent linen sheath, sliding it from her supple figure in one motion.

Her body was a thing of wonder, its beauty such that a single glimpse might drive a man to madness. Her breasts were lush as ripe fruit, her nipples erect and begging to be tasted. Below the slope of her belly lay the dark, moist shadow that concealed her most potent magic.

Maahes stripped off his belt and kilt, bunching the linen and concealing it behind the couch. His member rode high and hard against his belly. Her gaze surveyed him, all in an instant, and her breath grew fast. Lust roared up in Maahes's chest, raging as hot as Sutekh's futile cries of fury.

She opened herself to him, and he eased down into the cradle of her parted thighs. She whispered his name. He hesitated, knowing that everything must change once he had breached this last of her defenses.

But there was no going back, even if he could have compelled himself to stop. He leaned his weight on his arms, found her warm, wet portal and entered her with a firm, deep thrust.

Tameri cried out, arching her back as she accepted him. He began to move inside her, withdrawing only to drive into her again and again as she clasped her legs around his hips.

At first there was only the pleasure and lust, scattering every other thought and sensation as the wind scatters chaff. It was only Tameri's green eyes he saw, her flushed face, her lips parted on moans of ecstasy. Only his own body he felt, the easy shift of muscle, the blood fierce in his veins, the hunger to brand her forever as his alone.

But it could not last. The other presence flowed into his mind: Asar, claiming what Maahes had freely offered. Instinct cried for him to resist, to guard his own soul against invasion.

Tameri saw the doubt in his eyes. She clasped her arms around his neck and drew his face close to her.

"We will never be parted," she whispered.

He saw the change in her as she let go, welcoming Aset into her soul. He, too, gave way. Asar became a part of him, taking hold of his limbs and his heart and his mind.

But he was still there. And as he loved Tameri, Asar loved Aset, moving in that most ancient of rhythms, bringing her to the very edge of a boundless river of joy and fulfillment. He was present as Aset-Tameri tightened her thighs about his hips, raking her nails across his back as he worked more deeply. The magic spiraled about them, cool and blue and impenetrable.

And yet not strong enough. Their enemy had not conceded defeat. Maahes heard his roaring, and the drumming of his bloodred sorcery against the barrier Asar and Aset had shaped out of their eternal love. It was like the scorching point of a spear striking a shield again and again, searching for the one weak spot where it could break through.

Sutekh's only hope was to prevent the final embrace that would bind the gods to their avatars and lend them physical form at last. And he was beginning to succeed. The coolness gave way to warmth, bright silver heated in a blazing fire.

Little by little Asar began to weaken. His spirit retreated, and it was as if a great hole had opened up in Maahes's mind, collapsing in upon itself, stealing far more than life. Tameri's eyes dulled as Aset lost her way.

Fight, Maahes told himself, told her. *Fight.*

Perhaps it was only the desire to live that gave him new strength. Perhaps it was something far more powerful, forged so deep within the heart that nothing so insignificant as fear could touch it. But the strength flowed back into Maahes, a mortal strength, at once fragile and invincible.

Tameri felt it. She held him, vulnerable and formidable, reaching for the great Truth that even the vast chasm of Sutekh's evil could not penetrate. Maahes reached beneath the couch and shook the scroll from his kilt. He got to his feet and unrolled it, beginning to speak the words of the final segment even before he could read them.

The earth shook, and the gods who walked the frescoed walls, hidden behind the figures of Sutekh that had been painted over them, came alive. They burst through the skin of new pigment, their flat figures swelling to three dimensions, and turned upon Sutekh as one, raising staffs and crooks and flails as they circled him with chants in tongues known only to the life-giving soil of the Nile itself.

Their intervention bought only a few precious moments. Maahes set down the scroll and returned to the couch. Tameri opened herself again, and Maahes thrust with greater and greater urgency. Tameri's gasps drowned the gods' chanting and Sutekh's howls of rage. She shuddered and cried out as Leo brought her to climax. The overwhelming pleasure took him, and Asar returned, sweeping through Maahes like a clean, bracing wind...a wind that scoured the tomb, carrying with it the rare blessing of rain. The fire of Sutekh's fury sizzled and went out.

Then there was silence. Asar embraced Aset as the sun embraces the earth, life united to life, the end of the long night of separation. Aset lay quietly, her breath coming more slowly as she stroked Asar's arms.

Through eyes no longer entirely his own, Maahes looked about the chamber. Sutekh was gone, and only a pile of ash lay where he had been standing. The other gods had returned to their walls, but there were subtle differences in their postures. Everything Maahes had seen was real. Sutekh had been defeated.

But Maahes knew his time, too, was ending. His and Tameri's. Soon there would be nothing left of them but a memory. That had been the bargain, the price for restoring Asar and Aset to their guardianship of the world.

Let me see her once more, he begged the god. *Let me see her with my own eyes.*

Asar withdrew. Not far, but just enough. Leo cupped Tameri's face in his hand and kissed her with infinite tenderness.

"Leo?"

"I'm here."

She smiled and stroked his hair. "It was beyond anything I could have imagined," she said.

"You are more beautiful than the lotus flower."

"And you are more powerful than the lion."

He closed his eyes. "I am only a man."

"My love." She touched his eyelids. "Do not weep. We may forget ourselves, but we shall never forget each other."

"If only I had known you when you were young. When we could have—"

Her finger crossed his lips. "We had an eternity."

When he opened his eyes, her own had grown dim and distant. Aset was taking her again, and this time there would be no retreat.

Leo kissed her one last time and released his tenuous hold on his body. Asar filled the shell that had once belonged to him, filled his mind with thoughts and emotions beyond those any mortal could hope to grasp. Leo slipped his hand through Tameri's and let himself die.

TAMERI WOKE SLOWLY, Leo's steady breathing close to her ear. His arm was sprawled across her breasts, his legs entangled with hers. Sourceless light permeated the chamber, the healing warmth of Re as his celestial boat rose from beneath the horizon.

"Leo?"

He murmured an unintelligible protest.

"Leo, wake up."

Her ear tingled as he teased it with his tongue. "What time is it?"

"Dawn."

He stretched, his hand coming to rest on her breast. "Where are we?"

For a moment Tameri couldn't answer. She *knew* this place. And as the light moved through the chamber, she remembered.

She sat up, earning another protest from Leo. "Tameri, come back to—"

"We should not be here."

With a rumble of exasperation he sat up, as well, twisting to gather her against him. "Where is 'here'?" But as he glanced at the walls and the ash and the square doorway, he stiffened and tightened his hold.

"Where are they?"

Tameri turned inward, seeking the goddess. "I don't know."

Leo breathed in the scent of her hair. "They let us live."

A great grief washed over Tameri. "But why? They have waited thousands of years for reunion, for the chance to—"

Do not grieve, my daughter.

"Aset?"

I am here. As Asar is here.

Tameri clutched Leo's hand. "Do you hear them?"

"Yes." He squeezed her fingers. "Asar." He lifted his head. "Why? Why didn't you take us?"

There was no need, Asar said. *It was your strength that defeated Sutekh, not ours.*

"But the scroll…" Leo began.

It was but a tool, said Aset. *A tool left for one who would understand when the time was right. Without your love, it would have been useless against Sutekh.*

"Then why are you here?"

This incarnation is a gift you have given us. A gift you may yet choose to reclaim.

"I don't understand," Leo said.

But Tameri did. The Good Gods spoke, not of sacrifice, but of the gift of life. The gift that would permit them to dwell in mortal bodies, not as usurpers, but as partners.

Tameri met Leo's gaze and saw comprehension wake in his eyes. If they permitted it, Asar and Aset would walk upon the earth as part of them, a part of their souls, never to die.

In exchange, Aset said, *you will have wisdom and abilities greater than those of mortal men. You will live long. You will stand for the good and fight evil wherever you may find it.*

And when Sutekh comes again, as someday he will, Aset said, *we will be there.*

The bargain they offered was generous. But the drawbacks were plain. Tameri and Leo would never be entirely alone.

"We were prepared to give up everything," Leo said, caressing her shoulders with his lean, calloused hands. "If you…stay with me—"

Tameri hadn't believed that there would be a future, let alone one with Leo. "Is that what you truly want?" she whispered.

"You little fool. I've loved you since you stood up in the lecture hall and told Elgabri he was wrong. And long before." He brushed his lips across her cheek. "This humble soldier asks the princess to be his wife."

All Tameri's doubts, all the fears of this life and the last dissolved like the darkness in the face of the sun. "This princess is pleased to accept."

"And the gods?"

"There are no boundaries to love, my soldier. Have we not enough to share?"

His answer could not have been more clear. And as he kissed her, the light expanded until it embraced the whole, wide world.

* * * * *

Look for Susan Krinard's
next thrilling paranormal tale
BRIDE OF THE WOLF,
available March 2010 from HQN Books

New York Times Bestselling Author

MAGGIE SHAYNE

Her last chance to live, her only chance to love…

Lilith awakens cold, naked and alone, knowing nothing—not even who she is—except that she has to run, run for her life…because someone is after her.

When Ethan discovers the terrified woman hiding on his ranch, he knows immediately not only *who* she is but *what*. He's never forgotten her, not in all the time since he escaped their joint prison, a clandestine CIA facility where humans are bred into vampires willing to kill on command. He refused to accept that fate, and since he won his freedom, he's become a legend to those he left behind. With her own escape, Lilith has become a legend, too, and now—together—they have no choice but to fight those who would become legends by killing one.

BLOODLINE

Available wherever books are sold!

REQUEST YOUR
FREE BOOKS!

2 FREE NOVELS
FROM THE SUSPENSE COLLECTION
PLUS 2 FREE GIFTS!